THE KID

A Reed & Billie Novel, Book 3

DUSTIN STEVENS

The Kid
Copyright © 2016, Dustin Stevens
Cover Art and Design: Anita B. Carroll at Race-Point.com

It's so much darker when a light goes out than it would have been if it had never shone.
–John Steinbeck

Sometimes, only one person is missing, and the whole world seems depopulated.
–Alphonse de Lamartine

Chapter One

The brakes were brand new, touchier than The Kid anticipated. Depressing the pedal caused the oversized SUV to lurch to a stop in a series of jolts, a far cry from the smooth deceleration he was expecting. With each spasm his upper body jerked forward a few inches before slamming back again, a small puff of air releasing through his nostrils, an audible expelling of the emotion balled within.

Under different circumstances, his angst would have been aimed at the shoddy handling of the vehicle he was now seated in. It was an expensive ride, one far too pricey to be experiencing such shortcomings.

Tonight, though, whatever mechanical failures there may have been did not even register with him. It was the first time he had ever been behind the wheel of it, the exorbitant asking price one that he had not had to pay.

Within an hour or two it would be cast away, nothing more than a prop, a tool needed for the completion of his task.

Instead, his emotion was a contorted mass of competing feelings, each just as strong as the others, all demanding to be realized and acknowledged. Anger, hatred, vengeance, even a bit of sorrow, all wrapped into a tight package and hermetically sealed in his nether regions, threatening to burst out at any moment, at the very least to consume him from within.

The SUV finally came to a full stop with a mighty squeal of rubber against rubber, the hulking mainframe of the car rocking forward a few inches before settling back onto its chassis. The moment it came to a rest The Kid jammed the gearshift into park, needing both of his hands free for what lay ahead.

Sweat beaded across his brow as he sat in the driver's seat, thick sunglasses on despite the late hour. Their purpose was explicitly for this moment, meant to protect his vision as he stared into the rearview mirror, a pair of fluorescent flashers passing from one headlight to the other in the automobile pulled off the road behind him.

In equal three second pulses they passed from end to end, making a quick revolution around all four corners of the square lamps before jumping to the opposite side. Above them a pair of silhouettes could be seen seated in the front seat. On the right was a short, squat man, his bulk dominating much of the space. Beside him sat a man so tall the top of his head was hidden from view, as if jammed into the hood of the car.

The Kid felt his pulse tick upward, staring back at them.

It was the right car. It had to be.

Sliding his right hand over to the passenger seat, The Kid extended his grip over the gnarled grip of a .9mm Beretta. Keeping his movement hidden from view, he pulled it over onto his lap and passed it into his left hand before reaching across and taking up the second of the matching pair.

Keeping his fingers outside the trigger guards, The Kid squeezed the handles on both tightly, the muzzles for each pointed in opposite directions as they rested across his thighs. Veins stood out on the back of his hands as he stared down at them, feeling the reassurance of cool resolve flood through him.

It was time.

The second part of his plan was finally here.

A light breeze passed through the interior of the SUV as The Kid sat and waited. He watched as the two men behind him seemed to be in conversation, their heads rotating toward each other and back again behind him. No doubt they were running the plates on his car and making sure there was nothing outstanding before approaching, making him wait in a way that only cops could.

It wasn't like they ever considered that the people they were pulling over had lives they needed to get back to or that their evening wasn't already ruined enough.

As each moment ticked by The Kid felt his animosity grow, the feeling only serving to reaffirm his actions.

Outside, an 18-wheeler sped past, laying on the air horn twice in succession as it went. With the windows rolled down, the sound reverberated through the interior of the car, rattling through The Kid's head, his pulse jumping just slightly.

Fighting the urge to raise his middle finger to the trucker getting a good laugh at his expense, The Kid remained completely stationary, only his eyes moving as he alternated glances between the car in his rearview mirror and the guns on his lap.

A full eight minutes after coming to a stop, he watched as both doors on the car behind him swung open. A bevy of misshapen shadows were visible as a man climbed from each side of the car, both adjusting their pants before slamming the doors shut and stepping toward him.

Once more The Kid felt his pulse rise. His breath caught in his throat as he slid his index fingers beneath the trigger guards, counting the seconds in his head as his targets walked closer.

It was time.

For Big.

Chapter Two

"Touchdoooooown!"

Reed Mattox drew the back end of the word out more than a half minute, raising his face toward the ceiling, letting his voice roll from deep in his diaphragm. The only other sound in the aging farmhouse was the commentator of the game prattling on, his voice completely drowned out by Reed's bellow of excitement.

When at last his lungs could take no more, his body aching for air, he lowered his gaze back to the television, a smile plastered across his features. Onscreen a wide receiver for the Oklahoma Sooners was accepting the congratulations of his teammates, the entire stadium a frenzied sea of crimson.

"Did you see that catch?" Reed exclaimed, on his feet in front of the couch, wringing his hands before him.

On the floor nearby his detective partner Billie, a 65-pound solid black Belgian Malinois, looked up at him beneath heavily-lidded eyes, her entire being a visual depiction of how little she cared.

For the first month of the season, she had ebbed and flowed with Reed on every trial and tribulation of the Sooners football team, spending three to four hours every Saturday pacing from her bed beneath the kitchen table to the couch by Reed's side. Now well into October, her enthusiasm for the sport had faded, watching Reed with a detachment that seemed to be equal parts amusement and disdain.

"Bah," Reed said, waving a hand at her as the screen cut away to a replay, the receiver running a perfect wheel route to gain a few feet of separation. From there it was on the quarterback to lay it into the back corner of the end zone, the receiver snatching it from the air with one hand, his other encased by the defensive back trying to cover him.

Drawing in a full breath of air, Reed raised his face to bellow at the ceiling again when his cell phone erupted on the coffee table in front of him. Stopping his movement cold, he rocked forward at the waist and reached down, snatching up the implement without looking at the screen.

"See, some people appreciate a good play," Reed said to his partner, the same smile in place as he took up the phone and pressed it to his face. "Did you *see* that?!"

A moment of silence met his ear, stretched out just long enough that the smile fell from Reed's face as he pulled the phone back and checked the screen. He had expected to hear the voice of his father on the opposite end, sending up a similar yell of adulation, the two performing the same two-part verbal dance they had all but perfected over three-plus decades of watching football.

Instead, the number was from someplace far less enthusiastic.

"Sorry," Reed said, a flush of heat rising to his cheeks. "Watching the game."

"Reed?" the familiar voice of Jackie, night dispatch for the 8th Precinct Reed worked out of, asked.

"Yeah," Reed said, taking up the remote and extending it toward the television, turning off the sound to the game. In the wake of it the house fell quiet, players continuing to move across the screen in muted silence. "What's shaking, Jackie?"

Another moment passed before Jackie whispered, "There's been an accident."

Still unfazed in his excitement for the game, Reed took up a half-full bottle of Heineken from the table beside him and swigged down a long drink. "I'm not on tonight, Jackie. I think Ike and Bishop are the call crew."

A low sob sounded out over the line, the smile falling completely from Reed's features. Leaning forward, he lowered the bottle back down to the table, Billie sensing the shift in his demeanor, her head rising from the floor as she stared at him.

In the 10 months Reed had been with the 8th, they had handled the full gamut of cases. He himself had worked a revenge killer and a truly bizarre case of someone targeting people for organ donation. Some of the other detective teams had covered everything from drug deals to grand theft.

Never once had Jackie batted an eyelash, much less shed a tear.

"What happened?" Reed asked, already feeling his mouth go dry as he waited for a response.

"I..." Jackie started, her breath coming in ragged bursts. She paused a moment, as if contemplating whether or not to continue, before simply saying, "They're at Mercy West, both in surgery right now. It's bad."

All thoughts of the game fell away. On the opposite end of the room Billie pushed herself to her feet, her eyes a pair of moist discs staring unblinking back at him, waiting for any sign of movement.

"We're on our way."

Chapter Three

The lights above Mercy West hospital stood out bright against the ambient glow of Columbus as Reed angled his truck into town. Bypassing his police-issue sedan, he sat up high behind the wheel of the aging rig, Billie on the passenger seat beside him. With her bottom resting on the cloth cushion, she braced her front paws against the dash, her tongue wagging out of her mouth as they made their way forward.

It had taken less than 10 minutes for Reed to transition once the call came through. In rapid fashion he had killed the television, swapping out his gym shorts for a pair of jeans and sneakers. The Oklahoma t-shirt he was wearing he left on, pulling on a zip-up hooded sweatshirt before heading out.

His gun and his badge he left behind.

He was not going to work. He was going to show support.

It was true that every precinct had a couple of guys that took it upon themselves to give new hires a rough time. As the longest tenured crew working out of the 8[th,] Pete Iaconelli and Martin Bishop had focused in on Reed with laser-like intensity, keeping him under close scrutiny for three solid months. Not until they had been forced together on his first major case did things begin to thaw, only recently approaching anything resembling collegiality.

Despite that, Reed held no ill will. This was his second precinct, and after more than a decade in law enforcement, he knew how things worked.

Ike and Bishop had given him a hard time to make sure he passed muster, not out of malice. Even if they had, moments like this rose far above any internal pissing matches. Law enforcement was often referred to as a brotherhood, and even though Reed was only child, he liked to imagine the depiction was apt.

They could pick on each other, but damned sure nobody else could.

Pushing the accelerator as hard as he dared, Reed pulled up in front of Mercy West, a gleaming structure of metal and glass in the western suburb of Hilliard. Standing more than a dozen stories tall, it towered over the surrounding neighborhood, parking lots spread wide around it.

Following the signs, Reed went straight for visitor parking and pulled into the first available spot, clipping Billie to her short lead and hopping out alongside her.

Hygienic facility or not, she was an officer and had just as much right as anybody to be present. So certain of that fact was Reed, especially given the events of the night, he almost dared someone to say something as they made their way to the front entrance.

An oversized pair of glass double doors parted for them as they stepped inside, the ambient temperature several degrees warmer than that outside. Despite it being half past 11:00 on a Saturday night the entire front lobby was nearly full, an even mix of officers in uniform and others dressed to match his civilian attire. It was clear at a glance who was still on duty and who was off for the evening, everybody besides essential personnel dropping whatever they were doing the moment the call went out.

Reed nodded to a small cluster of officers in street clothes from the 19th Precinct – his old unit – as he passed, wading through the crowd in search of familiar faces. As he did so a handful of folks glanced in his direction, taking in both he and Billie before dismissing them and returning to their conversations.

A subdued vibe hung in the air as they moved forward, born of equal parts concern and anger. The faces of nearly every person wore the obvious internal conflict on their features, people vacillating on the proper response, no doubt asking each other for the slightest bit of information that might make some sense of what had happened.

Knowing that at this point anything he did pick up would be nothing but hearsay, Reed continued pushing forward, finally making his way to the far side of the room. There he found a cluster of men from his new home, all grouped tight, intermittingly tossing furtive looks at the double doors standing closed nearby, a sign for the operating suite hanging over them.

Officer Adam Gilchrist was the first to notice Reed and Billie. He turned to face them full, his thumbs looped into the front pockets of his jeans, a plain grey t-shirt covering his upper body. The last time Reed had seen him was a week before, a group from the precinct going out to celebrate the completion of his first year on the force. Now he seemed a far cry from the joyous young man he had been then, his boyish features pulled tight into a solemn look.

"Detective," Gilchrist said, extending a hand.

"Officer," Reed said, returning the shake. Beside them Gilchrist's partner Derek Greene turned, a black man just north of 40 with grey starting to show at the temples, and shook Reed's hand as well.

"How bad?" Reed asked, bypassing any pleasantries besides the handshake.

"Bad," Gilchrist said.

Greene glanced in his direction, a momentary shadow of disapproval passing over his features at his young partner's candor, before saying, "They're both in surgery now. Word is Bishop took a round in the knee. Non life-threatening, but a lot of damage."

The knot in Reed's stomach grew a bit larger, pressing against the pizza he'd eaten just a short time before.

"And Ike?"

The two officers exchanged a quick glance, their faces both managing to grow a bit more grim at the same time.

"Touch and go," Greene finally offered, adding no more.

Reed knew better than to press it, now not being the time for open discussion of such matters.

The feeling grew even more pronounced as Billie settled to a seated position against his leg. Without thinking he lowered his right hand and furrowed the hair between her ears, no sound escaping her as they stood and watched the crowd.

"Any word from Grimes yet?" Reed asked.

"He's back there now," Gilchrist said. "The waiting room is pretty tiny, so they're only letting a couple people go back. Ike's sister is in there, Bishop's wife and daughter. Aside from them, it's just Grimes and Jackie."

Never before had Reed given much thought to the family situation for either Ike or Bishop, though it made sense. Everything Reed had ever seen of the former, from his manner of speech to choice in clothes, seemed to scream bachelor. His counterpart, different in just about every way, seemed much more the family man sort, in a henpecked sort of way.

"Jackie seemed pretty shook when she called," Reed said. "You see her?"

Greene nodded once, his gaze moving past Reed, taking in the shifting crowd around them. "She got here about five minutes before you, was a complete wreck. I'm not sure I would have let her go back myself, but she refused to take no for an answer."

Reed nodded, adding the information to what little he knew. He allowed it to stew for a full two minutes, the humanist side of his mind controlling the thought process, thinking first of his fellow officers and their families. From there he shifted to Grimes and Jackie, captain and den mother of the precinct respectively, and what they must be going through in the waiting room.

Finally, once that was completely sorted out, the other half, the undeniable, detective half of his brain went to work.

So far he had learned that both men had been shot. Bishop's was non-life-threatening, Ike's much more serious. That ruled out a car accident, a stray bullet, or any of 100 other smaller things that could have put them in the hospital.

It still did very little to actually tell him what occurred.

With his hands shoved into the pockets of his sweatshirt, he leaned forward a few inches, dropping his voice just slightly as he looked at Greene and Gilchrist in turn.

"Okay, what happened?"

Chapter Four

The impromptu circle stood seven strong in the parking lot outside of Mercy West Hospital. Now that the clock was well past midnight, most of the non-essential cars parked outside had vacated, the sodium lights overhead casting down a harsh yellow glow illuminating nothing but bare asphalt. On the freeway nearby a few errant headlights could be seen rolling by, the world as quiet as a suburb of a mid-level city in the fall could be.

At the head of the group stood Wallace Grimes, captain of the 8th Precinct, a post he had assumed after moving over from the 19th. Familiar with Reed from their time together there, he had suggested Reed make the move when his partner Riley was killed in the line of duty 10 months earlier, even going as far as to create the K-9 position for him.

It was an offer Reed had accepted with reluctance, though with each passing week he found his gratitude for the invitation growing exponentially.

Approaching his 50th year, Grimes's black hair was fast sliding toward grey, his midsection just beginning to show the strain of taking up a permanent desk position. Dressed in slacks and a pullover, dark circles underscored his eyes, and deep parentheses framed his mouth.

By his side stood Jackie, her normal level of vivacity toned down by a factor of 10. Her usual plume of white blonde hair was pulled back into a ponytail, most of her trademark makeup having been wiped away with tears. She stood with hands shoved into the front pockets of a jacket two sizes too large, the garment seeming to swallow her up, her gaze aimed at the ground.

Third and fourth in line were Gilchrist and Greene, both wearing the same somber expressions they had since arriving. Joining them was a detective named Jennings that Reed had met a few times in passing, though had yet to work with. Like Iaconelli and Bishop he looked to be fast approaching retirement age, his thin blonde hair receding and pushed to the side in a long swoop. Wire rimmed glasses framed pale blue eyes, his jaws beginning to sag a bit.

Making up the rear of the crew were Reed and Billie, Reed assuming his standard pose of hands shoved into the pockets of his sweatshirt, Billie on her haunches beside him. From where they stood they had a good view of everyone present, all waiting in silence for the captain to begin.

"Thank you all for being here," Grimes said, his tenor sounding a bit more graveled than usual. "I know the families of Pete and Martin have been very touched by the overwhelming show of support this evening."

A dozen retorts sprang to Reed's mind, though he very carefully pushed them to the side.

Now was not the time to be cracking wise, or even stating the obvious, when both men we're in such a poor state of health.

"Martin is now out of surgery," Grimes said, keeping his gaze aimed at the bare patch of concrete in the middle of the group. As he spoke he made no attempt to make eye contact with anybody, stating the information in an even din that bordered on monotone.

"A bullet struck his right knee, shattering the knee cap. At some point he will have to have a replacement, though for the time being they have stabilized the joint."

He paused there as if there was more he wanted to add before clearing the thought away with a twist of his head.

Again more questions came to mind for Reed, though he forced himself to remain silent. He could tell by the way Jennings shifted his weight from one foot to the other beside him that he was going through the same thought process, though he too opted not to voice anything.

"Pete," Grimes said, pausing a moment at the sound of the name. Beside him Jackie's eyes slid shut, a quiver passing through her entire upper body.

"Pete was struck four times," Grimes said, raising his voice as if he needed the boost to get out what he was about to say. "One to his right arm, three to center mass."

Reed could tell there was a significant amount more he wanted to add, but again decided against it.

"There was a lot of internal bleeding," Grimes said, "which they've been able to get stopped. Aside from that, though, there's still a tremendous amount of damage. The doctors are now removing what's left of his spleen, trying to do some other clean up."

The skin around Reed's eyes pulled into a wince as he listened to the report, Billie nudging a bit closer against his calf. Each of the men beside him seemed to have similar reactions, Jennings continue to shift his weight from side to side, Greene and Gilchrist both tightening their expressions, moving their focus from Grimes to the ground and back again.

"As far as we can tell, this was a routine traffic stop," Grimes said. "They were about to clock out at the end of their shift when they spotted an SUV driving recklessly. Upon falling in behind it they noticed a taillight was also busted, so they pulled it over."

For the first time he raised his gaze, looking to each of the men around the circle.

"The run on the plates came back clean, no priors or outstanding warrants. At that time both men exited their vehicle and began to approach."

With each word his voice seemed to get a bit lower, every person in the circle knowing what was coming. Jackie seemed to retreat even further back into her jacket as he moved toward the climax, clearly not wanting to hear what was about to be said.

"Halfway there the driver opened fire, without provocation. Iaconelli was on the driver's side, much closer to the shooter, and took a total of four rounds. Bishop only took one, the height of the SUV and Martin combining to create an odd angle, the round hitting him in the knee."

Picturing the scene in his mind, concern, angst, dread, all drifted to the side of Reed's consciousness. In their place anger flooded in, imagining the detectives walking up to the SUV, seeing the muzzle flashes as a weapon began to discharge.

"Who called it in?" Reed asked, the question out before he even realized it, the first person besides Grimes to speak.

At the sound of his voice Gilchrist and Jackie both looked his way, Greene and Jennings each looking to Grimes for the answer.

"A man on his way home from a football game saw the driver speed away, noticed two bodies along the road and pulled over," Grimes said. "He called 911 and stayed with them until the ambulance arrived."

"The scene?" Greene asked.

"McMichaels and Jacobs," Grimes said. "They were the closest units. Earl and the crime scene crew are out there now."

"Any ideas on shooter? Motive?" Reed asked.

Grimes fixed him with a hard stare, his face revealing nothing for a long moment. "Have you been drinking?"

The question set Reed back a bit, his eyebrows rising on his forehead. He'd had a couple beers earlier while watching the game, though that was many hours before at this point. Certainly nothing that was inhibiting his speech or actions, would prompt the question from the captain.

"A beer earlier while watching ball," Reed said, a hint of an edge appearing in his voice. "Why?"

Grimes held the same expression for a moment before nodding just slightly. "Right now all we have is the license plate number that our guys ran before this took place."

He kept his attention aimed at Reed and said, "Your investigation starts now. The rest of you, give him whatever backup is necessary. If they can't help, call and I'll see you get what you need."

Chapter Five

Pure, unadulterated adrenaline surged through The Kid's system. It heightened his senses, brought about a euphoria that far outpaced anything he'd ever gotten from the occasional toke with his friends.

The Kid was just 13 the first time he ever held a gun. Growing up in a place like The Bottoms it was an inevitability, a question of *when* rather than *if*.

The first time he ever actually fired one he was 15, taking a rusted Beretta to a field outside of town to shoot at beer bottles. Even at such a young age, a complete novice with a weapon, he had shown an aptitude that his buddies still bragged about. Six out of six on his first go-round, a byproduct as much from luck as any skill he might have had.

From there the sense of excitement, both from the feel of the weapon and the knowing of his proficiency with it, only grew.

The first time he ever pointed a gun at someone he was 18, using it to obtain $83 and a case of beer from the Buckeye Gas and Go a few blocks from The Bottoms. At the time the lady working the counter - a black woman with silver in her hair - had barely batted an eye at him, cleaning out the register and handing over the meager contents without the slightest hint of fear. The odds were The Kid's heart rate climbed higher than hers throughout the ordeal, though that did nothing to diminish the effect it had on him.

Still, despite more than a decade passing since the first time he'd ever touched a firearm, this was the first time he had knowingly, intentionally, pointed and fired at another human being.

The effect was nothing short of intoxicating as it surged through The Kid's system, his body still coiled behind the steering wheel, a smile on his face as he replayed the events of the evening.

This was the last step, the final thing he must do, before putting the evening behind him and moving on to the next phase.

He just wasn't sure he wanted to just yet.

One time after another he played the scene back in his mind, the encounter lasting just under 10 minutes in real time but seeming much longer with each rehashing. On perpetual loop, he thought of how he obtained the car, how he circled the blocks of The Bottoms, identifying exactly who he was looking for, making the errant swipe of the steering wheel to get their attention.

Once they had him alongside the road was where things really got interesting, the visual replay slowing. With each subsequent viewing his mind filled in a few more details, whether they be real or his own imagination not much mattering.

The facial expressions on the pair as they approached, the lights of oncoming traffic spotlighting them, the splash of bright red blood as his bullets found their mark.

He had done it. No longer was it all just preparation for some distant goal.

Big would be proud.

The thought of Big pulled away a bit of the smile from The Kid's face, his features softening. A stab of something uncertain hit him deep in his stomach, roiling through his body, ebbing away some of the adrenaline.

In its place flooded in a renewed sense of purpose, the realization that he had done well, but still had a long way to go.

Twisting in his seat, The Kid reached into the back and drew up a black duffel bag. Unzipping the top, he took out a can of lighter fluid and set it in his lap, loading his two weapons into the bag and fastening it closed.

Taking up both items, he stepped out of the SUV, leaving the door open as he passed the strap of the bag over his shoulder.

The lot was one he knew well, the very same place he and his friends had come to shoot bottles years before. He knew there was no need to worry about anybody seeing him, the location far from the edge of town, the closest neighbor over a mile away. Little more than a gravel embankment near an old fishing hole, forest pushed in tight on three sides, the clearing just over 50 yards square.

There was even less concern for any of his friends from back then catching wind of the dump and fingering him, all of them either perished or in jail at this point.

Again, the kinds of things that were a question of *when*, not *if*, in The Bottoms.

The windows of the car were still down as The Kid flipped open the top on the can of lighter fluid and leaned inside the SUV. He reached out and jammed down the automatic cigarette lighter on the dash before shooting a heavy stream of the fluid around the interior of the SUV, the scent finding his nose, bringing a sheen of moisture to his eyes.

Moving in a sweeping arc, he expended the entire contents of the can into the space, wet stripes visible on the cushioned fabric seats, the odor so strong it almost caused him to gag.

When it was empty, he flipped the can down into the foot well of the passenger seat before grabbing up the lighter and inspecting the glowing red tip in the moonlight. Content that it was ready, he took a step back and tossed it in through the open window.

Just moments later flames became visible, growing ever stronger in intensity, until they stood out like bright orange fingers against a darkened night sky.

Chapter Six

If Reed had even the slightest indicator that he would be instantly beginning an investigation into the attempted murder of two fellow officers, he wouldn't have brought the truck. He wouldn't have had a beer with dinner, even if it was long since out of his system.

He damned sure wouldn't have left his badge and gun on the nightstand in his bedroom.

As it were, it took him nearly 40 minutes to make the trek home and back to the precinct. The entire way he went heavy on the gas, saying every last question that came into his head out loud, Billie sitting stone still and listening intently.

Based on what little information Grimes had, nothing seemed to make sense. There was absolutely no reason for someone to open fire over a potential moving violation. That meant that either the person themselves was wanted for something more or that there was something in the car they could not risk the detectives seeing.

Even at that, it begged the question of what could be important enough to warrant the attempted double homicide of police officers. No drug charges, no kidnapping arrest, not even the body of a civilian in the trunk, would possibly add up to the final sentence handed down for going after two officers.

As such, Reed had to believe that meant whatever motivated the shooter was either something that scared the shooter more than the threat of prison or that he had simply wanted these two particular officers dead.

The thought of going through their entire case backlog, more than two decades each, did little to raise Reed's mood as he wound his way back to the station. Switching from the truck back into his police issue sedan had removed concern for his colleagues as the preeminent though, his instincts as a detective taking over.

As much as the heinous nature of the act gnawed at him, both personally and professionally, he had to shove the feelings aside and focus on what he was doing. Right now that meant running down the plates on that SUV and seeing where it took him.

Everything else could wait.

At the end of the block, the 8th Precinct came into view, the front of it lit by a pair of small spotlights pointed upward over the front façade. Constructed from brick, the building had faded from years of exposure to the elements, the exterior now closer to pink than its original red, even under the harsh glare of the lights. Perfectly square in dimensions and rising three stories in height, the place looked to be a brick cube that had been retrofitted, a roundabout and flag pole out front completing the ensemble.

Reed pulled in without giving any of the structural components a second thought, finding the parking lot as deserted as was to be expected for 2:00 on what was now a Sunday morning. Angling for the front door, he slid to a stop in the handicapped stall closest to the entrance and parked at an angle, just two other cars visible.

Reed recognized them as belonging to Greene and Gilchrist, having requested that they meet him before heading home for the night.

"Stay here, I'll be right back," Reed said to Billie, pushing out of the car and jogging to the front. He found the door unlocked and swung through the first floor, ignoring the empty desks stretched out to either side, the executive suite behind frosted glass on the back half of the building.

Instead he jogged up the stairs, taking them three at a time, following the only lights in the building to the second floor.

A perfect match in layout to the ground level, detectives desks were housed on the left, all of them sitting quiet. The back half of the place was reserved for the evidence locker, also completely void of life.

The entire amount of human activity in the building was clustered around the dispatch desk to Reed's right, Jackie, Gilchrist, and Greene all standing alongside it, staring back at him expectantly.

Joining them behind the waist-high desk was Lou, the longtime dispatch operator for the day shift, a man that Reed had heard say no more than two dozen words in his entire 10 months with the 8th. One of the older employees in the CPD system, his head was void of hair, what little was left reduced to white tufts around the base of his skull. Most of his muscle mass had also deteriorated, leaving his facial features sagging and the collar on his shirt gapping more than an inch from his neck.

The expression on his face revealed there was a good chance he may be sick at any moment.

Reed knew the feeling.

"Did you run it?" Reed asked, his voice clipped and even, loud enough to be heard.

A moment of silence passed, nobody taking the lead.

"Jackie," Reed said, stopping himself just short of snapping, "were you able to retrieve the plate on the vehicle they pulled over?"

Jackie's mouth dropped open, her face a mix of shocked at having been brought into the conversation and surprise at his tone, before she collected herself. She closed her jaw and drew herself up a few inches higher, the same oversized jacket still enveloping her.

"Yes. The plate is registered to..." she paused, aiming her attention down at the counter beside her, "Jonas Hendrix. The address is in Grove City."

Reed nodded, pausing just a moment. He was a bit surprised that the address on the car was outside The Bottoms, the area comprising the majority of the 8th Precinct's jurisdiction. The mailing address for it was Franklinton, and a small sliver nudged into Hilliard, but Grove City was a good piece further south.

Not that it mattered in the slightest at the moment.

"Okay," he said, his attention on her. "Call Grimes and ask him to get on the horn with Grove City. Have him tell them we will be entering their jurisdiction to inquire about an attempted homicide on two police officers. If they could have a couple units on standby just in case, that would be great."

For the first time since Reed had met her, Jackie accepted a directive without saying a word. She offered only a nod, a short, curt gesture that moved no more than an inch in total.

"Also, can you call in a BOLO for Hendrix's car?"

Once more she nodded in assent, remaining silent.

Shifting to his left, Reed looked to Greene and Gilchrist, both appearing as antsy as he felt, their faces drawn tight.

"You guys ready to go pay Jonas Hendrix a visit?"

Chapter Seven

Pulling up in front of the house of Jonas Hendrix, Reed had a feeling. Somehow, deep inside, he just knew they'd been sent on a fool's errand.

It might have been the neighborhood, a full mile off the freeway, far enough not to catch a single residual sound from the outer belt encircling Columbus, even in the still night air. It could have been that every house on the street was built within the last two decades, their exteriors made of brick or white siding. Yards were clipped neat and uniform. Newer cars were parked in the driveways.

More than anything though, it was the collection of pumpkins sitting out on the front stoop that shifted Reed's demeanor in an instant. One moment he was amped up, adrenaline, anger, surging through his system. Despite the cool temperatures outside, sweat had plastered the t-shirt he wore under his sweatshirt to the small of his back. Veins stood up on the backs of his hands, running up his forearms before disappearing beneath the thick cuffs of his hoodie.

Just a single glance at the quartet of carved pumpkins arranged on the concrete steps leading to the front door pushed all that aside, though. Sloppy and uneven, they were clearly the work of amateurs, children no more seven or eight.

Seeing them there, the tension bled from Reed. He still had no idea what he might find inside the house, but he knew that nobody that displayed the handiwork of their kids on the front step spent their free time out shooting police officers.

Jamming the gear shift of his sedan into park, Reed grabbed the radio off the dash in front of him. He raised it to his lips, pressed the lever on the side and said, "Gilchrist, Greene, you there?"

A long moment of static passed through the car, filling the space. Behind him Billie nudged her nose up between the seats, her breath warm and foul.

"Yeah Reed, go ahead," Gilchrist replied.

"This isn't the place," Reed said, not adding any preamble at all. "This might have been where the car came from, but this isn't the guy that shot Ike and Bishop."

Another moment passed, Reed flicking his gaze to the rearview mirror. Pulled onto the curb behind him, he could see both their silhouettes looking to the house before Gilchrist came back over the line.

"Agreed," he said. "How do you want to handle it?"

As certain as Reed felt, as sure as the sense in his gut seemed, he wasn't about to do something foolish. They did still need to determine why the car belonging to this address was 15 miles north and why it was firing at police officers over moving violations.

"We've got more than probable cause," Reed said. "We're still going in." He paused and added, "Billie and I will breech. You guys stay back and keep an eye out for runners, watch the windows for any sign of life."

"Roger that."

Reed replaced the mic without another word, taking up his Glock from the passenger seat beside him. He slid the holster from the outside out of it and checked the slide, racking a round into the chamber as he rested a hand on his door.

"You ready?"

There was no need to open the rear, Billie darting between the seats and following him out behind the steering wheel. His feet had no more than hit the pavement when she spilled out behind him, her solid black form nothing more than a shadow as she circled to the front of the sedan, waiting for him.

Ten feet away, both doors to the second sedan opened, Greene climbing from the driver's side, Gilchrist opposite him. Both had already drawn their weapons, each moving to take up positions on either end of their car.

Once they both had a clear vantage of the front of the house, Greene raised a hand and motioned Reed forward, quickly returning it to the base of his weapon, using it for support as he kept the muzzle pointed at an angle toward the ground.

"Come," Reed said, dropping his voice a few octaves, calling on the tone reserved especially for commands. Upon hearing it Billie's body snapped rigid, her nose pointed straight ahead, every movement done with practiced efficiency.

Despite the deep-rooted feeling that the house was empty, Reed felt his pulse surge, his breathing growing shallow in his chest. Twice he gave soft squeezes on the handle of his weapon, feeling the gnarled ridges in the grip dig into his palm.

Eschewing the driveway and front walk, he cut a diagonal path across the lawn, the grass soft and springy beneath his feet. In 10 quick strides he was across it and up to the concrete steps, wasting no effort as he came upon the door and balled his hand into a fist, slamming it into the thick wooden barrier.

"Jonas Hendrix!" he yelled, his voice carrying out through the neighborhood. "Columbus PD, open up!"

The command was followed by a second pounding on the door, the blows echoing back through the house, no doubt heard by half the homes on the block. Within minutes lights would begin coming on around them, the telltale sign of onlookers curious to see what the commotion was about.

"Jonas Hendrix!" Reed yelled again, giving the door one last trio of knocks before stepping back. He waited there a full 15 seconds, listening close for any sounds of movement from within.

His knock-and-announce requirement satisfied, he took a step back and looked over his shoulder to the officers standing behind him. "Anything?"

At the rear of the car Gilchrist gave a terse twist of his hand, glancing over to his partner.

"Nothing," Greene said, his form having not moved an inch since taking up position.

"Prepare to breach," Reed said, not waiting for a response as he turned back to the front door. Beside him Billie bounced lightly in place, having been through this procedure a time or two before, recognition, anticipation, rolling off of her.

"On three," Reed whispered, as much for himself as his partner beside him. "One...two...*three*."

Pushing forward off his left foot, Reed drove the heel of his right foot through the narrow expanse of wood between the brass handle and the doorframe. The cushioned sole of his running shoe connecting flush, the deadbolt resisted just a moment before the thin wood fleshing outlining the frame gave way. Two long strips tore away, the sound of them sheering free finding his ears, a shower of wooden shards hitting the floor right behind it.

The smell of sawdust found Reed's nostrils as he let the momentum of the kick carry him forward, pushing the door open with his shoulder. "Clear!"

The word was still on his tongue as Billie bolted past, darting into the house and disappearing from sight. Reed could hear the sound of her toenails clattering on hardwood floors as he raised his gun to shoulder level and moved in behind her, swinging his weapon from side to side.

The interior of the house matched the exterior to the letter, the place having a comfortable, lived-in feeling, despite it being dark and silent. Heavy rugs covered large swaths of the floor and overstuffed furniture was placed around the living and dining rooms.

Piled high in the corner was a mountain of children's toys, the predominant colors being pink and purple. A bevy of photos hung on the walls, many featuring two smiling girls with blonde curls, confirming the motif of the toys, neither child appearing to be more than six.

Just as fast as she had gone, Billie reappeared, some of the tension released from her body. In quick order Reed made a pass over everything she had just been through, seeing three bedrooms, a kitchen, and a single bathroom before making his way back to the front door.

"Still clear?" he asked, raising his voice a bit to be heard. On the opposite side of the street he couldn't help but notice a trio of lights had come on in various houses, a direct response to his pounding and yelling just a few moments before.

"Clear," Greene said. "Inside?"

"Nothing," Reed said, lifting his sweatshirt and tucking his weapon into the small of his back. "Come on in."

He paused a moment, watching as both officers holstered their guns and began to walk forward, before disappearing back into the house.

At a second glance, the place was a bit more lived in than he had previously noticed, the sofa bearing a large stain of an indeterminate origin, bits of crayon and puzzle pieces cast to various places on the floor.

While he had never had children of his own, had never been especially close to anybody having young ones, it seemed to fit exactly with what he would anticipate. The place was as clean as could be expected, the house very much meant for comfort and not show.

"Yeah, no way the owner of this house did that," Greene said upon entering, his voice low and even. The soles of his shoes echoed across the floor as he stepped in, Gilchrist bringing up the rear.

"Nope," Reed agreed, casting one more look around the place. "Garage?"

"Mhmm," Greene agreed, falling in beside Reed as they circled through the living room and back into the kitchen.

Aside from the smell of wood just inside the front door, Reed could notice no other scents in the house, not from food having been cooked or disinfectants having been recently used.

"I get the impression nobody's been home for a while," Reed said.

"No way a family with kids that young is still out for the evening," Gilchrist replied.

Reed nodded in agreement, coming to the door in the rear of the kitchen. Using the bank of switches on the wall beside it, he flipped all three up, twin bulbs blazing bright overhead, the third becoming visible through the curtain on the top half of the door.

Reaching into the small of his back, he drew his weapon, hearing both men behind him do the same as he clutched the door handle and paused for just a moment.

In one quick motion he jerked the door open, the hinges moaning slightly in protest. He considered issuing the command for Billie to clear the space again but pulled up short, there being no need.

The garage was one large square, extended out almost 20 feet, measuring half that from front-to-back. A row of wooden shelves and a freezer were lined along the far side and a door stood against the back wall, though otherwise the place was empty.

Casting a glance to the other two, Reed returned the gun to his waistband and stepped into the garage, the brushed concrete smooth underfoot. He gave a quick look over the place before moving toward the door along the back wall, bending and placing his elbows on his knees to get a closer vantage.

"Looks like somebody's jimmied this thing," he said, his voice coming out a bit pained from the awkward position. "Crowbar, large screwdriver maybe."

"We've got some glass over here on the ground, too," Greene said.

Pushing himself to full height, Reed turned to look at him, seeing the senior officer in a crouch in the far corner of garage. After a moment he stood, all exchanging glances.

"Well, this certainly expands things," Reed said, thinking aloud, feeling his stomach somehow grow even tighter than it had been a short time before.

"Two attempted murders and grand theft?" Gilchrist asked, following the line of thinking.

"Maybe more than that," Greene said beside him.

"Yeah," Reed said, "where is the Hendrix family?"

All blood seemed to drain from Gilchrist's face as he looked between Reed and Greene. "No sign of a struggle, no other indication of forced entry."

Reed nodded, his mind already pushing forward. Despite the late hour there were things that needed to be done, regardless who they might wake up or annoy in the process.

"Still, until we find them, we have to consider the possibility," Reed said. Once more he lowered himself to look at the door casing, careful to touch nothing before pushing himself upright and moving a few steps back toward the kitchen.

"I'm going to call this in to the local precinct, tell them we've had a certain B & E and grand theft auto, potentially kidnapping or worse, have them send their crime scene techs out to gather whatever they can. In the meantime, can you guys go hit those houses across the street with the lights on, see if anybody noticed anything, if they happen to know of the Hendrix's whereabouts?"

Greene nodded, saying nothing.

"Where are you off to?" Gilchrist asked.

"I'm going to visit our crime scene guys," Reed said. "I'll be back as soon as I can."

Chapter Eight

Road flares began more than 100 yards from the scene, starting at the edge of the road and angling out across the far right lane. Laid on their side, the flares were interspersed every 10 yards, laid end-to-end in a jigsaw pattern so that the moment one burned out it automatically ignited the next in order.

The flares were already three deep, the remains of the first two nothing more than ashy outlines on the asphalt, as Reed arrived. He ignored the glowing red markers trying to push him out to the side and pulled to a stop off the shoulder of the road, fourth in a line that included two blue-and-white cruisers and a large white paneled van.

The cruisers were self-explanatory. One would belong to McMichaels and Jacobs, there to secure the scene. The other would be a pair of officers set to direct traffic, most likely unneeded for the time being, maybe at all given how light things tended to be in the area on Sunday mornings.

The van belonged to Earl and his crime scene crew, the doors on it standing open, the interior light illuminating stacks of equipment stowed tight in the back.

"Stay," Reed said, climbing out to the sound of Billie emitting a low whine from the back seat. It was the same exact way she reacted every time she was left behind, something Reed made a point of doing as little as possible.

As an officer of the law, she was entitled to go wherever he went.

Still, there were certain realities that didn't always make that practical. Despite her expert training, first with the Marines overseas and now with the department, there was no way to get around the fact that she was a dog. With that came a certain degree of contamination that could occur at a fresh crime scene, especially where blood or bodily fluids were present.

As much as Reed hated the thought, pushed it aside as fast as it entered his mind, he held a deep-rooted certainty that there was about to be plenty of the former present.

The smell of sulfur found Reed's nose as he walked toward the scene, the effects of the flares burning bright nearby. They sent up a hazy red light that shielded all else from view until he was past them, the glare replaced by crime scene lights 50 yards ahead, a few silhouettes moving between them.

With his badge swinging from the chain around his neck, Reed walked with his hands extended by either side, careful to let every person present see he wasn't a threat as he approached.

The first person to spot him and step forward was Officer Tommy Jacobs. On duty when the call came in, he was dressed in his full black uniform, the cooler weather causing him to switch from the short sleeves back into full length. Several inches shorter than Reed, he had an open, fleshy face and a mouth encased by a thin goatee.

"Mattox?"

"Officer," Reed said, sliding his hands into his pockets.

A moment later his partner Wade McMichaels appeared by his side, the same grim expression Reed had seen on every single person for the last six hours on his face. Taller and leaner than Jacobs, his face was clean shaven, his hair buzzed short on the sides.

"You working it or you here to take a look?" McMichaels asked, the tone indicating the question was far less hostile than it might have seemed.

Reed took no offense in the slightest. The events of the evening had everybody on edge.

"Grimes assigned me a couple hours ago at the hospital," Reed said. "We ran the plate they pulled over and went to the house first, then came straight over."

Both men nodded, content with the explanation for the passage of time before his arrival.

"Anything?" Jacobs asked.

"The house had been broken into, nobody was home," Reed said, recalling the events of just a few minutes before. "At the very least the car was stolen..."

"At the most, a kidnapping or worse on top of all this," McMichaels finished, bitterness creeping into his voice.

"Christ," Jacobs muttered beside him, turning at the waist to glance over his shoulder at the criminalists working behind him.

Reed nodded once, in agreement with both, though he said nothing.

"Anything turn up here so far?" Reed asked.

The question pulled Jacobs back to face forward, the partners exchanging a quick glance.

"Lot of blood," McMichaels opened. "*Lot* of blood."

Reed nodded again. Given what Grimes had explained at the hospital, he had expected as much, the very reason he had left Billie in the car. A litany of questions sprang to mind, his subconscious wanting to start fitting things into place, to visualize everything that had happened. In careful order he tamped them down, waiting until he spoke with Earl, got a good look at things for himself.

As much as he trusted the two officers before him, having worked with them more than just about anybody in the precinct given their shared roles on the night shift, he still wanted his own impressions to be clean when he first saw things.

"How's the scene at the hospital?" McMichaels asked.

He didn't bother to ask if Iaconelli or Bishop were going to make it, Reed picking up on the insinuation, knowing neither side wanted or needed to hear the words out loud.

"Bishop is out now," Reed said. "His knee is wrecked, word is he'll need a new one before long."

"Christ," Jacobs muttered again, glancing down at the ground.

"Ike?" McMichaels inquired.

"Still on the table," Reed said. "They had to remove his spleen, get a lot of internal bleeding slowed. The details were pretty thin, but I get the impression he's going to be touch-and-go for a while yet."

Both men fell silent, Jacobs continuing to stare down at the ground, McMichaels raising his face to the sky and pushing a long breath out through his nose. They remained that way for several moments, Reed eventually nodding and stepping past them, patting Jacobs on the arm as he went.

It was the same way he felt, the same way everybody in the precinct felt.

"Hey, Reed," McMichaels said, his voice low, causing Reed to turn back. "I know those two kind of gave you a hard time when you came over, but..."

He let his voice trail off there, the implication clear.

"I know," Reed said. "And it wouldn't matter anyway. These are ours."

McMichaels nodded once as Reed turned back, covering the last 15 yards to the scene.

A quartet of spotlights were set up on all four corners, each aimed inward, casting down a brilliant fluorescent glow over a space almost 20 feet in length. On one end of it Iaconelli and Bishop's sedan was still parked, Reed assuming they had been taken by ambulance to the hospital.

In front of it on the asphalt was a pair of blood stains, McMichaels initial assessment being pretty spot-on. Tucked up along the edge of the road was the first, the patch more than two feet in diameter before disappearing into the grass abutting the pavement.

Six feet away, room enough for the width of an SUV, was a second spot, the edges of it distorted and uneven, as if the source had been moving or tried to crawl away. The thought of it caused Reed to wince slightly as he tried to measure the total length, his best guess being that it was more than five feet in total.

Small pockets had settled into the rumble strips engraved along the edge of the roadway, the surfaces of the pools already congealing, flies and mildew just a few hours away.

Stretched out between the two blood stains were a series of fresh skid marks, the faint scent of scorched rubber still noticeable in the air.

"Damn," Reed whispered, taking it all in, his gaze sweeping over everything in quick order. He ignored the two techs covered in white paper suits as they collected samples and instead focused on the scene itself, trying to visualize how everything had played out.

From what he could tell, it seemed a pretty straightforward incident, much in line with what Grimes had said hours before.

"*Damn* is right," a voice said, drawing Reed's attention up from the scene in front of him.

Sliding his hands from his pockets, Reed extended his right in front of him, taking a few steps to his left to meet Earl Bautista, head of the crime scene unit for the west side of Columbus.

At first glance there was no way anybody would have guessed what the man did for a living, his appearance lending itself more to someone on the other side of the law.

By any feasible definition Earl was a big man, standing a few inches taller than Reed and weighing in somewhere close to twice as much. His tremendous bulk he kept hidden perpetually under a pair of bib overalls, his ensemble for the evening completed by a long-sleeve thermal beneath them. His bald head shined bright under the harsh crime scene lamps, offset by a heavy beard outlining his jaw.

He clamped Reed's hand in his and pumped it twice before releasing, turning to face the scene and running a hand back over his scalp. "Damned awful, I tell you."

"Looks like it," Reed said, shifting to the side as well, their shoulders a few inches apart. Together they stood in silence a moment, each assessing, before Reed asked, "You want to go first or should I start and you correct any mistakes?"

Beside him he could sense Earl glance over, though he made no effort to meet the look.

"Forgive me for being brusque," he added. "Obviously..."

"This gets top billing and a full rush job," Earl finished. "I get it. No worries."

At that Reed glanced over, nodding, letting it be known that his question was not malicious in any way.

"Best we can tell," Earl said, "place plays out just the way it looks. Ike and Bishop pulled over a vehicle right here. Judging by the tire treads and the space between them it was large, most likely a truck or SUV."

"Car registration showed it to be a Chevy Tahoe," Reed interjected.

A small grunt slid out from Earl as he watched his guys work, processing and accepting the information in short order. "That fits, for sure.

"Anyway, after calling it in, both detectives exited their vehicles and the shooting began."

Raising his right hand, he motioned for Reed to follow, drifting over to the left. "We found three shell casings that had rolled into the rumble strips up here, all on the driver's side of the car."

"You thinking single shooter? Or the man in the passenger seat was firing a weapon with a side ejection feed and the brass stayed inside the car?" Reed asked.

Earl opened his mouth to respond before pausing. He considered the question a moment, then raised his eyebrows. "Truth, right now we don't know. If I were to guess I'd say single shooter, but that's pure speculation."

Having worked with him a number of times before, Reed knew that if Earl had a strong supposition, there was probably good reason for it. He also knew it was a reasonable bet that it could be trusted.

"What makes you say that?" Reed asked.

"Logistics of it," Earl said. "You can tell by the blood present, by the injuries sustained. Bishop was hit once, most likely went down, was out of sight from the driver's side. Someone on the passenger side would have just leaned out the window and continued firing."

"Meaning multiple gunshots and at least one shell casing," Reed said, thinking out loud.

"Right," Earl agreed. "Instead, he went down, the driver focused on Ike."

Again the two men considered the twisted amoeba of blood left behind by Iaconelli.

"You think maybe it was personal?" Reed asked. "Maybe they just wanted to subdue Bishop so they could go after their real target?"

Again Earl chewed on the question, his face contorting itself a bit as he rolled it around in his mind. "I mean, yeah, it's possible. I don't buy it, but until we can do some more digging, I just don't know.

"Right now we're still looking at everything here on the asphalt. After that we'll start going through the weeds over there. Hopefully we can find another casing, get the metal detectors out and find an errant bullet buried in the mud, something that will give you a better heading."

A final time Reed nodded, his hands back in the front of his sweatshirt, taking in the horrific scene before him.

"I appreciate it."

Chapter Nine

The call had come in the moment Reed got back to his car. Judging by the tenor of Gilchrist's voice and the way Billie was pacing in the back-seat, he got the impression it was far from the first time such a call had been placed, though neither side pressed the matter.

The message delivered was simple enough – one of the neighbors had been put on notice by the Hendrix family. They were going to be away for the week and asked the couple across the street to collect their mail for them.

For the second time in just over an hour Reed found himself moving quickly down the outer belt toward Grove City. Despite his nerves pulled taut, his every inner thought telling him to surge forward, to move while things were still hot, he opted against running with the siren on. Instead he kept his speed a steady 15 miles above the posted limit, covering the ground between the two sites in just 12 minutes.

Greene and Gilchrist's sedan was still parked on the curb in front of the Hendrix home as he arrived, a panel van similar to the one driven by Earl and his team now pulled up behind it. The front door of the house stood wide open and a bevy of lights could be seen pouring out onto the front lawn, though Reed didn't give them much more than a passing glance.

His attention was focused on the small cluster of folks on the opposite sidewalk, the group staring as he pulled to a stop just a few feet away and hopped out, Billie pressing into his side and spilling onto the street before he had a chance to even contemplate leaving her behind.

Together they circled around to the group, Greene and Gilchrist standing to either side, who Reed presumed to be the couple Gilchrist had alluded to between them. Neither looked to be much older than 30, most likely either newlyweds or well on their way toward it. On the right was a woman with blonde hair hanging to her shoulders, her blue eyes a bit puffy. She wore red and black flannel pajama bottoms and an Ohio State sweatshirt, the cuffs of the sleeves pulled down over her hands.

Standing by her side, an arm around her shoulder, was a man with hair buzzed short and a square jaw, the kind of look that hinted at some sort of military background. Dressed in gym shorts and a fleece pullover, he openly appraised Reed and Billie as they approached.

"Keith, Dawn," Greene said, taking the initiative, "this is Detective Reed Mattox, his K-9 partner Billie. They have the lead on this case."

"Reed, this is Mr. and Mrs. Rollins."

For a moment Reed considered reaching out to shake each of their hands before thinking better of it, reading their stiff body language as a sign that they were anxious for the entire affair to be over.

Given the time of night and the ambient temperature, it was a more than fair stance to take.

"Good evening," Reed said. "I know it is late, so I'll keep this as brief as possible. I understand you are friends with the Hendrix's?"

A muscle quivered in the man's neck, though he remained silent, deferring to his wife beside him.

"That's right," she said, her voice sounding much stronger than her appearance would indicate. "We've lived across the street from each other for about a year and a half."

Reed nodded. "Do you happen to know where they are now?"

"Florida," she replied. "Disney World. Their oldest daughter is on fall break, so they decided to head down for a few days."

Glancing to his right, Reed noticed a notepad clutched in Gilchrist's hand. Strewn across it were several lines of dark blue ink, undoubtedly every word he was now hearing having already been transcribed.

There was no need for him to slow things down by taking notes himself, knowing he could get a full workup of whatever he needed later.

"When was this?" Reed asked.

"They flew out Wednesday evening when school released," she replied, adding just enough of a tinge to her voice to let it be known she had already answered all of these questions, did not particularly appreciate doing it again.

Even still, Reed pushed forward. He had a job to do.

This is what they got for being the nosy neighbors that turned on their lights to see what was happening across the street.

"And when do you expect them back?"

"Tomorrow evening," she replied. "School is back in session on Monday, Jonas and Amy both work."

It was the first time Reed had heard the name Amy, his mind filing it away as the blonde woman he had seen in the photos on the wall inside the house.

"Do you happen to know where they're staying or how to reach them?" he asked.

"Don't know where they're staying," she said, shaking her head, her hair just brushing against the tops of her shoulders, "but we have their cell phone numbers we can give you."

"Good, please do that," Reed said, nodding.

Across from him both people paused for a moment before Keith peeled himself away, heading back toward the house. His body language seemed to indicate he wasn't especially glad to be doing so, though he went anyway.

"Mrs. Rollins, do you happen to know what kind of cars the Hendrix family drives?" Reed asked.

A small vertical line appeared between her brows as she thought a moment, folding her arms across her chest. "Um, they have both have SUV's. Amy's is smaller, a RAV4 or something like that, red. His is bigger, solid black, not sure what kind of make or model."

Reed flicked his gaze to Greene a moment before shifting it back to face forward. "Do you know if they drove to Florida?"

"No," she said, again shaking her head. "I was out in the yard when they left for the airport. I think with only a couple days, it didn't make sense otherwise."

"And they took...?" Reed said, letting his voice fall away.

"Amy's car," she replied. "The RAV4."

Once more he cast a glance to Greene, the officer meeting his look, both already thinking the same thing. Jonas Hendrix's black Tahoe had been left unattended in the garage. Somebody must have known that and entered through the rear door, instantly accessing a vehicle with a clean back story free from fear of anybody reporting it missing for a couple of days.

"Did you happen to notice the other SUV, the black one, since then?" Reed asked. "Anybody coming or going since they left?"

The wrinkle between her eyebrows grew more pronounced as her husband exited the front door and walked toward them, an iPhone gripped in his hand. She thought on the question a moment before turning to him and saying, "I haven't seen any movement since they left. Have you?"

Pressing his lips into a tight line, he thought a moment before shaking his head. "Nothing. But we both work full time, get up early most mornings."

The last line was added with just a bit of emphasis, enough to let Reed know that ending things soon would be appreciated.

"Okay," Reed said, "just one more question. Do you happen to know of anybody else that would have access to the house?"

Again Dawn looked to her husband, her features twisted up in thought.

"I mean, we met a few random family members over the summer at their daughter's birthday party, but if any of them have access, I don't know."

At that Reed nodded and thanked them for their time, collecting the contact information for the Hendrix's and releasing them back to their house.

As they retreated Reed drifted across the street, Greene and Gilchrist flanking him, watching as a pair of shadows continued to move about within the house.

"They say anything else useful before I got here?" Reed asked.

"No," Greene replied. "It took the crime scene crew a while to arrive, we'd only just started talking to them when we called you."

Reed grunted, not knowing how much more could have been gleaned anyway. It was apparent that they knew very little, did not want to be involved any more than was absolutely necessary.

Just getting the contact information from them was about the best that could be hoped for, all things considered.

"Kind of surprising they didn't notice the garage door going up and a car driving away," he said, thinking out loud. "I can't see somebody having the stones to pull that off during the day and they were pretty quick to wake up when we showed tonight."

Both men nodded to either side of him, neither saying a word.

"Any word from in there yet?" Reed asked, thrusting his chin forward a couple of inches, motioning toward the Hendrix's house.

"No," Greene said. "We told them what we had found, insinuated they should start there, but whether they heard us or not I'm not sure."

Jurisdictional pissing matches were not something CPD, or any other law enforcement agency in the country, was immune to. Reed knew these guys would do their job, and do it well, but that didn't mean they had to be happy about someone else showing up and handing them more work.

"Even after you mentioned it was in connection to two cops being shot?"

"They softened a little," Gilchrist said. "Not as much as you'd expect."

Reed's eyebrows rose a tiny bit, though he said nothing. For a moment he contemplated everything that had transpired on the evening, everything that still lay ahead to be done.

"You guys can go on home," he finally said. "I'll sit on this, call you if anything else comes up."

"You sure?" Greene asked.

"We don't mind waiting," Gilchrist added.

47

"Yeah," Reed replied. "There's not much more we can do until morning. First light I'll call the Hendrix's, track down the witness from the scene." He paused a moment, his mind racing to process everything before them.

"Maybe come morning, you guys can come back out here, see if any of the other neighbors saw anything?"

Chapter Ten

A full 24 hours had passed since Reed had been to bed. He'd certainly pulled many, many such stints in his time, some much longer, but very few carried with them the combined weight of the last day. What had started with complete contentment – doing yard work, training with Billie – had evolved into elation during the Oklahoma game. From there it had been a veritable spiral, beginning with the call from Jackie and going through his visits to the Hendrix home and the crime scene.

When Grimes had handed him the case the night before, his initial hope was that things would be simple, or at the very least linear. He could run the plates on the SUV, get an address, go pay them a visit. There he would either find the shooter or something that would give him a direct line on where to find them.

A to B. Linear.

Instead he was just a few hours in and his case resembled something more like a spider's web. The home of the SUV belonged to a family that, based on initial appearances, was the American Dream. Nice house, two small kids, probably had a dog that was staying at a nearby kennel.

Whether or not they were merely a target of opportunity or there was some connection, Reed had no idea. The fact that they had not been abducted was a tremendous relief, but it still did little to explain how their car ended up on the side of the road when it did.

There was also the question of the detectives themselves and whether or not they were being targeted or simply had the misfortune of pulling over the wrong car. If it was a personal connection, Reed could be looking at decades of back files, all of them rife with potential suspects, people that the detectives had put away and would be out for revenge.

There was also the question of the blood spatter at the scene, of the initial thoughts of Earl. The damage inflicted on Iaconelli did seem excessive, though if there were only a single shooter that could have just been circumstantial. If Bishop had been driving, there was no way to know if he would have been on the receiving end of a handful of bullets.

The assorted pieces of data swirled through Reed's head as he pushed in through the back door to his house. He left it open behind him, Billie in the yard doing her business, as he walked across to the kitchen table and unloaded his badge, weapon, and keys in quick order. A heavy sigh crossed his lips as he wrestled his sweatshirt off his shoulders, revealing the same Sooners t-shirt he'd been wearing while yelling at the television 10 hours before.

Ten hours. Seemed like a lot longer than that.

The thought of sinking into the padded chair alongside the table occurred to Reed, though he pushed it aside. He knew if he succumbed to that the odds were good he wouldn't be rising again, lowering his head to the table in front of him, not to move until noon.

Rather than subjecting himself and his neck to that torturous agony, he crossed over to the cabinets beneath the sink and extracted a 25 pound bag of kibble, filling one of a matching pair of stainless steel bowls on the floor. He took up the other one and filled it with cold water from a pitcher in the fridge, placing both on the floor as Billie entered behind him.

Her toenails beat out a steady rhythm on the hardwood floor, the pads of her paws leaving behind wet smudges and bits of grass clippings as she went straight for the bowls. The sound of her lapping water found Reed's ears as he closed the door and stood watching her a moment.

She'd been assigned to him nine months prior, coming on the heels of the death of his partner and best friend Riley. The two had graduated from the same class at the academy together, going with separate senior officers during their training year before being paired up again.

As the sole woman uniform in the precinct, the occasional snicker had been made over the years, both toward Reed and Riley, but neither had ever outwardly reacted to the barbs. Over time the jabs had fallen away as they both ascended quickly, having graduated to detectives in record time.

On New Year's Day Reed had been in Pasadena, a trip instigated by Rose Bowl tickets from Riley for Christmas. When the call came in that Riley had been in an accident he was still half-drunk in a hotel room in California, the results of too much tailgating and celebrating the night before.

His father had been completely passed out on the bed beside him.

The news had been a nuclear bomb, turning everything in his personal and professional life on its head. Overnight he became a hermit in every sense of the word, renting the farmhouse far outside of town, limiting his entire interaction with the world to work, essential stops like the gas station and supermarket, and home. He switched from the 19th Precinct to the 8th, even volunteering to take over the midnight shift to further minimize his contact with anybody.

Six weeks after Riley's funeral he had been given Billie, a former bomb sniffing dog with the Marines in Afghanistan. She too was on the backend of a tragic loss, her handler having stepped on an IED outside Kabul.

The word in her file was that even after he was gone she had covered the remains of his body with her own, waiting until rescue transport arrived to take him home before she would move an inch.

Whether that was true or a romanticized retelling Reed would never know, though it seemed to fit with everything he had seen from her thus far.

The going was still tough, and they both knew it. Never did a day pass when he didn't think of Riley and on occasion he could still see moments of hesitation in Billie that reflected similar thoughts inside of her. For the most part, though, they were both getting by, using each other to heal, to reacquaint themselves with the world.

The fact that Reed felt so compelled to find whoever did this to Iaconelli and Bishop now only served to confirm that.

"Sleep well, girl," Reed said, watching as she continued to shove her nose into the bottom of the bowl, attacking the food with so much vigor it scooted across the floor. "We're back on in three."

Chapter Eleven

The Kid was parked in the fourth row of the parking lot, far enough back that there was no chance of him being noticed. In the busy shopping center he was just one of 100 indiscernible customers, an aggrieved boyfriend or husband, waiting for his lady to finish her business inside and come out.

For his part he played the role to the letter, lowering the driver's side window and propping his elbow up on the sill. He rested his hand along his brow and stared at the grocery store, every so often pushing out a loud sigh, timing them with the passing of anybody that might remotely be within hearing distance.

As he sat and stared at the front entrance to the shopping center, a host of competing emotions fought for top billing inside him.

The frontrunner at the moment was actually surprise, both at how well the events of the previous evening had played out and how easily he had assimilated into the role. Those pieces were far and away the biggest hurdles he'd had to overcome in the lead-up to this undertaking, having convinced himself that his targets were just short of invincible.

Getting their attention, executing his plan, had almost been too easy. It threatened to take away a bit of the enormity from the moment, might even potentially taint the very reason he began in the first place.

Riding shotgun after surprise was elation, for the very same reason. Now that he was well on his way, had proven to himself, and everybody else for that matter, that it could be done, that it wasn't too difficult, his confidence surged.

Despite the fact that the incident was just hours old, already he was seated in the parking lot, ready to kick off the next step. There was no reason to delay, nobody that could stop him even if they wanted to.

Knowing that brought with it a feeling of equal parts euphoria and invincibility. To anybody that were to walk by, the only outward sign of any of the events from the previous evening were his bloodshot eyes, a product of smoke from the torching of the car he'd swiped and a lack of sleep.

Otherwise he was as faceless as all the other schmucks shuffling back and forth from the supermarket in front of him. He was younger than most, in better shape than almost all, but otherwise there was nothing discernible about him.

He was a ghost. A lethal, predatory, ghost.

The thought caused the right corner of his mouth to curl upward as he continued to watch the entrance to the market. It was nestled in the front of his mind, pushing all other notions aside, as the object of his presence stepped outside.

As it did, the smile fell away from his face, his hand lowering itself from his brow. His heart rate increased just slightly, his attention aimed on the figure before him.

Her name was Deidra Weston, though she insisted on being called Didi by anybody that had known her for longer than a minute. Four years above 50 in age, she could have easily passed for a decade younger, the result of a posh lifestyle and spare capital to be spent on cosmetic and surgical enhancement.

Hidden beneath oversized sunglasses and an outsized hairstyle, she pretended to be oblivious to the world around her. She wore a dress and heels despite the cold, her bare legs on display for all to see. In a slow and easy gait she moved away from the store and cut a path toward the front row of the lot, unlocking the rear door of her Audi S3 and depositing the lone small bag in her hand. From there she looked around the lot twice, her head on a swivel, perpetually on the watch for whoever might be nearby.

Only once she was content that nobody of consequence was in the vicinity did she climb into her car.

From his vantage in the fourth row, The Kid watched everything, forcing himself not to smirk at the pompous nature of it all.

It was the fifth such day he had spent following her, the end result of countless hours spent in internet research. On every single occasion before she had conducted herself in much the same manner, the actions at first a cause for concern, worry that she might spot him and think to act on it.

Not until the third day out did The Kid realize not once had she even seen him, his lower-class car and physical attributes being of the kind that never registered in her mind. He could have been parked in the stall beside her and she wouldn't have glanced his way.

Would never glance his way.

The brake lights on the Audi flared as Didi put the car into reverse and backed away, The Kid watching the entire thing. He waited as she eased out of her parking spot and was almost clear of the lot before starting his own ride and pulling forward in her wake.

Things were coming together. They had worked beautifully the first time.

There was no reason to believe the next would be any different.

Chapter Twelve

Reed had told Billie they were back on in three, and he had forced himself to lie in bed for all 180 minutes, though the number he actually slept could be counted using only his fingers and toes. Despite the deep-rooted exhaustion that seemed to grip his body, his mind refused to quit working, trying to piece things together, to make sense of everything.

The simple fact was, though, there were still many holes, too many moving parts, to make it all fit just yet. Until all those things were nailed down there would be no way to form a coherent narrative in his mind. Trying to do so was just an exercise in futility or even worse, an excuse to start creating information that simply wasn't there.

At exactly 10:00 Reed sat up in his bed and rolled his feet to the floor. He took up his cell phone from the nightstand and checked to find there were no new messages, scrolling down a couple of spots in his call history to the dispatch desk and hitting send.

Lou answered on the third ring, his voice just as detached, tinged with a bit of sadness, even fear, as it had been eight hours earlier. "8th Precinct."

"Lou, this is Mattox. Has anything come back on the BOLO for Hendrix's car yet?"

Several moments passed, Reed picturing the aging man's face twisted up on the other side, fighting to discern who was on the phone and what the request had been.

Given the situation, Reed decided to help him along.

"Detective Reed Mattox, requesting any information on the Be-On-The-Lookout that was posted last night for the automobile of Jonas Hendrix."

He slowed his cadence and raised it two octaves, the sound echoing through the house. On cue he could hear Billie roust herself from her bed beneath the kitchen table, working her way down the hallway toward him.

"Oh, yes," Lou said, a flicker of recognition in his voice. "Sorry, Detective, I did not hear you the first time."

Reed waited out the apology, saying nothing.

"And no, there has been no word yet on the BOLO. I will keep you posted."

Holding the phone a few inches away from his face Reed blew out an angry sigh, careful not to curse out loud, not wanting Lou to sense what he was thinking. He held it there as Billie appeared in his doorway, her dark eyes two iridescent discs flashing in the half-darkness of the house.

"How about our guys?" Reed asked. "Any word from the hospital?"

He could hear the rustling of papers on the other end as Lou searched for an answer, probably having been updated that morning and jotting down the information.

The fact that he didn't know by heart, or hadn't been asked about it enough times already to have it memorized, was a bit disconcerting, if not entirely surprising.

Cops were quite superstitious about such occurrences. While they would go to the ends of the earth to track down whoever had done this, that didn't mean they needed the omnipresent reminder of what could happen to them every time they went to work.

"Bishop's awake," Lou replied. "Ike is out of surgery, though they're keeping him in a coma right now."

A moment passed as Reed contemplated the news. He was glad Bishop was awake, though his status had never really been up in the air. He was much more concerned for Iaconelli and the way Lou had mentioned that they were keeping him in a coma, though he didn't feel the need to press it.

The odds were Lou knew little beyond what he had already shared. Asking any further questions would probably only make for an awkward conversation on both sides.

"Okay," Reed said, pushing out a sigh, his mind already working forward to the next thing on his list. "Can you send the information on the witness from the scene last night to my phone?"

"Will do," Lou replied, both sides signing off without another word.

When the call was disconnected Reed tossed the phone onto the bed beside him, raising both hands to his face and rubbing vigorously. Stars appeared behind his eyelids as Billie came closer, resting her chin on his thigh. Dropping both hands to her ears, Reed worked at the thick hair behind them, hearing the dog let out a low groan of approval.

"You about ready to get going?"

Another sound from somewhere deep in her throat rolled out as Reed stood and walked to the kitchen, opening the back door. He filled Billie's bowls and set a pot with three eggs to boiling on the stove before heading back into the recesses of the house. Ten minutes later he emerged showered and changed to find Billie working on her breakfast, his ready and waiting for him on the stove.

Less than 20 minutes after rising they were on the road, headed toward town.

Chapter Thirteen

The man's name was Harold Baldwin, a teacher at Hilliard Darby high school that moonlighted as a Sunday school leader at a nearby church. The first time Reed tried to reach him the call had gone straight to voicemail, a full half hour passing before a response came. When it did the man explained that church rules dictated his phone be off while teaching but that he now had lunch and a planning period back-to-back, giving him just over an hour of availability.

After that, he would be inaccessible until the end of the day at 3:00.

Given that Reed was already almost to the outer belt, he jumped at the opportunity to meet, turning north and finding the school in short order. Less than 10 minutes after hanging up he parked in one of three open visitors stalls out front. There was no thought of leaving Billie behind as he clipped her to the short lead, almost wanting some overbearing hall monitor to comment on her presence.

The badge he left tucked deep in the pocket of his sweatshirt.

There were a number of ways Baldwin would be able to explain a man and a dog visiting with him on church grounds. No such luck existed for trying to calm the gossip mill if he was seen meeting with a police officer in private.

Harold Baldwin was waiting for them the moment they stepped through the front door, the building bringing back a bit of déjà vu for Reed. Despite many years passing since he spent much time in either a school or church, the place had an odd familiarity about it that seemed to remind him of both.

Same brick walls, same narrow metal lockers that made the same sound when being slammed, same droves of children all dressed and acting the same way, each trying to prove they were just as cool as everybody else.

Assorted banners and pictures hung from the walls around the front foyer as Reed stepped right up to the man and asked, "Harold Baldwin?"

"Yes, sir," Baldwin replied, extending his hand. "Detective Mattox?"

"Reed," Reed said, accepting the handshake. He motioned to Billie pressed tight against his knee and said, "My partner, Billie."

Baldwin raised his head in understanding, his mouth parting as he did so, though no sound came out.

Much like the building itself had an odd familiarity, Baldwin did as well. He reminded Reed of a handful of teachers he'd had over the years, his height measuring a few inches below six feet, a paunch starting to protrude over wrinkled khakis. His blonde hair was thinning and combed to the side on top, a trimmed moustache underscoring a bulbous nose.

"Is there someplace you'd like to talk?" Reed asked, his gaze drifting past the man to the flow of students moving by. Many were blatantly gawking as they went past, dismissing him in a moment, their attention focused on Billie by his side.

Bearing the appearance of a wolf in midnight hue tended to have that effect.

"Certainly," Baldwin said, nodding. "We can go to my classroom if you'd like."

"Absolutely," Reed said, falling in behind the man as he led them in the opposite direction of most of the foot traffic. Reed kept a tight grip on the leash as they went, ignoring the stares of people less than half his age, before making a right down the first hallway.

At the third doorway Baldwin pulled up, extending a hand. "Please."

Nodding in thanks, Reed stepped inside, the room bringing back a flood of memories from a lifetime ago. The chalkboards on the walls had been swapped out for dry-erase, but otherwise the place was just as it had been in the 90's. Combination chair and desks still sat in even rows, the floor underfoot still contained the same checkerboard tile pattern.

The only noticeable difference at all was the wooden crucifix hanging on the wall, the hollow eyes of Jesus staring down at them.

The symbolism was not lost on Reed as behind him Baldwin closed the door and stepped over to his desk, an oversized relic piled high with various stacks of paper. He pulled out a matching hardback chair and settled into it, waving a hand at the desks around the room.

"Feel free to have a seat."

The comment tugged the left side of Reed's mouth upward as he glanced back before turning to face forward. "Thanks, but we're good. I'll try to keep this short anyway."

Flicking his gaze to the clock on the opposite wall, Baldwin said, "I have almost 45 minutes. Ask away."

"Down," Reed said, using his command tone. Beside him Billie lowered herself flat to the ground, allowing him to drop the leash.

"Mr. Baldwin," Reed began, "I understand you were the first one to arrive on the scene the other night."

A shadow passed over Baldwin's features, the previous affability falling away, replaced by a look bearing equal parts horror and sadness. He remained silent a moment, his eyes glossing over, before shaking the images from his mind.

"I was," he said simply, barely more than a whisper.

"Can you walk me through it?" Reed asked. "That's probably the best place to start, then I can target any areas of uncertainty I might have."

"Sure," Baldwin said, his face beginning to bear the look of someone that might be sick at any moment. "Can I ask before we start though, are the two men I found okay? Did they...make it?"

For a moment Reed cursed his own foolishness, forgetting that Baldwin had been the first to arrive. There was a decent chance that Iaconelli owed his life to the man, if not Bishop too.

"My apologies," Reed said. "Yes, they are both alive. One of them is awake this morning, I will be heading over to speak to him later this afternoon.

"The other..." Reed paused a moment, contemplating how much to share, before pushing forward. "The other spent most of the night on the operating table, but he's hanging in there."

He left it at that, hoping the man across from him picked up on what was being said without pressing it any further.

"I'm guessing that's...the, uh..." Baldwin said, holding his hands out to either side, making the universal sign for girth.

"Yes," Reed said. "Detective Iaconelli."

"Iaconelli," Baldwin repeated, his voice bordering on reverent. "He was in awful bad shape when I got there. I almost passed out just seeing him."

Reed paused there, remaining silent, waiting for the man to continue. In his experience it was far better than a series of leading questions, allowing a witness to pick up a story wherever they saw best, telling it in the way that matched how they had constructed it in their mind.

"I was on my way home from my nephew's game," Baldwin said. As he spoke he fixed his gaze on the back wall, his voice, his features, taking on a far-off tenor.

"He's a defensive back for Capital, and I was swinging back around the outer belt from Bexley." He flicked his gaze to Reed and said, "I live not too far from where we're sitting."

Reed nodded in understanding, saying nothing.

"Anyway, there was some pretty heavy construction on the south end of town, so I got off the freeway and cut up through Grove City. I grew up down there and know the area pretty well. Figured I could catch 104 straight up into Hilliard, avoid all the work crews and delays."

Again Reed nodded. He had been lucky to avoid most of the construction in his run down to the Hendrix's house the night before, but he knew that things got dicey just south of there.

"I was coming up through the edge of Franklinton, just about to Hilliard, when I saw that a car was pulled over."

He paused there, his eyes squinting slightly. "The automobile that had them pulled over wasn't a traditional squad car with red and blue lights up top, but I could see the front beams flashing, so I slowed down."

"It was a detective car," Reed said. "Unmarked sedan."

"Ah," Baldwin said, raising his chin a few inches. He paused again, collecting his thoughts, before saying, "I was a good ways back when I first noticed it, so I drifted into the other lane, dropped my speed.

"Ahead of me I could see doors on either side of the cop car – I'll just call it that for now – open up. Two men emerged, both of them outlined by my headlights."

Again he took a moment, casting his gaze over to Reed.

"To be honest, I didn't think a whole lot of it at the time. Maybe a little bit of excitement they had gotten somebody that wasn't me, but not much more than that."

A look approaching guilt passed over his features as he forced a smile and said, "You know how it is."

His mind deep in the story Baldwin was telling, Reed had to force himself back to the present. He tried in vain to plaster a half-smile on his face, the look resembling something closer to pained.

He did know the exact thing Baldwin was talking about, had seen it 1,000 times before, had even felt it himself back before joining law enforcement.

"Anyway, I was going along, listening to scores on the radio, when I saw several flashes of light," Baldwin said, the same sick look crossing his face. He opened his mouth to continue but no sounds came out, his face fast becoming pasty, sweat creasing his brow.

"Gunshots," Reed whispered, putting himself in Baldwin's position, trying to imagine coming up on the scene.

Baldwin nodded and said, "At first I had no idea what they were. Five or six in a row, they came out pretty quick – bam bam bam bam bam."

Each time he said the word he smacked his right hand into the palm of his left, the sound echoing through the room, causing Billie's ears to perk on the floor beside Reed.

"I hit the brakes hard," Baldwin said, "screeching to a halt, not sure what the heck was happening. By the time I got to a stop the car was peeling out of there, the tires making a God-awful sound, pushing a puff of smoke up before taking off."

Any bit of color the man's face had held just minutes before was gone. His pallor was chalky as he reached up and tugged on the collar of his shirt, the garment twisting a bit to the side.

"Must have sat there a full minute before I realized that the two silhouettes I'd seen earlier weren't there anymore. Wasn't until then that my mind starting piecing things together, caused me to start moving again."

Reed could tell there was no small amount of guilt in the man's tone, though there was no reason for it. He had seen police officers, people trained for such situations, react in much worse ways. This was a man that had just been taking a shortcut home on a Saturday night.

To stumble across something as horrific as the scene he'd been to the night before would shake anybody.

"I called 911 before I got there," Baldwin said. "I don't know, but I just kind of knew something was wrong. After that I rolled up even with the cop car and parked, got out."

His eyes slid shut on the last two words, Reed envisioning the man climbing out, seeing the carnage that was sprawled on the street, the smoke burning his eyes, the scent of charred tires in the air.

An all-out sensory assault if there ever was one.

"Blood," he whispered. "So much blood."

His eyes opened a fraction of an inch as he raised his hands before him, staring down at them. "I had some old towels and blankets in the back of my car. I tried to stem what I could until the ambulance got there."

He raised his focus to Reed, his fingers still outstretched in front of him. "But there was so much. It seemed to be coming from everywhere."

Reed met his gaze a long moment. "You did well, Mr. Baldwin. You probably saved his life. Everybody in the precinct, all of us, are very grateful to you for what you did."

Baldwin nodded as if he heard the comment, though it did nothing to change the expression on his face. Slowly he lowered his hands back to his lap, saying nothing.

"I don't suppose you were able to get a look at anybody when you pulled up?" Reed asked. Already he had the make, model, and license plate on the car. He knew that was essentially a dead end.

The likelihood of him having seen anybody, especially from that distance at that time of night, was almost non-existent, but he still had to ask.

"No," Baldwin said. "It was dark and I was a good ways back. If not for those flashes from the gun, I wouldn't have even looked over."

Reed nodded, again placing himself in Baldwin's position, trying to imagine what he might encounter upon approach.

"You said *gun*, singular," Reed said. "You only saw the one?"

Raising a hand to his chin, Baldwin pinched his face in thought for a moment before nodding. "Yes. Like I mentioned, I was in the left lane, coming up on the outside. There might have been another on the opposite side, I just couldn't see it."

He paused again, the same look in place, as he continued chewing on it. "I mean, I guess there must have been, both detectives getting hit like that, but I didn't see anything."

The answer seemed to track with the initial assessment of Earl the night before. This was most likely a single shooter, firing through open windows. The fact that Bishop had gotten off with only a single shot, that no brass was found on the passenger side, seemed to confirm as much.

Raising his gaze up to the clock on the wall, Reed noticed that Baldwin's recount of the story had taken most of their allotted time. Down to just his last few minutes, he scrolled through everything again in his mind, careful to cover every last crack before releasing the man from the uncomfortable conversation.

"Mr. Baldwin, when you arrived, were either of the detectives conscious? Did they say anything?"

"The taller one was," Baldwin said, extending a finger toward Reed. "Twice he told me to help...well, I thought he was saying *Mike*."

"Ike," Reed said. "We call Detective Iaconelli Ike around the precinct."

"Right, makes sense," Baldwin said. "He was weak, fading fast.

After he saw me start pressing towels on his partner I thought he said one last thing, but I can't be certain."

"What was that?" Reed asked, feeling a slight tremor in the pit of his stomach.

"Back?" Baldwin asked, phrasing it very much like a question. "I know it doesn't make sense, but I'd swear that's what he said."

Chapter Fourteen

The man on the opposite end of the line sounded frightened, just short of petrified. His voice was lowered and his words clipped, as if he was standing just out of earshot from someone, a hand cupped over the receiver on his phone.

"I'm sorry, you say our house was broken into?" Jonas Hendrix asked.

In the background Reed could hear commotion – children laughing, water splashing, people in conversation. The combined effects of the noises made him think the Hendrix family was posted up beside a pool somewhere, milking the last few hours of Florida sunshine before heading home later that night.

"Yes," Reed said, "and I am very sorry to be breaking this news to you over the phone."

"No," Hendrix replied, the word terse. "I appreciate you making the call. I apologize for missing your message earlier this morning."

The man had in fact missed two messages that morning, Reed making a point of calling right after leaving his house and again upon exiting the church. It wasn't until now, as he worked his way back toward Mercy West, that the man had gotten back to him, a full two hours after the initial request to speak.

Despite all that, Reed opted to let it go. What had happened already would have the man's hackles raised. The events that had occurred at his house in the preceding day, from the theft of his car to a crime scene unit scrubbing it down, were bound to push his ire even further.

There was no need to add to it by giving a lecture on the amount of time needed to respond to a message.

He was, after all, on vacation.

"Not at all," Reed said. "I just wanted to contact you as soon as possible and let you know everything that has happened."

He paused, debating how to most delicately state what he was thinking, before adding, "And to let you make arrangements before your arrival back in Ohio."

The ambient noise over the line disappeared. In their stead was only the sound of flip-flops slapping against bare skin, Hendrix most likely relocating somewhere to be alone before saying another word.

Reed waited in complete silence as he did so, counting off almost 30 seconds before the man came back on the line.

"Okay," Hendrix said. His voice was pinched, as if trying to put on a tough exterior, though Reed could tell there was just a hint of cracking present around the edges.

It was far from the first time he had encountered the reaction, stock responses from witnesses and victims both when speaking to the police.

"Start at the beginning."

Outside, the early-afternoon traffic was thin. It being Sunday, a great deal of the flow was home in the suburbs, watching football or having barbecues. They were far from the congested industrial portions of the city, allowing the streets to be clear as Reed headed toward the hospital.

As much as he appreciated the easy path, he would have given anything to be home with Billie doing either of those things, or a dozen other, for the afternoon.

Just the same, given what had happened to Iaconelli and Bishop, there was nothing else in the world he would be doing until this was figured out.

"Last night your car was pulled over near Franklinton by a pair of detectives from the 8th Precinct," Reed said. "The infractions were a busted taillight and erratic driving."

"My...wha..." Hendrix sputtered. "But that's impossible."

"We know that, sir," Reed said, careful to keep his voice just a degree or two away from placating. "We spoke to Mr. and Mrs. Rollins and were told that your family is in Florida until tonight. They were also the ones to provide me with your cell phone number."

He added the last sentence as a throw-in, the kind of thing nobody ever thought to ask in the moment, but would certainly wonder about later.

A moment passed as Hendrix blew out a breath. "So if you talked to the Rollins's..."

"Yes, we've been to your house," Reed said. "Or rather, *in* your house. Given the information we had at the time, we had probable cause to enter, believing you to be the driver of that car."

"You went in my house?" Hendrix asked, his voice beginning a slight transition, moving past abject shock, a bit of incredulity creeping in. "Over some moving violations?"

"No," Reed said. "We went in because your license plate was called in by two detectives that were then shot before your Chevy Tahoe fled the scene."

He knew the statement was a bit off-sides, the kind of thing meant as much for shock value as to deliver a message, but he needed to stem any growing animosity before it threatened to take over the conversation.

"Again, at this point we have cleared you of any suspicion. Earlier today I spoke to your hotel and confirmed you have been on site for three days now and that a shuttle is already arranged to take you and your family back to the airline.

"Ten hours ago we knew none of that though, so we entered."

For a moment Reed considered apologizing before deciding against it. Despite it being an ingrained human response, doing so was something Riley had always cautioned him against, stating that it gave the victims the impression that he had done something wrong.

The offense, she reasoned, was on the perpetrators. Any blame should be directed their way, not at the officers investigating it.

When Hendrix didn't respond Reed pushed forward, adding, "We entered your garage and found signs of forced entry, confirmed that your car had been stolen. Unfortunately, none of your neighbors saw anything, though we are still canvassing the neighborhood."

"Oh my God," Hendrix whispered, the life having seemingly bled from his voice. "Oh, my God."

"Yes," Reed agreed. "And again, I do apologize for delivering the news like this. Obviously, a crime scene unit was brought in to search for fingerprints and forensics."

He paused just slightly, hoping the lifelessness he heard on the other end of the line would be enough to bypass getting berated. "Which means we can't release the scene just yet. Is there somewhere your family can go for a day or two, just until we make sure the place is scrubbed clean?"

A sharp inhalation found its way to Reed's ear, so loud it brought an image of a man standing in stunned silence on the other end, the color draining from his face.

"Somewhere to go? You mean..."

"A hotel, a family member, anything," Reed said. "We don't believe you are in danger in any way, more a target of opportunity than anything."

"But...but..." Hendrix sputtered. "How would they even know?"

Reed had asked himself the same question many times.

"We're not sure yet, Mr. Hendrix. These days, could be any number of ways, social media being the most common."

"Oh, my God," Hendrix repeated, the voice just barely audible.

Sensing that he was losing him, Reed moved on with his last request, wanting to get to it before the man slipped into catatonia.

"Also, if possible, I would like to speak with you once you land here in Ohio tonight. I will meet you wherever you'd like so you can shield your daughters as much as possible from all this."

Chapter Fifteen

Bishop had been moved to the critical care unit. It was determined moments after his surgery that his life was not in danger, the need not existing for intensive care. Instead he was positioned in a separate wing, high on the 8th floor, the place just as well staffed but lacking in the manic energy that seemed to resonate in other places throughout the hospital, areas where life and death still hung in the balance.

Places like where Iaconelli was currently housed.

Exiting the elevator, Reed pocketed his badge. He didn't want Bishop's wife or daughter to see it, to make things any worse for them than it already was. There was no way he could hide Billie from them, the oversized animal obvious as a police dog on sight, if not for her look then for the fact that she was being allowed to roam the halls of the hospital.

Still, in his limited experience with such matters, every little bit helped.

Stepping forward to a waist high desk, he rested his palms atop it and waiting for a middle-aged nurse in pink scrub pants and a multi-colored top to finish a call. When she was done she glanced up at him, a look of resignation already on her features.

"Room 818," she said, the undercurrent of a sigh in her voice.

For a moment Reed opened his mouth, wanting to make sure he was pointed in the right direction, before thinking better of it and nodding his thanks.

The nurse returned the nod and extended a single finger out to her left, Reed tapping the desk with his knuckles twice before setting off in that direction.

Given her response, and the turnout that had been in the lobby the night before, it was a safe assumption that he was far from the first officer she had seen on the day.

Keeping the looped handle of the short lead gripped tight in his hand, Reed led Billie down the hallway, her toenails and his running shoes making for a unique two-part concerto. Side by side they made their way forward, a pair of uniforms coming into view up ahead. Without even bothering to check for room numbers Reed walked straight toward them, feeling his pulse pick up just slightly.

Reed's initial appraisal of Bishop had been that he was Iaconelli's flunky and little more. He laughed at every bad joke his partner made, did his best to insert his own whenever possible. At times the bravado seemed forced at best, the kind of thing brought on by someone trying way too hard for acceptance.

Over time that assessment had diminished somewhat, Reed finally resigning himself to the fact that the men meant well, in their own misguided way. A few cases had caused their paths to cross in significant ways, and like most professionals, any petty personal strife had fallen by the wayside.

In recent months something approaching a begrudging respect had begun to surface between the two sides, a fact aided considerably by the fast-approaching day when the older duo would be hanging up their badges.

"Officers," Reed said as he approached, nodding to a pair of fresh-faced uniforms that couldn't have been more than a month out of the academy.

Both turned and openly stared at him for a long moment, taking in his attire and Billie by his side, before the young man on the left said, "Detective."

His face was void of any stubble, his blonde hair buzzed close to the scalp. Glancing past him into the darkened room, Reed asked, "Is Detective Bishop awake?"

A moment passed as the officer again gave Reed a once over before saying, "He was just a little bit ago. Your captain came by to see him."

On the opposite side of the door the second young man leaned forward and said, "Been a pretty steady stream all day. I'm sure he appreciates your support, but you guys might want to set up some kind of visiting hours so he can get his rest."

Fire flashed behind Reed's eyes as he glared at the young man, his dark hair shaved tight on the sides and left long on top, slicked straight back in the newest hipster style. "I'm not just here to show support, and trust me, he won't be getting much sleep until I catch the asshole that did this."

In unison the jaws of both men fell slack, a flush of blood coloring the second guard's cheeks. Reed made no effort to hide the disdain on his face as he stepped between them, Billie on his hip, and closed the door behind him.

Without the ambient light from the hallway, the room was almost completely dark. The only sources of illumination were a pair of computer monitors, one tracking heart rate, the other vital statistics. Together the screens cast a pale glow over the room, bathing Bishop in a chalky light.

Even on his best day the man had a complexion that trended toward albino, his excessive height and lack of body weight giving him the appearance of a skeleton. His pale skin and close-cropped hair tended to accentuate the look.

Lying in the hospital bed, every one of those attributes seemed to be emphasized, save the normally gaunt face. In its place was a puffy ball, the result of bags of saline fluids being pumped into his system, causing his deep-set eyes to appear almost cavernous.

"Well played," Bishop said, his voice low. It was so unexpected Reed flinched a tiny bit at the sound of it, Billie clenching, her striated muscle pressed against his leg.

He paused a moment before answering, feeling foolish as his heart rate slowed, before asking, "They been like that all day?"

"All day," Bishop replied. "My family got sick of them two hours ago and decided to head home for food and a nap. I thought the captain was going to shoot them."

Despite the gravitas of the moment, Reed couldn't help but smile, easily able to picture Grimes doing just that.

"How you feeling?" he asked, stepping forward, the light from the monitors rising up his chest, stopping just short of his chin.

On the bed before him Bishop was laid completely flat, a thin white blanket covering his right leg and upper body. Extended out from beneath the side of it was his left leg, the entire appendage encased in a heavy air cast.

"Not feeling a damn thing," Bishop said, rolling his head over to glance at Reed a moment before returning his focus to the ceiling above. "They have me on a time-release morphine drip, so about every 90 minutes or so a new jolt floods the system, knocks me out for a while. Then I wake up, lie here a bit, talk to whoever might stop by, do it all over again."

Reed nodded, unsure how to respond. He had been fortunate enough never to have been in a major accident before, nothing requiring a hospital stay since he had his wisdom teeth extracted as a teenager.

"Any update on the knee?"

"What knee?" Bishop responded, the combination of morphine and exhaustion pushing aside any bit of inhibition, his true feelings on the matter ebbing into his voice. "Damn thing is basically a mash of spare parts right now, they just have to wait a while before they can put in a new one."

Reed felt his features draw up into a wince, though he remained silent. Given the man's unique dimensions and his advancing years, such a procedure would be tough, most likely the first of many just like it.

The force would give him an early retirement, would take care of all related expenses, but it was still a far cry from how anybody would want to kick off their post-work life.

"Any word on Ike?" Bishop asked.

"Came up here first," Reed said. "Wanted to see if you were awake, talk to you about what happened last night."

Again Bishop rolled his head to the side to look at Reed, his face impossible to gauge. The two men held the pose several moments before Bishop nodded, his chin dipping just a fraction of an inch.

"You know, I was glad when the captain said he'd assigned you to this. Some of the cases you've handled since coming over were...impressive."

Heat flushed Reed's face and back, drawing a sheen of sweat to both. For a moment he remained silent, unsure how to respond, before pressing his lips together and nodding slightly.

"I will find who did this. I promise you both that."

To that, Bishop said nothing, staring at Reed. He held the pose a long time, long enough that Reed wondering if fresh morphine was being pumped into his system, before saying, "I know Ike and I, we gave you a hard time when you first came over. You need to know, we didn't mean anything by it."

More than once Reed had suspected it wasn't quite that innocent, though he was far past caring, especially given the circumstances.

"I know," Reed said, "and even if it was, this is different. We would be throwing ourselves at this anyway."

Bishop swallowed hard, a lump traveling the length of his throat. "I mean, I know what some of the people think about Ike, but he's been my partner for 19 years, you know?"

Without realizing it, without knowing why, Reed reached forward and grabbed Bishop's hand. He squeezed it twice and said, "I do know, Martin. More than you or anybody else will ever realize."

There was no effort by Bishop to return the gesture, though he made no attempt to pull away either. Instead he continued to stare at Reed, moisture pooling at the bottom of his eyes.

"What was it like to lose a partner?" he whispered.

For an instant Reed thought he too might tear up. He raised his face toward the ceiling and took a deep breath, extending his right hand down and finding the thick hair atop Billie's head. "Hell. It was nothing short of Hell."

Bishop drew in a breath through his nose, snorting a bit of phlegm in, the sound loud in the enclosed room. "That's what I thought. That's why it had to be you, it *has* to be you, on this."

Taking one more pull of air, Reed pictured Riley. He envisioned the last time he'd seen her, dropping him off at the airport, wishing him a good trip to California.

He thought of her gravestone that he and Billie still visited frequently.

"I will find him," Reed whispered. "But first, I need to know every single thing you can remember from last night."

Chapter Sixteen

"Dispatch to Unit 225, over."

Reed could just make out the sound of his radio squawking through the locked doors of his car, fumbling fast for his keys. As he did so they slipped through his grip, landing in a misshapen heap on the ground, the clatter of a half-dozen metal implements hitting concrete finding his ears.

Beside him Billie stood with an impassive look on her face, the tiniest bit of animal judgment aimed in his direction.

"Dispatch to 225, over."

The voice definitely belonged to Jackie, having come in early to relieve Lou after a very long shift. An obvious edge was apparent as Reed grasped the proper key and jammed it into the lock on the door, going headfirst across the seat without letting Billie into the back first.

"Reed, you there?"

This time the words came out sharp and harsh, an obvious response to everything that had happened in the last day.

"Go ahead, Jackie," Reed said, resting a knee on the front seat and holding the mic to his face.

The sound of his voice seemed to surprise her, a moment passing before she spoke again, her tone having retreated back to normal. "Everything alright over there?"

"Yeah," Reed replied, his own annoyance starting to rise. For his first three months with the 8th Jackie had appointed herself as his unwanted guardian, checking on him at all hours while he worked the graveyard shift. At the time he knew it was in response to what had happened to Riley, though he still didn't appreciate the insinuation that there was something wrong with him.

In the time since she had backed off a bit, though she still let it be known that she was the overseer of the precinct.

Moments like these Reed found himself wanting to point out he had a mother - a damn fine one at that - though each time he managed to bite it back before saying something he would inevitably regret.

"We were speaking to a witness. What's going on?"

He intentionally left out the part about which witness he was speaking to, not wanting to have to give a full rundown of his investigation at the moment. He himself was still processing what Bishop had shared, not yet up for articulating everything.

"We just got a call from the Madison County Sheriff's Office. They found Jonas Hendrix's car."

A jolt of adrenaline passed through Reed's chest as he squeezed the lever on the side of the mic and said, "Tell them I'm on my way and send the address to my GPS if you would."

"You've got it."

Reed lowered the mic, about to hang it back on the stand, then snatched it back up. "Jackie?"

"Yes, Sugar?"

"When you talk to them, can you ask if they would mind our crime scene guys taking a look at it? Earl was on-site, already has a familiarity with everything."

Even as he said the back half of the statement, he knew it sounded like bunk. The truth was, Earl and his crew was the best in the city, a fact widely known and accepted. On the flip side was a rural county office with limited manpower, the very definition of understaffed and overworked.

This was too important to let something that might be a crucial detail fall through the cracks.

"Will do," Jackie said. "Should I get Earl up and ready on standby?"

Reed mulled it a moment, the right side of his face squinted up as he considered the question.

"How far to the site?"

"Looks to be about..." Jackie said, her voice trailing off as she went to check her numbers. "Eighteen miles."

"Tell him to go on out," Reed said. "I'll clear it again with whoever's there and call him in the first chance I get."

Chapter Seventeen

The differences between Reed and his partner were many. The most pronounced of those, something he had encountered a dozen times in their work together and was only still beginning to fully appreciate and utilize, was her extreme sense of smell. Armed with more than 220,000,000 scent receptors, her ability to detect aromas was more than 45 times more attuned than his own.

Even at that, his nose did just fine picking up the distinct smell of smoke and lighter fluid in the air.

The directions of the GPS unit on his dash had deposited him on the bank of Big Darby Creek, the location little more than a turnout from a country road. Six miles from the closest throughway of any size, Reed had spent the back half of the drive thinking that the sheriff or Jackie or both had gotten the location wrong, not believing he was on the right path until a pair of Madison County cruisers came into view, parked nose-to-tail on a gravel drive extended away from the road.

In front of them stood two men, both wearing brown pants and shirts, tan hats balanced on their heads. They each turned and stared as Reed eased his sedan to a stop in line behind them, looping his badge over his head before stepping out.

"I'll just be a minute, girl," he said as he exited, immediately picking up on the odor in the air. Unlike barbecue, it was distinctly free of any appetizing properties, carrying a twinge of something chemical with it.

Stepping forward past the cruiser, Reed could see the drive open up into a gravel lot leading down to the riverbank. Parked in the center of it was Jonas Hendrix's Chevy Tahoe, or rather the remains thereof.

Resting more than 50 feet from the closest foliage, the automobile had been burned to nothing more than a shell, a circle of black soot staining the pale gravel in a wide arc around it.

"Great," Reed muttered, wondering why nobody had mentioned that the thing had been charred beyond use, but remaining silent as he stepped forward.

"Detective Mattox?" the man on the right asked, a tall, rawboned man in his late 40s. In total he couldn't have weighed more than 150 pounds, parts of his hollow cheeks hidden beneath a heavy moustache.

"That's right," Reed said, extending his hand. "Sheriff..."

"Monterey," the man replied. "I have a first name too, but everybody just calls me Monty."

"Alright, Monty," Reed replied, "and I'm just Reed."

He released the grip and moved to the man beside him, someone several years younger than Reed. He was a bit thicker than his counterpart and was free of any facial hair, but the resemblance was uncanny.

If forced to guess Reed would peg him as a son, though wouldn't rule out a nephew.

"Howie," the young man said, pumping Reed's hand once before releasing it.

"Appreciate you guys calling me in," Reed said. "We've had every officer in the state looking for this car for 16 hours now."

Motioning toward the wreckage, Monty led the trio a few steps closer, a faint bit of heat still emanating from it. "Sorry there isn't more to see. About the only thing we got of any value from it was the license plate number."

Glancing at the mess before him, Reed nodded with the assessment. For a moment he wondered why the shooter had left the plate before dismissing it, reasoning he had kept it on for the same reason he had stolen the car.

He had known it was clean and that it would go nowhere.

"Anything inside?" Reed asked.

"Not that we could see," Monty replied. "Howie made one trip up and peeked in, walked back out the same way. We didn't want to track things up any more than that."

Given that the ground was gravel, it would be impossible to pull a footprint, though Reed nodded anyway.

Better to have them slow play things than risk corrupting a scene.

"How'd you guys find this thing, way out here?" Reed asked.

"We didn't," Howie replied, his voice bearing the candor of a young man not long on the job. "Couple fishermen came down looking to put in and spotted it."

"They just left a few minutes ago," Monty added. "We have their information if you want it, but it sounds like they didn't know a thing beyond being a little pissed their fishing trip got ruined."

In another time Reed would have laughed out loud at the comment, though at the moment it barely registered with him. Instead he forced himself to bite back the bile that was threatening to crawl up the back of his throat about the situation that he was facing.

Thus far every potential lead had turned out to be nothing. The Hendrix family was out of the state, the car was torched and dumped. The shell casings at the scene were generic .9mm and Bishop couldn't really remember anything after the shooting started.

If something didn't break soon he was going to be looking at a blank slate, unsure where to go next. The thought caused his stomach to tighten, intensifying the acidic liquid traveling in the wrong direction through his chest.

"I asked my crime scene crew to be on standby," Reed said, jumping ahead, his mind already piecing together what he needed from the scene stretched out in front of him. "You guys want this one or you mind if I have them take a look?"

The men exchanged a quick glance, the younger man deferring to the older.

"Figured you might," Monty said. "Tell them to come on in. One of our deputies usually does that sort of thing for us, if he can. After that we have to call on your crews from the city.

"Probably end up being the same guys down here either way."

Reed nodded, glad for one less hurdle to clear for the time being. At that he moved forward a few more steps, careful to stay clear of the dark outline on the ground. He raised himself up onto his toes and peered into the remains of the car, not especially hopeful for what he might find.

All that remained of the SUV was the rough outline of the frame, most of the interior having burned away. What was left behind had melted into a twisted mess of rubber and vinyl, the entire thing looking like a black candle that been left to burn overnight.

"I might have my partner take a quick run around the place too, see if she can pick up anything," Reed said as he stared into the gaping maw of the car frame another moment.

Content that there was nothing more for him to see, he lowered himself back to flat feet, turning to see the men staring back at him.

"Your partner?" Monty asked, confusion clear on his face.

Chapter Eighteen

The sun was long since below the horizon, the outside temperature dropping more than a dozen degrees with it. As the calendar inched steadily closer to Halloween, long gone was the oppressively hot summer that had enveloped the region, ceding to what promised to be another brutal winter. Just into the second week of October, already the overnight lows were touching 40 with no reason to believe it would get better for a long, long time.

Reed did his best to ignore the chill as he leaned against the side of his sedan, the cool metal of the exterior pressing against the back of his sweatshirt and jeans. In his hand he held the last part of a pulled pork sandwich, the wrapper still encasing the bottom of it, protecting his hands from the thick barbecue sauce threatening to pour out at any moment.

As hungry as he was, showing up to interview a witness with dinner all over his hands was still bad form.

At his feet were the two smaller plastic bowls Reed kept in the car for days such as these, emergency provisions for times when the job kept them out far beyond the traditional eight hour shift. The one on the left had been picked clean of every last morsel of kibble, the one on the right with just a half-inch of water remaining in the bottom.

Many times over the years Riley had chastised him for not taking better care of himself on the job, his tendency to become overly focused often pushing aside even the most basic of necessities, such as fuel or sleep. Over the years it had turned into a bit of an inside joke between the two of them, the kind of thing that only friends seasoned by time and experience can talk about.

Now that she was gone and in her stead was Billie, it was something he had taken much more interest in. For as capable as his new partner was, there were certain things she still required from him.

Taking the time to make sure she was well-fed and able to relieve herself was one of them.

The last of the sandwich went down as Reed wadded the paper into a ball in his hands, turning and placing it atop the hood beside him. Still chewing, he bent at the waist and tossed away the unwanted portion of Billie's water, the bottom mostly just drool and slobber. Using a napkin, he wiped it clean and stowed the bowl away before pursing his lips and whistling a two-note call into the night.

On cue Billie emerged before him, beginning only as a pair of glistening eyes before becoming a silhouette and finally a full body.

"Good girl," Reed said, rubbing the fur behind her ears before attaching the short lead to her collar and grabbing up the garbage from the top of the car.

Circling around the back of it, he led them forward to their last stop of the night.

The Holiday Inn was located on the southern edge of Grove City, a couple miles off the interstate, on the far outskirts of town. Nearby the glow of restaurants and chain hotels could be seen, though unlike most areas of town there was open space visible between them, the signs of urban sprawl just beginning to take hold.

Jonas Hendrix had called less than an hour before and said his family had arrived and was settled for the evening. There was absolutely zero enthusiasm as he did so, Reed able to tell in an instant that the man would rather do nearly anything else in the world.

For as much as he would like to give the guy a break for the night, he also pictured Bishop lying back in his hospital bed, remembered the words he had said when he spoke about his injured partner.

Recalled the way he had felt when he first heard about Riley.

He would be as non-intrusive as he could be, but the fact remained that Hendrix had information that he needed. Even if he didn't, that could tell Reed a lot too, his only hope being that by the time they headed home for the night, a new direction had revealed itself.

The front door to the hotel operated on a sensor, sliding silently to the side as Reed and Billie passed through. Inside the temperature was almost 20 degrees warmer, bringing a rush of heat to Reed's cheeks as he stepped into a subdued lobby.

Built to match every single other like-kind establishment in the country, the tile underfoot was square and white, the walls painted taupe. Generic artwork hung at even intervals, the recognizable green logo of the chain splashed across anything that would hold it.

On the right was a counter extended more than 10 feet in length, behind it a young man in a vest sporting a mop of curly hair. He glanced at Reed and then Billie, a look of alarm passing over his features as he opened his mouth to object to an animal being inside.

Already knowing where things were headed, Reed reached into his sweatshirt and extracted his badge, letting it bounce against his chest. "Detective Reed Mattox, my partner Billie, CPD."

Just as fast as it had arrived, the look receded from the young man's face, a bit of curiosity flooding in. "We're here to meet with Jonas Hendrix."

The young man kept his attention on Billie as he nodded once and said, "Right. He's in the conference room down the hall. Can't miss it."

"Thanks," Reed said, pushing past the desk without once stopping. At the edge of the front lobby the flooring switched from tile to carpet, the thin material surprisingly soft, absorbing all sound as they made their way to the end of the hall.

It was the first time Reed had ever been to the place, the first hotel he had stepped into since Pasadena 10 months before, but the layout was simple enough. On his right a space for continental breakfast, a restroom, and a small fitness center passed by, each standing dark and silent, the only light coming from a single door at the end of the hall.

Knocking once on the frame of it, Reed paused just momentarily at the threshold, peering inside.

The space was of medium size, more than a dozen feet in either direction. A trio of white wooden tables was arranged in a horseshoe pattern, chairs pushed up tight against them, a projector screen on the opposite wall, everything positioned for easy viewing.

Standing in the center of the arrangement was Jonas Hendrix. Based on the photos at his home Reed had estimated him to be somewhere around 40, though at the moment he appeared to have aged more than a decade. Large bags hung beneath his eyes and deep trenches were pushed back through his thinning hair, no doubt the result of having run his hands through it one time after another since they last spoke.

Several inches shorter than Reed, he wore wrinkled khaki shorts and a pullover with the sleeves pushed up, sweat visible on his skin.

The sound of the knock pulled his attention over to Reed, his mouth dropping open.

"Detective Mattox?"

"Reed." He motioned to his side and said, "My partner, Billie."

A look falling somewhere between surprised and uncertain passed over his face as he nodded, saying nothing.

"Thank you for meeting with me," Reed said, entering the room. He released his grip on the leash, dropping it to the floor, and said, "Down."

Beside him Billie acted in concert, her head remaining upright, her ears pointed straight up above her.

Stopping just short of the edge of the closest table, Reed pushed his hands into his pockets. "I spoke to the crime scene folks earlier this afternoon. They said they want to make one more quick pass through in the morning, then they will have the place cleaned and put back to normal."

Hendrix appeared as if he barely registered anything Reed was saying, his face blank.

Just like with the Rollins's earlier, Hendrix was fitting directly into one of the more standard responses. Some became angry, some went into denial. This man appeared to be in shock, a state that could last anywhere from a matter of hours to weeks or more.

Given that he was the sole male in a house featuring two young daughters, Reed feared Hendrix might linger much closer to the latter, though he didn't comment on it.

"We appreciate you being so cooperative about this," Reed said, hoping to pull the man forward just enough to interact with him.

The words hung between them for a moment before Hendrix raised both hands to his face. He rubbed his palms over his cheeks before pushing them back through his scalp, his face bearing a red hue from the movement.

"*Cooperative*," he whispered. "As if we had a choice."

Reed remained silent a moment, allowing the man to have the floor, as much to see if we would mention anything useful without being prompted or if we has simply rehashing things in his mind.

"Longest damn flight of my life," he said, beginning to pace. He made it no more than a few steps before having to turn, covering the ground in long strides before reversing course and heading back again.

Watching him go, Reed decided to hold off on mention of the car just yet. He had just a few questions he needed to get to first. Seeing how the man was reacting, it was clear he was already teetering on the brink of sanity, a perfectly acceptable response, but not one Reed could do a great deal with at the moment.

"Mr. Hendrix, like I mentioned earlier, we do not believe you or your family had anything to do with this," Reed said.

The statement stopped Hendrix momentarily, his jaw again falling slack as he stared over at Reed.

"Well, of course we didn't. We don't even own a gun."

Reed already knew that, having run the records that afternoon for any signs of a permit, but nodded as if it were of paramount importance.

"What we would like to know is how this individual knew your family was going to be out of town," Reed said. "The fact that this occurred while you were away was not a coincidence."

The look on Hendrix's face grew even more pronounced, all color bleeding from his cheeks. "Oh, my God," he whispered, echoing the line he had used repeatedly that afternoon. "Do you think he was *watching* us?"

For a moment Reed considered the notion, assessing it and dismissing it in quick fashion. The neighborhood they lived on was situated such that any sort of surveillance would have had to be conducted right along the street. Given the number of homes nearby and the speed with which neighbors had responded to his breech the night before, it seemed very unlikely that anybody could have spent extended periods of time observing and gone unnoticed.

"Not necessarily," Reed said. "Like I said, most likely your SUV was a target of opportunity, not something personally aimed at you.

"Tell me though, do you happen to have any new neighbors? Anybody out of town that might be employing a house sitter?"

The pacing stopped as Hendrix backed himself up to the closest table, resting his bottom against the edge of it. He folded his arms across his chest, his entire form seeming to shrink in size, as he raised a hand to his chin and pondered the question.

"No, we're the newest family on the block, been there more than two years. As far as I know, nobody else has been gone recently."

"How about lawn care companies, dog walkers, anybody else that might be familiar with your habits?"

Another moment passed before Hendrix shook his head to the side. "Nothing like that. We've been saving almost six months for this trip. Bought our cars on credit. No luxuries like those of any kind."

Glancing down to Billie, Reed nodded. The information seemed to fit with what he expected, the home and the street neither one seeming affluent enough to make use of such services. Any family that would ask a neighbor to collect mail seemed unlikely to hire someone else to cut their grass.

"How about social media?" Reed asked. "Are you guys active on Facebook? Twitter? Anywhere that someone might have seen a posting about your impending trip?"

"I'm not on anything," Hendrix said. "I work in sales, barely have time to make it home for dinner and baths every night."

He paused, before adding, "I know my wife has Facebook, though I don't think she's real active. I mean, we're 40 after all."

There was no further explanation, though there didn't need to be. Some things just seem a bit frivolous after a certain age. Raising kids becomes far important than sharing photos with people they hadn't seen in decades.

Just the same he made a mental note to have someone take a look, determine if anything was out there that someone might have seen and taken advantage of.

"Have you found it yet?" Hendrix asked. "My car, I mean."

A bit of familiar dread flushed just briefly into Reed's stomach, a conditioned response to having to be the bearer of bad news. On the grand scale of things, this wasn't quite as awful as having to share the loss of a loved one, but it would still come with an impact, especially for someone in the state that Hendrix was before him.

"This afternoon the Madison County Sheriff's Department found your car at a put-in along Big Darby Creek," Reed said.

Every part of him wanted to pause there, to not heap anything more on this poor man for one day, but he knew he couldn't do that. It was better to get everything in the open right up front, to let him know the enormity of the situation so he could begin making plans, take his first steps to returning things to normal.

Just as surely too, even as harsh as it sounded, Reed also knew he needed to be pushing onward himself. He felt for the Hendrix family and their plight, but right now his entire concern was focused on the man that had shot Iaconelli and Bishop.

They were partners. He would not abide them having to go through something similar to what he had.

"I'm sorry, Mr. Hendrix, but the car was burned beyond repair. Tomorrow it will be transported to our crime scene garage and held for the duration of the investigation in case anything further could possibly be pulled from it.

"After that, the easiest thing for you would be to just let us send it to a junk yard."

Remembering the charred shell of the vehicle he had seen that afternoon, Reed knew there was no way any insurance company would ever pay to put that SUV back on the road. It would be a losing proposition, no matter how valuable or how much sentimental attachment there might have been.

Several emotions passed over Hendrix's face in quick order, running the full gamut, before his features contorted themselves into a crinkled heap. His mouth opened and shut twice as if he might respond before he gave up on the notion.

His hands again rose to his face, covering his entire visage as his shoulders began to shake, Reed tapping his leg and leading Billie away.

Jonas Hendrix had been through enough. He didn't need to suffer the added indignity of someone watching him cry.

Chapter Nineteen

The full ski mask The Kid wore was hot. He had bypassed wool for cotton, but still it felt exceedingly warm against his skin, stuck to his face as droplets of sweated beaded up, saturating the material, causing it to cling to his cheeks and forehead.

Of everything he had undertaken, would undertake moving forward, it was the part he disliked the most. It was the one thing that seemed at odds with his mission, with his goals, a lone blight of cheesiness on an otherwise perfect plan.

The single thing that Big would never let him live down, wearing a ski mask like a robber in a bad heist film.

Still, for as much as he disliked the feel of it, hated the very notion of it even more, it was a necessary evil. If everything went as planned tonight, there would be a survivor.

Survivors had eyes. They remembered faces.

Especially someone as attuned to staring at her surroundings as Didi Weston.

There was no way to know for certain that she would be the one to survive until morning, though if not there was a decent chance The Kid would leave nobody behind. If it wasn't her, that meant her husband had acted in his own best interests, sacrificing his wife, an act that The Kid knew he could not abide.

If the man was so vile that he would give up Didi to save himself, then he deserved the same fate as hers.

Glancing down to the glass of water in his hand, The Kid considered dumping the entire thing over his head. He craved the cool refreshment from the oppressive heat of the garment, aching to have it lower the temperature of his scalp by a few dozen degrees, bringing it closer to something approaching normality.

For a moment he stared down at it before dismissing the idea and lowering his knee onto the spine of Dennis Weston. Two vertebras popped under his weight as he moved, positioning himself just so, halfway down the man's thorax.

Three feet away from them, Didi Weston watched the entire scene. Seated in a straight back chair The Kid had drug in from the kitchen, her wrists and ankles were secured with thick bands of duct tape, the metallic silver material catching bits of overhead light. Another wide swatch was stretched across her mouth, a tendril of blood sneaking down from her left nostril over the top of it.

The Kid had had no original designs of hurting her, though now that he stared her way he had to admit it added a sense of urgency to her appearance. Coupled with the hair that was now teased out above her head, a telltale feature of the brief struggle that had occurred, she looked the part of a proper victim.

From this moment on her presence was to be used as more of a prop, a means of leverage, than anything else, though The Kid needed the threat of violence to be very real in order for things to work.

Now, it most certainly was that.

As much as he would have liked to take a few moments and admire the good work he'd done – slipping into her vehicle, waiting until they were back at her home before overtaking her, lying in wait for her husband to get in hours later – now was not the time. Most of that had been nothing more than preparation and any celebration of it would be premature.

The real object of his ire, his angst, was now pinned to the floor beneath him.

Dennis Weston was officially the next target for The Kid, the second step in a sequence of retribution. Things might never be made right again, but at least they could be made whole.

The Kid knew Weston to be the same age as his wife, though he looked much older up close. Whether it was from a life in the field he had chosen or decades of trying to keep Didi in the lifestyle to which she was accustomed he wasn't sure, and didn't much care.

All that really mattered was that the man had been much easier to subdue than anticipated, had seen his wife tied up and walked straight toward her, never once thinking of the corner as he passed or even seeing the butt of The Kid's gun before it smashed into his temple.

In the time since he had laid completely motionless, allowing The Kid to tie his hands behind his back, linking his feet together at the ankles. From there the rest of the configuration had been pretty simple, pulling his heels back almost to his bottom, looping a rope through his feet and around his neck.

When he was done the older man had resembled a giant misshapen pretzel, the top of his head and the bottom of his feet just a short distance apart.

With his weight pressing the man down, The Kid tossed the glass of water at his face, the liquid hitting him square. It had the intended effect as Weston's eyes burst open, his mouth gaping as he drew in deep breaths of air.

Shifting onto his haunch, The Kid used his weight to keep the man in place, pulling Weston's feet back a couple of extra inches to keep him from choking himself just yet.

Beneath him the man began to struggle a bit, realization setting in.

"Wha? What is this?" he gasped. "Who are you?"

The Kid didn't bother to respond. Instead he simply stood, allowing the man's feet to lower themselves back to their natural position. As they did so the rope around his neck grew tighter, a low gurgling rolling out of him, his body fighting for air.

"Here's how this is going to play out, Mr. Weston," The Kid said. "I could sit here and slap you and tell you to shut up and do a lot of other unnecessary things that would be great fun for me, and which you very much deserve, but I won't.

"That's what this little contraption I've outfitted you with is for."

Pacing back and forth in front of his foe, a smile curled up behind the ski mask The Kid wore. For so long he had imagined something like this, envisioning finally being able to get even, to give these people what they had coming.

Adding to his satisfaction, the feeling of deep-seated joy that was pulsating through him, was the tear soaked face of Didi across from him. One time after another she attempted to lift her body from the seat of the chair, hoping to nudge the piece of furniture closer, wanting in some way to be of aid to her husband.

It was easily the most humane thing he had seen her do in the duration of the time he'd spent watching her.

Twice more The Kid walked the length of the Oriental rug his victim was laid out on, watching as he flopped around, gagging, his face growing red. Only once the buildup of blood became such that Weston's features passed over into purple did The Kid again drop himself unceremoniously into place, pulling back on the feet to ease the tension.

As he did so the rope grew slack, Weston's face rolling forward toward the carpet as he tried to pull in ragged gasps. Every few seconds he spit, his throat already too sore, too swollen, to bother swallowing.

"Why?" he panted, the word just barely audible.

The Kid smiled again. Already the man was past wanting to know who he was. He didn't try to negotiate, made no attempt to talk his way out of the situation.

He was now grasping that the situation he found himself in was a finality, that his endpoint was already determined.

"Choices, Mr. Weston," The Kid said, rotating so he faced toward Weston's head, able to see the man and his wife both clearly before him.

"You are a man that has built a career off of making, and in some instances presenting, choices. So this time, I have one for you."

Reaching into the small of his back, The Kid drew his weapon. He held it up for Didi to see, watching her eyes grow wide, before extending it and wagging it on the edge of Weston's field of vision.

"This right here is a standard .9mm handgun with a full magazine of bullets."

With his opposite hand he tugged on the rope pulled taut between Weston's ankles and throat. "And this is a little something I designed that can and will choke the life out of you. Do you understand?"

It took a moment for Weston to respond, his body still fighting for precious oxygen. Over the sound of his garbled panting Didi could be heard sniffling, her eyes puffy and bloodshot, tears running across the smooth surface of the duct tape and dripping from her chin.

"Okay," The Kid said, his voice belying almost glee as he held their lives in his hands, people that had never given him the courtesy of a passing glance, that had held so many lives in their hands before.

Lives like Big's.

"The way this works is, one of you is not walking out of here tonight," The Kid said. "Who that is is entirely on you, Mr. Weston."

He leaned forward and lowered his voice, fighting down his every inner desire to pull back his mask, to let the man see who his tormentor was.

"Either I shoot your wife now, cut this rope and walk away," The Kid said, "or I hop off of you, and your wife and I both watch you suffocate to death."

Another moment went by as The Kid paused, relishing the situation and his control over it. "So, what's it going to be?"

Wrapping a hand around the man's feet, he pulled them back a bit more, allowing just an inch more slack, enough so the man could provide a response. "Come on now, we don't have all night here. It won't bother me to just end you both right now, but I'm trying to be sporting about this."

Every bit of The Kid tingled with anticipation as he leaned forward, cocking his ear to the side, anxious to hear what he already knew the man would say.

"Go to hell," Weston whispered.

"You first," The Kid replied, releasing his grip. Below him Weston's feet snapped back into place, his body pulling itself into a tight half-arc, flopping on the floor like a beached sea creature.

"You wanted to know why?" The Kid said, watching the scene play out, seeing the muted emotion of Didi as she clamped her eyes shut and turned away, unable to watch any longer.

"Payback, Mr. Weston. Choices have consequences."

Chapter Twenty

The pressure was starting to mount. Reed could feel it squeezing in on him, even if nobody else had actually voiced the words. They all saw how hard he was pushing, the way he was running himself and Billie both ragged, being omnipresent for every discussion that took place. There was certainly nobody blaming him for anything, just over 36 hours having passed since the incident took place.

Still, Reed could feel it all around him, at moments so thick he felt as if he should reach out and push it away from his face. Two cops were in the hospital, one with the very real possibility of never waking, the other maybe never standing up under his own power again.

Taken alone, those injuries were serious enough. To have occurred to two detectives on duty, especially ones just months from retirement, had the hackles raised of every last person on the force.

"So where do things stand?" Grimes asked, seated in his customary position behind his desk. He was back in his starched uniform, the same thing he wore every day, the other night at the hospital being a rare aberration, the first time Reed had seen him in street clothes in ages.

"This morning begins follow up," Reed said, leaning back in his chair directly across from Grimes, one of two matching pieces with blue cloth coverings, Billie flat on the ground beside him.

Along the wall to his left stood a narrow table, a few plaques and frames resting on it. Otherwise the office was almost void of personal touches, the standard-issue furniture filling the space and nothing more.

"Get with Earl and see if anything came from the car, talk to Grove City and find out if they were able to pull anything on their second pass through the Hendrix house."

Grimes nodded, the skin under his neck folding up as he laced his hands atop his stomach.

The meetings were something that had started almost immediately after Reed transitioned over from the 19th. They had originated as a way for him to brief the captain of anything that transpired over the night, prepping him to distribute new cases to the daytime crews that did most of the investigating.

Over time he and Billie had transitioned into a floating team, their home still on the graveyard shift but given the autonomy to vacillate whenever new cases arrived.

This morning's meeting had not been planned, Reed simply unable to sleep, his mind refusing to slow down. Instead he had rousted Billie early, taking her into the backyard for a quick workout before heading into the precinct to do some research. Upon entering he had seen the captain's light on and stopped in, the visit a courtesy to let his superior know where things stood.

"So the car was a wash?" Grimes asked.

"From start to finish," Reed replied. "Was spotted by a couple fishermen that were just trying to get on the water, hadn't seen a thing. Completely torched beyond recognition, no way any fibers or DNA survived."

Grimes's response was the same as Reed's had initially been, his face twisting up a bit in anger. "Damn."

"Yeah," Reed agreed. "I let Billie have a go around the place, just so she could pick up any scent that might have lingered in case we come across him again, but overall it was kind of a losing battle."

At the mention of her name Billie raised her head from the floor, glancing up to Reed. Her ears stood for a moment before dropping back into place, her chin returning to the top of her paws.

"Have you spoken to Hendrix yet?" Grimes asked.

"Last night," Reed said, adding a slight nod, recalling the events from the previous evening. "Taking it exactly as you'd expect a man with a wife and two small daughters to."

"Angry or shook?"

"The latter," Reed replied. "Never voiced the usual questions, but he was weeping when we left."

"Mm," Grimes replied, the response free of asking what the usual questions were or judgment of any kind.

They had both been down the path enough times that there was no need.

"How about our witness?" Grimes asked.

The right side of Reed's face scrunched up slightly as he shook his head. "Not really. I think his arrival scared the shooter off more than anything."

"Sounds like that might have been a good thing," Grimes said.

"For sure," Reed agreed. "Guy definitely did us a solid, probably saved Ike's life. I just mean he didn't get a visual on anything we might be able to use."

On the opposite side of the desk Grimes made the same grunting noise, offering nothing further.

"He did mention that when he arrived Bishop was still awake, told him to go help Ike and said something like *back*, but he couldn't be certain," Reed added.

"Back?" Grimes asked, squinting as he said the word, folds of skin appearing around his eyes.

"Something like that," Reed said, raising his palms before dropping them down to his thighs. "Right after that Bishop passed out, couldn't remember any of it when I talked to him yesterday."

A moment passed as Grimed used his foot to rotate his chair a quarter turn, shifting his attention to face out the window. In the distance the morning sun was just beginning to rise, a pale white disc sitting above the horizon, promising another chilly and overcast day.

"Back," he whispered, tapping the pads of his thumbs together, thinking on what Reed had said.

More than once Reed had seen the stance before. Something had caught deep in the recesses of his mind, was preoccupying his thoughts, even if he couldn't quite articulate it just yet.

When those moments arose Reed knew better than to interrupt, giving the man all the time and space he needed.

"You going to be around here for a while?" Grimes asked, flicking his attention over to Reed, keeping his torso aimed toward the window.

"I can be," Reed said, meeting the gaze. Again he wanted to ask what the captain was chewing on but kept the urge at bay, knowing there was something to it and that he would be brought in when and if he needed to be.

"Give me..." Grimes said, his voice trailing off as he snapped his left wrist up before him, pushing back the cuff of his dress shirt with his right hand to reveal a watch on a battered black leather band. "One hour. Let me make a few calls."

Chapter Twenty-One

Reed was three pages deep into Earl's report from going over Hendrix's car, the initial details just as thin as he had feared. An accelerant, most likely basic lighter fluid, had been applied liberally over the interior of the vehicle. The resulting flame had burned hot and thorough, destroying all organic matter.

The only thing of any real value that had survived was a single shell casing that had rolled under the passenger seat, the driver most likely not noticing it before taking off. Ballistic testing had confirmed it was the same make and model as those found at the original crime scene, though the firing pin marking indicated it was a different weapon.

A diagram of the interior of the car illustrated what Reed and Earl had discussed the night before, that most likely it was a single shooter using two of the same gun.

So focused on the report was Reed that he didn't hear the captain approach, making his way into the detective's bullpen and walking clear to the back corner without being noticed. Not until he flipped a thin file on the desk beside the crime scene report did Reed know he was there, flinching just slightly before looking up.

Grimes said nothing as he pulled over a chair from an adjacent desk and dropped down into it, facing the opposite direction as Reed.

"That was fast," Reed said.

"Yeah, well," Grimes said, motioning to the file between them, "things like that tend to get top billing around here."

Without knowing why, Reed felt his stomach clench, a bit of the same feeling he'd had a few nights before returning to him.

"Oh, shit. What's up?"

Raising his head a few inches, Grimes motioned with his chin toward the file. "Read it. There's not much there, won't take a second."

The clench in his stomach grew even more pronounced as Reed pulled the file over a few inches and flipped back the top. Inside it were three pages affixed with metal fasteners at the top, the ink on all three thick and a bit distorted, as if the sheets had been faxed over.

Dark writing filled the bulk of the pages, done in a slanted hand across the premade forms.

Before he had a chance to begin reading, Grimes narrated aloud.

"Last night Dennis Weston was murdered in his home," Grimes said. "It seems someone broke into his wife's car and she drove them there, was lying in wait when he arrived."

He paused there, his gaze fixed the length of the empty second floor, at 10 minutes after 7:00 the entire station still sitting empty.

"He walked in and saw his wife tied up, went to help her, was hit in the head by the killer. From there he was tied up in an elaborate configuration, basically ensuring that he strangled himself while the killer and his wife both sat and watched."

Reed drew a sharp breath in through his teeth, the sound audible, pulling Billie's gaze up to him. She raised herself from her stomach to her front paws, her neck pressed against his thigh, as he waited for the captain to continue.

"The killer remained until Weston was dead before turning and walking out. Even dialed 911 from the house phone on his way."

Questions upon questions sprang to Reed's mind, the conditioned response of a detective already in the midst of an investigation.

Still, he remained silent.

"They arrived and found the wife, Diedra, passed out in the chair, shock having set in. On the floor at her feet was her husband, long past the point of saving."

"Damn," Reed whispered.

The sentiment was genuine, even if the relevance to anything they were now doing was still unclear.

That was a hell of a way for anybody to die, an even worse thing to have to sit and watch.

"Who are Dennis and Diedra Weston?" Reed asked. Never before had he heard the names, though from the way Grimes was acting he should have.

The question pulled Grimes's attention away from the room, his focus moving to Reed.

"Dennis Weston has been the warden at Franklin County Medical Corrections for 18 years."

He stopped there, waiting as things began to align in Reed's mind.

"Oh, shit," Reed whispered, ideas going off like fireworks in his mind. "You think this was connected?"

"I don't know," Grimes said, "but the BCI is handling the investigation. They sent that around to every precinct in the city early this morning, a veritable call for help without saying as much."

Reed glanced down at it, knowing there was something in there he would soon need to read, but trusting the captain to fill him in in the meantime.

"When the investigators spoke to the wife, she told them the last thing the killer said before leaving was it was about payback."

Reed's lips parted a fraction of an inch.

Payback.

He should have seen it earlier, should have put things together right after Baldwin first mentioned it to him.

"Do we know anybody at the BCI?"

"Not really," Grimes said, "but I don't think it matters. They sent that out basically asking for help, remember?"

Reed nodded, again looking down at the thin file before him. It wasn't a certainty that the two cases were connected, though the fact that two attacks had been made on law enforcement personnel in as many nights, even as disconnected as two detectives and a prison warden might be, was too much to ignore.

"You want to make a few more calls just the same? Maybe open some doors for me before I arrive?"

"Already done it," Grimes replied. "They're expecting you just as soon as we get done here."

Chapter Twenty-Two

Franklin County Medical Corrections served as the hub for all major medical needs for the various state facilities in central Ohio. It housed inmates that required more attention than could be provided at the site infirmary in each location, reserved more for chronic diseases or the occasional severe attack than the traditional flu or head cold. Parsed into two separate buildings, it provided both primary care and behavioral health care, the latter serving as a psychiatric ward for a geographic area covering more than half of the state.

Located just outside of German Village on the south end of town, Reed had been by it a few times, though never actually inside. As the facility was meant to cater to patients that were already incarcerated, his roles in the uniformed division and later as a detective had never required him to make the trip.

The place looked exactly as Reed remembered it upon approach, chain link fencing rising two stories tall around it, coils of razor wire spooled in lazy loops throughout. In total the facility looked to cover the better part of 15 acres, each of the buildings inside appearing squat and square, constructed of concrete block and brick.

A guard house stood at the end of the only public drive into the place, a thick man with a bull neck and shaved head stepping out as Reed pulled close.

He seemed to communicate only in grunts as Reed flashed his credentials and gave his and Billie's names, waving them through two minutes after stopping. Not once in that time did he enunciate a single coherent word, barely looking up from the clipboard in his hand.

Allowing the engine to idle, Reed rolled forward to the closest building, following a stenciled sign toward the administrative offices. From there he eased into the first visitor stall and parked, glancing once through the windshield before exhaling and climbing out.

If forced to guess, Reed would put the construction date on the facility at somewhere in the 1940's, the building looking more like something that would have once served as an observation post on a nuclear testing site. The outer wall was made entirely of rough cut concrete block, the surface dimpled and textured, filled in only nominally by decades of paint.

A row of small windows was spaced evenly across the ground floor, all a little too small for the massive expanse of the building, like beady eyes on a wide face.

Billie waited on the backseat as Reed attached the short lead to her collar before hopping down. Together they made their way over the curb painted red and up a narrow walkway, past a row of juniper bushes in dire need of pruning.

Clearly, unlike most prison facilities, the inmates that were housed here were not the kind to spend their days performing manual labor.

The sidewalk extended along the edge of the building for almost 30 yards before making a turn, leading through a set of double doors painted the same dusty brown as the exterior of the building.

The doors opened into a wide hallway, the corridor extended straight out in front of them. To the left was an oversized window beginning at waist height and extending nearly to the ceiling. A vertical line cut the partition in half, the pieces of glass resting in a stainless steel tract, capable of being pushed to either side.

Behind the window sat a dowdy woman with silver hair and a

cardigan sweater, her lips pursed below a pair of thick framed glasses. She openly stared at Reed as he took a step forward, not sure what the correct protocol was, waiting for her to initiate the interaction.

She did not. Instead she merely stared at him, an expectant look on her face.

"Uh, hi," Reed said after a moment, glancing down the hall. Aside from the complete lack of movement anywhere nearby, it bore a striking semblance to the church corridor he had been in just a day before. "Detective Reed Mattox with the 8th Precinct. My captain called over earlier, you folks should be expecting me."

The woman continued to stare at him, the same look in place, before saying, "I wasn't expecting anything." She made a point of scanning him once over and added, "Still don't."

Warmth spread to Reed's face and neck as he willed himself not to react. No doubt she was just a few hours removed from finding out her boss had been murdered in a most gruesome fashion, Reed trying to tell himself her demeanor was just her way of dealing with things.

Something told him that wasn't quite the case, though.

"I'm here to meet with the BCI team investigating things," Reed said, pushing past her comment, just wanting their interaction to end.

Extending it a few extra moments, the woman held her gaze before sniffing once and jerking the top of her head toward the opposite end of the hall. "Big office with Warden stenciled on the door. If you can't find that, just follow the sound of all that racket she's making down there."

Thus far, Reed had yet to hear a single sound beyond the voice of the woman behind the glass.

Still, he said nothing of it.

"Thank you," he said, tapping his leg and leading Billie down the hallway. To either side a series of wooden doors filed by, all with various names and titles stenciled on them in gold filigree, extending the gamut from Medical Director to Chief Financial Officer.

Most of the lights inside them were dark, the offices empty, though if that was in response to events of the previous night or just the standard MO around the place, Reed had no way of knowing. If this was his case to work he might think to check into it, but as it wasn't, he let the thought pass.

Three-quarters of the way down the hall a sound found his ears, resembling an empty box hitting the floor. Beside him he could sense Billie tense just slightly, his own nerves rising a tiny bit as they walked forward.

The last door on the left stood open as they approached, yellow light extending out over the black and white tiled floor before fading, blending in with the outside sunshine coming from the window at the end of hall. The sound of more movement could be heard as they grew closer, Reed circling into the doorway and swatting his knuckles at the metal frame.

Standing in the center of the room was a woman with straight brown hair hanging just past her shoulders, sunglasses resting atop her head. Her eyes flashed as she jerked toward the sound of his knocking, her face bordering on malevolent before softening a tiny bit.

"Morning," Reed said, making no attempt to move into the room.

"Morning," she replied, remaining rooted in place as well.

"Detective Reed Mattox, my partner Billie," Reed said. "My captain called over earlier, said I would be coming by."

The woman held the pose a moment, her body completely rigid, before lowering the box she held in front of her a few inches. As she did so, some of the tension she was carrying bled out as well, her features slackening a bit more.

"Sorry," she said, "been a rough go since I got here."

Without thinking about it, the right corner of Reed's mouth curled upward as he flicked a glance down the hall toward the front reception counter. "Yeah, they didn't exactly roll out the welcome wagon for us either."

The woman offered a slight smirk as she tossed the box she was holding to the floor, just one of a half-dozen empties that were strewn about the place. Behind her was an oversized desk without a single thing on it, not a computer monitor or even a calendar blotter. A few framed paintings hung from the walls, Rockwellian scenes that made the entire place feel more like a doctor's office than the place a warden would work from.

"Cassidy Glenn, BCI," she said. She pushed out a loud breath before bracing her fists on either hip, continuing to stare at them. "Tell me Detective Mattox, do you drink coffee?"

Chapter Twenty-Three

Reed could count the number of times he had willingly consumed coffee on both hands, finding the taste revolting, hating the roller coaster effect it had on his equilibrium. Spending most of his time on the graveyard shift was bad enough, but swallowing down gallons of liquid caffeine exacerbated the effect to levels that tended to keep him reeling for days on end.

Despite that, he accepted the invitation from Glenn, a move made as much to get himself far away from the antiseptic administrative wing of the facility as to build inter-agency collegiality.

The beverages were obtained from the onsite cafeteria, Glenn leading the way with a practiced familiarity that intimated it wasn't her first such trip on the day. They both ordered plain black and took their cups to go, more than a few curious stares following them as they swept outside and found a picnic table on the grounds, posting up across from each other.

Around them the day was promising to be exactly as the sunrise had hinted, the sky overcast, the world awash in the same white light that would be present for much of the next six months. The temperature hovered somewhere in the upper-50s, the lack of wind making it bearable, if not quite pleasant.

"So," Glenn began, opening the discussion, "your captain said you might have something connected to this."

She had tied her brown hair back behind her neck, the sunglasses now resting on her nose. When Reed first arrived she had been in shirt sleeves and slacks, now wearing the matching suit coat.

"Possibly," Reed said, "though that was based on a very preliminary look through the notes your office sent out this morning."

"Which were themselves preliminary," Glenn added.

"Right," Reed said. He paused there, picking up on her insinuation, and said, "Not your idea, I'm guessing?"

A single eyebrow rose above the edge of the sunglasses. Reed was unable to see her eyes behind the mirrored lenses, though he could surmise they too bore a similar expression.

"This thing is a jurisdictional nightmare," she said. "We've got the warden of a prison facility. Normally that would fall under the Bureau of Prisons, meaning it's an FBI case, only this particular one is state run."

Reed nodded, lifting his coffee and taking a small swig. The caustic liquid burned his tongue as it passed through, both from the excessive temperature and a composite makeup that could chew rust from a fender.

"Making it worse, this place is clearly within CPD control, but the warden lives out in New Albany."

"Giving the local police jurisdiction," Reed said, following her reasoning. He thought for a moment of the Madison County crew he had encountered the day before and said, "Which I'm guessing they're not quite equipped to handle."

"Uh-uh," Glenn said. "All too happy to hand it off too, though whether that's because they know they're in over their head or if they just want no part of this thing is anybody's guess."

Bitterness seemed to practically drip from Glenn's words as she spoke, pulling up just long enough to take a quick drink of her coffee. If she found the substance to be as revolting as Reed she gave no indication, placing the cup down and staring into the distance.

Around them the sound of traffic on the roads framing the facility could be heard, large trucks releasing their air brakes and cars playing the bass on their stereos way too loud. Reed pushed them from his mind as he sat and thought, trying to balance what she was saying with her tone.

If the local police weren't giving her an issue, he couldn't quite place where the obvious anger she felt was coming from.

"So it went to you guys?" Reed asked.

"No, it went to me," Glenn said, twisting her head back to look at Reed, "because nobody else in the place wanted it."

A bit of dawning hit Reed as he shifted his focus down to the coffee before him. In his limited experience with the organization, he knew the Bureau of Criminal Investigation was an organization housed in the Attorney General's Office, designed to aid in any investigation involving a state agency. By and large, that meant forensics or prosecution assistance, the investigative wing of the division being quite small by comparison.

For them to be handed the lead, especially in a case such as this, was quite unusual.

"This was a dead end, so it came your way?" Reed asked, piecing together things out loud.

"Exactly," Glenn said. She jerked her head back toward the building behind her and said, "And what you saw in there was visual proof. No computer, no files, just some empty boxes that were labeled like they should have been something but not worth the time it took me to drag them out."

Once again understanding settled in, Reed grasping the vitriol that seemed to be pouring out of her.

At the moment none of it seemed to be aimed in his direction, a point that was close enough to a victory.

"Alright," Reed said, "knowing all that, I'll go first, lay out what I'm working with. After that you can do the same. If at the end of it we think there's overlap we'll discuss things further.

"If not, thanks for the coffee, and best of luck."

Behind her sunglasses there was very little Reed could discern. Based on her earlier comments, he had assumed her to be much like him, wanting to push straight ahead, to get moving on things as fast as possible.

They both were facing uphill climbs and as good as the occasional vent session could feel, it didn't aid either in accomplishing their goals.

Raising her free hand a few inches from the table, Glenn flicked her fingers back toward herself, motioning for Reed to continue.

In short order Reed went through the sequence of events, beginning with the basic traffic stop and filling her in through the discovery of the car. He provided a bit more detail than the thin file he had read of her case that morning, highlighting that Hendrix was exonerated and that the car was dumped.

He held off on what Baldwin heard from Bishop, not wanting to twist her thoughts, cause her to force facts to fit a theory.

"Okay," Glenn said when he finished, a bit of uncertainty clear in her tone. "This morning at around 2:00 a.m. a 911 call was placed from the home of Dennis Weston, the warden here. Nobody on the other end, but they left the line open, making sure the call stayed active.

"Local patrol in the area swung by to check it out, found Weston dead, his wife unconscious, duct taped to a chair beside him. Apparently the killer had worked her over pretty good, too."

Reed kept his face impassive as he listened. More than once muscle memory told him to raise the coffee and take a drink, though the actual taste of it kept him from doing so. Instead he kept all 10 fingers wrapped tight around the paper cup, drawing warmth from it.

"Paramedics were able to revive her, though Weston was long since passed. Choked himself out using some sort of homemade noose."

Having read the file beforehand, Reed had a general idea of what she was referring to, her description being as good as anything he could have come up with.

"You've read the synopsis that went out, right?" she asked.

"I did," Reed said, having gone through it a handful of times, committing the entirety of it to memory.

"So then I don't need to cover the back story," Glenn said.

"No," Reed said, shaking his head to either side. "I can tell you're a little uncertain though about how things line up and why I'm here.

"In that report, it was mentioned that Mrs. Weston was coherent just long enough to give a partial statement."

"Right," Glenn said. "That's actually why I'm here now. The minute they untied her last night, she ran upstairs and started self-medicating. Damn paramedics didn't think to ask when they arrived and gave her valium."

"Oh, damn," Reed said, drawing the words out to sound just short of a groan. "So she's been comatose ever since."

"Just about," Glenn said. "Tried speaking to her this morning and got nothing. Bunch of drooling and eyelid fluttering. Going to try and head back out there shortly, but who knows if that'll get me anywhere."

Reed winced, getting a sense even more for the frustration that was rolling off of Glenn in undulating waves.

"Well, the last thing she said of any relevance was that the killer mentioned this all being about payback, or something close to it," Reed said.

"Right," Glenn said, continuing to work on the coffee, oblivious to whatever harm it might be doing to her digestive system.

"Before Detective Bishop passed out, our witness believed he heard him say *back*," Reed said. "He thinks there was more to it, but it was the last gasp of a fading man."

Deep parentheses formed around Glenn's mouth as she considered it a moment. "And you think maybe he was saying *payback*?"

"Maybe," Reed said, unwrapping his fingers from around the cup in a bit of a shrug. "But given that our guys were detectives, and yours was a prison warden, thought it might be worth looking into."

There was no vocal response from Glenn as she considered the reasoning. She shifted her focus past Reed, back to the traffic crawling by outside the walls of the facility, and pondered things for a moment.

"Your guys that were hit," she asked, "how long have they been on the force?"

Already Reed knew where it was going, had thought of the same thing on the drive over.

"Two months shy of hanging it up."

"And Weston was four years past when he should have done the same," Glenn said.

119

Reed nodded. "So if there is a connection, we could be looking at 20 years of overlap."

"Right," Glenn said. "I mean, there can't be *that* many people that your guys arrested that ended up in here, but 20 years is a long time. Some of that stuff is probably still on paper somewhere, not even logged into the system."

Reed had considered that as well.

"Still," Reed said, "I've got two ranking detectives in dire medical condition. You've got a long standing warden murdered in his own home.

"Is there any way we don't look into this?"

Reaching up, Glenn slid the sunglasses from her face and dropped them upside down on the table. She pressed her opposite hand over her eyes and kneaded her thumb and forefinger in slow circles, pushing out a long sigh.

"What's your jurisdictional clearance look like on this?"

"Far as I know, whatever it needs to be," Reed said. "Things tend to become more relaxed when there's an attempted cop killer on the loose."

He paused, watching as she nodded, before adding, "Besides, so long as I'm with you, I can go wherever the BCI can."

The kneading stopped as Glenn slowly pulled her hand away. The skin around her eyes was red as she looked at Reed, her expression somber.

"Well then, you ever been to New Albany?"

Chapter Twenty-Four

Part Two was complete. Just like Part One, and even the task before that, it had gone off without the slightest hiccup, the end result of meticulous and painstaking planning.

As with the night before, The Kid couldn't help but feel a bit of mixed emotions as he thought back on it. He was elated that everything had gone to schedule, that his original design, nothing more than some amateur scheming, had proven so infallible. The traps he had created were working, the ability to hold life in his hands bringing with it a power that was nothing short of intoxicating.

Even now, as he was hours removed from his incident, he couldn't help but feel the strong pull of it lingering in his system. The Kid could see how some people became addicted to it, craving it the way a junkie might need their fix.

At the same time, the underscoring melancholy of everything was too much to be ignored. It provided a lead lining to each event, marred his victories in a way that would never allow them to be true successes.

A single thought was all that kept The Kid on the level, tying everything together, keeping either extreme from becoming too pronounced.

Big would be proud. Of that, there was no doubt.

A smile grew across The Kid's face as he laid flat on his back, his fingers laced behind his head. He allowed his vision to blur as he stared at the web of shadows playing across the dimpled stucco ceiling, the same thing looping through his head over and over again.

This one had required far more from him than the previous. Sure, he had obtained a car, drawn the attention of the detectives, even had to conjure the nerve to fire on someone for the first time, but it didn't compare to the events of hours before.

There had been a detachment to those activities. Not once had he been within more than 10 feet of either person, never did he see their faces, sense their fear, watch as any injury was done to them.

The second target had been on an entirely different level. He had spent time with Diedra Weston, had studied her patterns, gotten a feel for her as a human being. He had done the same with Dennis Weston, discovering the only thing he truly cared about was the woman that stayed with him solely for the lifestyle he provided her.

More than that though, The Kid had gotten dirty, had shown a willingness to get down in the mud when the need arose. He had assaulted them both, had stared them in the eye as he tied them up.

Watched as the life seeped out of Weston, as his wife wept for him.

There had been no need to watch the news or scan any websites, The Kid trusting he had performed perfectly. Nobody had seen his face, not a single fingerprint was left anywhere. Not a person alive knew who he was, had any reason to suspect who he might be.

At this point, he doubted anybody had even strung together why he was doing what he was doing.

They would, though.

Soon.

The smile faded from The Kid's features as he considered the notion, his face receding into a stony visage. He kept his attention focused upward, thinking that as wonderful as it had been, as vindicating as it all felt, it was time to move on.

It was time for the third step to start. Tomorrow was the day, the anniversary that felt like it had been so long in coming, a box on the calendar he had stared at with manic intensity for months on end.

Removing his hands from behind his head, The Kid rolled over onto his side, the satin sheets he laid on smooth against his exposed flesh. Propping himself up on an elbow, he rested his head against his right palm. Using his left hand, he slid his laptop closer, using his index finger to navigate the cursor, pulling a live camera feed up onto the screen.

The image was relayed to him in grainy black and white, untold shades of grey providing depth and texture. There was no telling how many times The Kid had sat and watched this very same shot, notating every movement, studying every pattern until he knew them better than his own daily routine.

The parallel of it all – of the camera, of the date, of the impending demise – was almost poetic. The first time The Kid had set down to plan it out it had seemed almost too perfect, the kind of thing that could be schemed but never actually accomplished.

Thus far, the first two steps had proven that theory wrong. He had done exactly as he wanted.

Tomorrow, the third would be the same. He only had to wait until then, just a few more hours, before finally putting to rest something that had started so long before.

Big would want it that way.

He would be proud.

Chapter Twenty-Five

The decision to drive separate wasn't much of a decision at all. Upon getting up from the picnic table neither one bothered returning to Weston's office, Reed trusting Glenn when she reported that there was nothing there to see. Until her witness came around, though, she had needed somewhere to start, the office being the obvious choice.

Their ensuing conversation had only confirmed that action. When someone like Weston was murdered it had to be assumed it was in connection to his employment and not just a random home invasion. The manner of death further seemed to indicate something personal, the possible connection to Reed's victim taking it a step further into a vendetta killer, or even worse a serial.

That thought seemed to hang heavy, albeit unstated, between them as they each climbed into their respective vehicles and headed out past the northeast corner of the city. Getting back later would be a nightmare for Reed and Billie, the work week now under way, but in the meantime traffic was thin.

Riding two car lengths behind Glenn, Reed spent the drive deep in thought, no sound coming from dispatch. A host of thoughts and questions he had no way of answering came to mind as he drove on, Billie pacing in the backseat, eager to be up and moving.

Reed knew the feeling.

Twenty minutes after leaving the Franklin County Correctional Medical Facility, Reed pushed past the airport and the opposite corner of the outer belt. All buildings taller than three stories fell away behind them, replaced by farms interspersed with occasional patches of small businesses, the land appearing more agrarian than urban, white board fencing lining the road.

Another 10 minutes passed before the speed limit slowed, a sign that looked to be the handiwork of both a professional artist and woodworker welcoming them to New Albany.

"Damn," Reed muttered as he passed through, noting that every last structure in the small town adhered to a strict construction code. Regardless of whether it was a McDonald's, an Exxon, or a Costco, the front façade was made from brick, the exterior professionally landscaped.

It being fall, floral arrangements with pumpkins, mums, and corn stalks were present on every corner. Bales of hay provided perches for artisanal scarecrows in most yards.

"One of *those* places," Reed muttered, turning on his blinker to follow Glenn, moving off the main strip and following a side street back into a bucolic neighborhood. Enormous lawns stretched out to either side, framing brick houses featuring what Reed figured to be at least six bedrooms each, the price tags he could only hope to guess at.

Not a single person could be seen as they rolled through, no cars parked on the street, none even sitting silent in the driveways.

The lone exception was at the end of the lane, a pair of police cruisers parked on the curb, a white van in the drive.

White Collar America or not, a crime scene was still a crime scene.

Reed followed Glenn forward and parked fourth in line behind the cruisers. They climbed out at the same time, meeting alongside her car and surveying the front of the house.

"Are we in Stepford?" Reed asked, the home appearing to be a near carbon copy of every one on the block, all significantly north of his farmhouse.

A sharp snort rolled Glenn's head back an inch. "Had that feeling on the way in too, huh?"

Reed grunted in response, the two falling in beside one another and walking to the foot of the drive before turning up toward the house.

"Your partner not coming?" Glenn asked, hooking a thumb back to the cars, rotating just slightly at the waist to motion toward Billie.

"Not until I've seen it first," Reed said. "She'll never do anything without my command, but I still like to make sure there's not a lot of blood or bodily fluids around before I bring her in."

Glenn nodded once, saying nothing.

"Besides, it's usually better to give a new crime scene crew a heads up first," Reed added. "My guys are cool with her, but nothing freaks out someone scrubbing for evidence like a dog showing up."

"I bet," Glenn said, leading them across the front walk and toward the door.

In front of it stood a pair of uniforms, the duo reminding Reed of the team that was standing outside Bishop's door. Neither looked to be more than a few months past their training period, both appearing a bit pale, like they would rather be anywhere else in the world.

"Good morning," Glenn said, sliding her credentials from her rear pocket and flipping them over. "Cassidy Glenn, investigator, BCI."

Beside her Reed raised his badge from his chest and said, "Detective Reed Mattox, CPD."

Each made a face bordering on relief as they stepped to the side, the young man on the right stating, "Head on in, can't miss it."

"I think they're expecting you," the other added.

Reed knew there was no way anybody was expecting him, the invitation to come being extended and accepted almost on a whim just a short time before.

The front door to the home led onto a wide foyer, an enormous stairwell extending straight up from it and opening into an open banister stretched to either side. Oversized openings led toward what appeared to be a formal dining room on one side, a parlor on the other.

Following the sound of voices and the spillover of bright lights, Reed and Glenn walked past the foot of the stairs and straight down a wide hallway, the corridor ending in a cavernous living space.

As far as crime scenes went, it was one of the more innocuous Reed had ever encountered. The body of Dennis Weston had already been removed, there being no blood spatter or bodily residue left behind that needed to be scrubbed away, not even the scent of anything in the air.

All that was present to indicate a crime had been committed was a few coils of used duct tape lying at random intervals around the room, a length of white rope on the ground, and a chair that had been pulled over so as to be in direct eyesight upon entry.

Otherwise, save the duo of criminalists painstakingly going over everything, there was nothing out of the ordinary.

"Thoughts?" Glenn asked, coming to a stop on the edge of the room and resting her fists on her hips.

For a moment Reed felt a pang of offense pass through him before pushing it down, remembering that this was not her first time in the house.

Maybe she really was just asking for his opinion.

"If this is the same guy, this is a major de-escalation," Reed said. He could feel her gaze on him, though he made no effort to match it, continuing to study the room around him.

"How so?" Glenn asked.

"The other one was messy," Reed said. "Ugly. Lot of blood, left behind a couple of shell casings. Felt violent, almost spur-of-the-moment."

He made a show of extending his face toward the ceiling, checking the crown molding above, looking for signs of any digital monitoring.

"This took planning. Not only did he manage to subdue both people without raising their guard, he also managed to get in and out of this neighborhood without being seen."

Shifting his gaze over to Glenn, he added, "Well, I assume anyway on the last part. Otherwise, I'm guessing we would have heard by now."

"Hmm," Glenn said, nodding. "I wasn't sure what the first scene looked like, but I agree on your assessment of this one. Whoever this is knew what they were doing. Wanted to make a statement."

"Which was?" Reed asked, his hands back in the front of his sweatshirt, watching the tech crew work.

"Million dollar question," Glenn replied.

To their left a man appeared, having come from what seemed to be the wall itself, Reed figuring there was another room extended out in the opposite direction. Dressed in a uniform matching the two officers out front, he was at least a decade older, a goatee encasing his mouth.

"Investigator," he said, stopping after a single word. He raised a single finger in front of himself and used it to motion back in the direction he'd just come from.

"We have Mrs. Weston here if you'd like to speak with her."

Chapter Twenty-Six

In another context, one Reed guessed was as recent as just a day before, Diedra Weston would have been an attractive woman. A bit older certainly, the type Riley used to jokingly refer to as a *country club grandma*, but immaculately well preserved. It was not hard to imagine that in a day, a week, or even a month she would be again.

That moment was just most certainly not now.

The kitchen was arranged in an open air style, the kind Reed imagined would be employed in a Greek or Italian dwelling somewhere high in the countryside. Spanish tile lined the floor, all of it shades of white that were just barely distinguishable, giving the room a light and airy feel.

An oversized island sat in the middle of it, a cooking prep station and stainless steel sink both present. Various appliances and kitchen utensils were perched on butcher block counter tops lining the outside of the room.

Everything was polished to a mirrored shine, as if the items had barely ever been touched or if they had, were meticulously cleaned after every use.

All of this Reed registered and dismissed in an instant, his focus moving past the working part of the kitchen to the far end. There the space opened up tremendously, a cherry table sitting on the edge of the kitchen space before the floor dropped six inches in height, a second level spread wide, encased by windows standing floor-to-ceiling.

In the summer, the glass would most likely be swapped out for screens, tons of sunlight pouring in, refracting off the floor, giving the space a quality that bordered on ethereal.

Now though, given the outside temperature and time of year, the windows stood closed, gray skies visible.

Three men were standing along the edge of the floor separating the two levels. One was the man that had called for them, a second in a matching uniform standing nearby, chewing on his bottom lip, his hands thrust down into his pockets.

The third man wore a tie loosened at the neck and a plain blue sports coat, his receding hair combed straight back above tortoise shell glasses. Had Reed seen him on the street he would have guessed him a high school teacher or small college professor, though given the context figured him to most likely be his counterpart with the New Albany Sheriff's Department.

Serving as the centerpiece for the arrangement, her body wrapped in a floor-length fur coat of an indeterminate origin, was Diedra Weston. Seated alone at the table, her chair was angled so as to face away from the living room, her thick blonde hair haloed around her head in a wide arc. Gone was any trace of makeup, the coloring on her face of a much more dubious nature.

Her left nostril was rimmed with red, open scabs lining it. A harsh crescent extended down from her opposite eye, the center of it black, the outside blue and purple. Based on shape and location Reed figured she might have been hit with the butt of a gun at some point, having seen similar wounds before.

The entirety of her visage was puffy, as if she'd spent most of the night crying, though for the moment her face was dry.

Side by side he and Glenn crossed the kitchen, stopping just short of the table. There they paused, Reed ceding the floor to Glenn, alternating glances between Weston and the men around the outside.

"Would you gentlemen mind giving us just a couple of minutes?"

Glenn opened, the question surprising Reed, though he gave no outward display.

It was clear the request had not been expected by the others either, both officer's jaws dropping open, each looking to the detective between them. A moment passed as he stared at Glenn, letting it be known he did not like or even appreciate the move, before he nodded.

"We'll be in the living room if you need anything."

Never had Reed heard his voice, though it was plain there was a clear edge to it. Maintaining his stance, he stared impassively as the men drifted away, listening until the sounds of their shoes faded away as they moved from tile back onto carpet.

Once they were beyond earshot, Glenn moved a few steps to the side so she was directly across the table from Weston.

"Ms. Weston," she said, "my name is Cassidy Glenn, I'm an investigator with the Bureau of Criminal Investigations with the state. Here with me is Detective Reed Mattox from CPD. I've asked him here to provide expertise."

The arrangement wasn't quite so spoke-and-wheel, though Reed let it pass. Already he could see the dynamic Glenn was looking to establish, from asking the other men to leave to positioning herself across from Weston.

The woman had been through the worst kind of trauma imaginable. Not only was her husband murdered, her home had been breached, as had her physical well-being. Given the nature of the acts, it was overwhelmingly likely that the perpetrator had been a man.

Glenn knew that, recognized it right off, and was looking to provide as safe an environment as she could.

Without thinking, Reed took a half step back, making sure he was just beyond the periphery for Weston. He kept his hands thrust into the pockets of his sweatshirt, the stance meant to be non-threatening, and waited for Glenn to continue.

"Ms. Weston, I understand you requested to come back here this morning, is that correct?"

Another moment passed, one so long that Reed couldn't help but wonder if the reason for her return was to gain access to her self-medication products again. If that were the case, she may very well already be beyond the point of any usefulness again, the careless nature of the sheriff's department having cost them the better part of a day.

"I requested to get the hell out of that office," Weston said, her voice much stronger, clearer, than expected. It bore the slightest lilt of a foreign accent, Reed guessing from her features the source to be Scandinavian.

"They brought me here."

Across from her Glenn nodded, sliding herself down into a seat. She did not ask to make the move, doing so quickly, as if it was completely natural.

It was a tactic Reed made a note to employ in the future.

"Mrs. Weston, I know this must be awful, but can you walk us through exactly what happened yesterday?" Glenn asked. "Start first thing in the morning, give us the full run through of everything you did."

In front of him, Reed could see Weston's head shift away from Glenn, her attention on the windows lining the outer wall. She remained that way a moment before saying, "Yesterday was Sunday, so I did exactly as I do every week. I met a friend for tennis, showered and changed at the club, and ran a few errands. Grocery store, dry cleaning."

"And when you say the same as you do every week," Glenn interjected, "you mean you follow the same general schedule, or you visit the exact same places?"

"Same places," Weston said, "like clockwork. Tennis, grocery store, dry cleaners. Dennis would go into the office for the afternoon, I would follow my schedule, we would meet in time for dinner."

There was a slight crack on the last words, Weston lowering her head. She raised a hand and pinched her nose between her thumb and forefinger, holding the pose for just a moment before drawing in a deep breath and raising her head to face forward again.

"Okay," Glenn said, "tennis club, grocery store, dry cleaners. Then what?"

"Then..." Weston said, her voice drifting for a moment. "I didn't even know he was there. I had no idea. I was so preoccupied when I came out of the dry cleaners I just jumped in and drove off. Didn't even think to check the backseat."

The last sentence caught Reed's attention, his focus shifting to Glenn. She flicked her gaze over to him, letting it be known she'd caught it too, before leaning in.

"Check the backseat for what?"

"*Him*," Weston said, a visible shudder causing her upper body to quiver as she said the word. "He must have been lying behind the front seat, stayed completely quiet. I didn't even know he was there until I was pulling into the garage."

Another quiver wracked her body, the thick robe doing little to mask the movement. She wrapped both arms across her torso and drew herself in tight, her entire form seeming to shrink before their eyes.

"Until I felt his arm snake around my neck, heard his voice in my ear."

Just as one question was being answered, a handful more sprung to mind for Reed. They now understood how the man had gotten to the house unseen, but it still left open the issues of how he gained access to her car without being noticed and how he had managed to leave.

"Were you able to get a look at him?" Glenn asked.

"Not really," Weston replied. "He wore a black ski-mask the whole time, black leather gloves. I did see his wrists a couple times and he was definitely white, average height."

She paused before adding, "Sorry, I know it's not much."

Standing alone, the information was precious little. Reed figured though that if they could get a look at files later, determine where Iaconelli and Weston overlapped, just knowing the race of the killer might be useful in narrowing things down.

He would have preferred something unique, such as a man of Asian descent or an identifiable scar, something that would really make the digging easy, but at the moment he would take anything.

"What happened then?" Glenn said, skipping over the thin personal description, Reed reasoning she did not want to lose any momentum they already had going.

"I struggled to get away, but after that, the lights went out," Weston said. She again raised a hand, this time motioning to the side of her face.

"I'm guessing that's where this came from because when I woke up I was taped to a chair in the living room."

"Any idea when that was?" Glenn asked.

"No," Weston replied, shaking her head just slightly. "But I know it was dark outside."

"You mentioned your husband usually joined you for dinner," Glenn said. "Was he back yet?"

"No," Weston repeated, "which is why I was preoccupied. He'd called while I was in the dry cleaners, said he had an annual review coming up and would have to stay later than usual."

Without realizing it Reed felt the skin around his eyes tighten, hoping he wasn't right in thinking where this might be headed. If even the slightest possibility of domestic troubles, of infidelity, was sneaking in, the investigation could get a whole lot uglier.

It also severely reduced the chances of their cases being connected.

"And you didn't believe him?" Glenn asked.

"No, I did," Weston said, "which was the problem. The man worked such ridiculous hours as it was, what little time I did get, I wanted."

A bit of heat flushed Reed's face as the statement came out, though he gave no other indicator.

Judging by the blush on Glenn's cheeks, she had had the same thought as well.

"I get what you're asking," Weston said, lowering her voice to just north of a whisper, so quiet Reed had to lean in to hear what she was saying. "And thank you for being more delicate than that asshole back there was, but this was not a case of a jilted lover or something.

"Yeah, I know I'm not from here, and I know my husband was not the most attractive man alive." She stuck her chin out and rotated it in a quick circle, encompassing the kitchen. "All this though, this is recent. When I married him he was a psychiatrist working with inmates making $48,000 a year."

She didn't bother expounding any further, though there was no need to.

"What happened after you woke up?" Glenn asked, choosing not to directly address the statement.

"Nothing," Weston said, "not for a long time anyway. He had wrapped my wrists and feet in duct tape, pressed it across my face. I was scared to death, wanted to cry, but was too afraid I wouldn't be able to breathe.

"Instead I just sat there, waiting, hoping to God my husband would come home and save me."

"Where was your abductor during this time?" Glenn asked.

Another moment passed, the back of Weston's head tilting down a slight bit. "I don't know. I couldn't see or hear a thing."

"Have you had a chance to look through the house yet? Is anything missing?"

"Just a real quick glance," Weston said. "My jewelry is all here, same for all the electronics."

She paused there, for the first time turning her head far enough to the side to see Reed. "Do you hear that?"

Again Reed and Glenn exchanged a glance. They both turned to the side and listened close, nothing unusual coming their way.

"You mean the men in the other room?" Glenn asked.

"Exactly," Weston said. "This is a big house, sound carries. The whole time I was sitting there, I didn't hear a single thing.

"I don't think he was going through anything. I think he was just sitting and waiting for Dennis to get home."

If that were the case, any previous concerns Reed had about the connection between the two was gone. Just the way the traffic stop with Iaconelli and Bishop seemed personal, this too was beginning to show similar signs.

Whoever this was was targeting specific people, and was not above being careful and patient to get to them.

"What happened once your husband arrived?" Glenn said. She still used the same tone, just a few steps up from placating, but Reed could tell by the increased cadence of her questions that she was getting anxious, she too putting together what they were being told.

Another moment passed. Reed could tell by the way Weston fidgeted in her seat that the closer she got to the end of the story, the more uncomfortable she became. He knew that retelling it couldn't be easy, especially so soon after the fact, sitting not 50 feet from where it happened.

Still, they needed the information. Already the killer was far out ahead of them, gaining more distance by the moment.

"When I heard the garage door open, my blood pressure skyrocketed. I started thrashing and trying to scream, but that damn duct tape had me silent and motionless," she said, her voice back to a whisper.

"I tried and tried to warn Dennis as he walked in," she said, her shoulders shuddering as she began to cry softly. "The look on his face, the sheer horror, shock, of seeing me tied up..."

Again she paused, her tears coming harder, louder. "He had no idea that guy was even there waiting for him. All he saw was me, his wife, in trouble. Walked straight forward, right into the knockout shot."

Rotating slightly at the waist, Reed glanced back out into the living room. He recalled the layout of the room, of the hallway that opened into the space.

If someone were lying in wait, they would have the perfect vantage, just off the hallway. They could remain concealed, catch someone unawares, especially someone that was focused on their wife tied up in front of them.

"After that, it's all a bunch of starts and stops," Weston said. "When he hit Dennis, I passed out too. A while later he splashed water on both of us, I guess wanting me to see what he was doing."

Both hands came to her face this time, brushing back over her cheeks, wiping away tears. One at a time she lowered them to her thighs, using the thick material of the robe to rub them clean.

"And what was he doing?" Glenn asked.

Weston's head snapped sharply over to Glenn, as if the sound of her voice shook her from the memory. Her lips parted and stayed in place a moment, staring, before saying, "He had tied Dennis up. Or, more accurately, twisted him up like a pretzel. His hands and feet were behind him, a rope had been looped around his ankles and neck."

Once before, Reed had seen something similar. A young couple had been experimenting with sexual bondage and had taken things too far, the young man choking himself to death before his girlfriend could get him free.

The scene he and Riley had arrived at was difficult to see, a far cry from some of the more gruesome things they'd encountered, but no less harrowing.

He hated to think what it was like having to watch one's longtime spouse go in such a way.

"Did the killer say anything?" Glenn asked. "Either before or after your husband arrived?"

"Not to me," Weston replied. "Like I said, my mouth was covered the entire time, so it wasn't like I could respond."

Again she paused, drawing in a deep breath, large enough it raised her shoulders an inch on either side of her neck. "To Dennis, he explained that he had a choice. He could either take his own life and I could live, or he could try to fight it and we both would die."

To her credit, Glenn didn't ask the obvious follow-up question.

The fact that Diedra Weston was sitting there with them answered it anyway.

"Anything else?" Glenn asked.

"Consequences," Weston whispered, rotating to look at each of them in turn before shifting back to stare out the windows, the expression on her face letting it be known that she was done with the conversation.

"The last thing he said was, actions have consequences."

Chapter Twenty-Seven

Billie scrambled down out of the backseat, legs splaying across the asphalt as she snorted her displeasure at having been left behind. Seeing the condition Deidra Weston was in, Reed was reasonably certain he'd made the right call leaving Billie behind, not knowing what affect her presence might have had. While she was not a male, there being no outward reason why she would scare the woman in any way, there was just no way to ever be certain.

A solid black wolf had a tendency to frighten even the most secure of individuals, something Weston was far from being at the moment.

Reed watched as she paced a few moments, waiting to see if her services would be needed, before moving past the cars and onto the front grass of the Weston's lawn.

"I don't think she appreciated being pinned up," Glenn said, a look of mild amusement on her face as she watched Billie go.

A handful of retorts came to mind, but Reed opted against voicing them, settling instead on a wan smile. "If we had any piece of physical evidence beyond just a few shell casings from the first crime scene, I'd set her loose here now. She'd be able to tell us within a minute if this is the same guy or not."

He glanced over to Glenn, watching as her eyebrows raised a fraction of an inch. "No shit?"

"No shit," Reed said. "I've only been K-9 for about 10 months and was a little skeptical when I came over, but she's incredible. Saved our asses a few times already."

Ten yards away Billie turned in a tight circle before lowering herself into a squat, marking her territory. "All present indications to the contrary."

"Ha!" Glenn said, the sound somewhere between a cough and a laugh. The exertion of it bent her forward at the waist just slightly, her hands hanging down in front of her.

A moment passed as the two watched Billie finish and continue moving about the front yard before Reed turned and rested his backside against the hood of his car. "So, what did you make of all that?"

Raising her arms before her, Glenn folded them across her waist, holding the lapels of her jacket closed. "Where to even start?" she muttered, shaking her head twice. "I'm assuming we can bypass the way those buffoons in there have handled her thus far?"

"We can," Reed agreed. There was no way they ever should have brought her back to the house already, both given her condition and the fact that the crime scene was still considered active.

It was also apparent from their postures standing in the kitchen and Weston's eagerness to get away from them that their bedside manner left something to be desired.

"Okay, first thing," Glenn said, "the guy gave Weston a choice. Actually told him he had to kill himself or they both died."

"Yeah," Reed said. "You ever see something like that before?"

"You mean outside of the *Saw* movies?"

The right corner of Reed's mouth ticked upward slightly. He could tell she was being facetious, but just slightly.

"I've heard of making someone choose," Reed said, "but never something where they actually had to do themselves."

"Not just that," Glenn said, "but do it by strangulation, while his wife watched, no less."

The same exact thoughts had appeared in Reed's head as he listened to Weston recount her tale, had played on loop ever since. "No way this isn't personal."

Glenn nodded twice, her jaw set. "You heard the officers on the way out. Nothing appears to be missing in the house, no signs of him searching for anything."

"Right," Reed said, shifting slightly over his shoulder to look at the front of the enormous brick home rising behind him. "And if he wanted to, he could have made out with quite a stash. It was all right there for the taking."

"Instead he touches nothing, calls 911 on the way out."

A gust of cool air passed through, pushing handfuls of leaves from the trees overhead. Already most of the orange and gold had floated to the ground, collecting in bunches along the curbs, leaving only the darkest red and brown behind.

Reed watched a trio float down toward the asphalt, his vision blurring as he thought things over. "So either he wanted to make sure she didn't die too or he wanted us to find Dennis Weston."

"Or somebody to, anyway."

Blinking his eyes back into focus, Reed flicked his gaze to Glenn. "Either way – personal."

"Personal," Glenn agreed.

For a moment neither said anything, each processing the information, fitting things into their minds, putting it up against what they were searching for.

"Okay," Reed said, "so where does this leave us? Do we continue to assume this is connected and dig a little further, or go our separate ways and keep the other apprised of whatever we find?"

The question came out a bit harsher than intended, but that didn't lessen the veracity of it. Despite the scene he was still standing less than 100 yards from, he had one of his own pressing him even more. He felt for Glenn, and for Mrs. Weston, but his responsibility was with finding whoever had shot Iaconelli and Bishop.

Across from him Glenn nodded, no sign of any anger or offense crossing her features, thinking it through.

"Give me your honest opinion on if these are connected," she said.

Bunching his cheeks up tight for a moment, Reed considered the question. He shifted his head a fraction of an inch to either side and said, "60-40 in favor, maybe as much 70-30. The MO's are drastically different, we have no physical evidence linking the two, but similarities are present."

"Most notably?"

"The personal nature of it," Reed said. "So far both scenes have involved people in the criminal justice system and both have employed words such as *payback, consequences, choices.*"

He paused there, waiting as Glenn considered the notion.

It took less than a minute, giving the impression she had already reached the same conclusion before asking the question.

"Okay, so we keep working together?"

The candor of the statement surprised Reed a bit. He paused, for the first time noticing she was working without a partner, remembering that she had only just been assigned that morning.

At some point he would need to ask about it, but now wasn't that time.

"Alright," Reed said, "though right now I wonder if dividing-and-conquering wouldn't be a better approach. I'm outside of jurisdiction, so you can start a search for Weston's car, coordinate anything you need from here."

Glenn nodded. "And you?"

"I need to check the reports from my guys, start pulling case files. My top priority is going to be figuring out how my victims and yours overlap. We do that, we might have a shot at determining who's behind this."

Once more Glenn nodded before raising her left arm and checking her watch. "Right now it is 1:30. Agree to speak again at, say, 7:00?"

Chapter Twenty-Eight

Three files were sitting on Reed's desk by the time he made it to the precinct. The start of afternoon traffic had made the going a bit slower heading back, the trip from New Albany taking nearly a full hour. That pushed the clock to half past 2:00, Reed becoming more aware of the time with each passing moment.

Even more so of the occasional glances every person in the precinct seemed to be throwing his way.

The top in the stack was from Earl, the full official workup of the shooting scene the night before last. Holding it open on his lap Reed scanned through it once, looking for any new pieces of information to jump out at him. He knew that if anything major had been discovered Earl would have called him personally to relay it, but couldn't help himself from looking just the same, a conditioned habit from years as a detective.

When nothing rose to the surface, he slowed down and read through everything a second time, making a point to go over relevant details a couple of times, committing them to memory so as to be ready for quick recall moving forward.

Just as had been discussed, preliminary shooting patterns indicated a single shooter sitting in the driver's seat. Recovered shell casings showed the weapon to be a .9mm Beretta, a common law enforcement issue, easily obtained in hundreds of different places. The shells themselves were for standard rounds, a fact that probably saved Iaconelli's life.

Parabellums were designed to mushroom on contact, to expand and create mass chaos upon exiting a target. Had the shooter been using them, there was no way the detective could have survived multiple hits to the torso.

Aside from that, there was nothing much of use. No DNA, no organic forensics of any kind.

All blood, fibers, and tissue that were found belonged to one of the detectives.

Closing the file, Reed set it aside and took up the second in the stack. Also from Earl, it was much thinner than the first, nothing more than a couple of sheets affixed at the top by a metal clip.

The car that was found along the Big Darby Creek had been burned to the point that most useful evidence was long gone. As with the first site, there was no organic matter, the interior seats reduced to ash, a process aided by a considerable amount of accelerant.

In the back of the vehicle was found the source of it, a metal can of generic lighter fluid.

Beneath the passenger seat they'd located a pair of shell casings, the make and model matching those found at the first scene, though the indentation from the firing pin was different.

Two guns in a matching set employed by a single shooter.

The vin number had survived the inferno, confirming that the vehicle did belong to Jonas Hendrix. No attempt had been made to swap the plates.

Sighing, Reed closed the file and placed it atop the first, a new stack forming alongside the original. Beside him Billie sat on her back haunches, her ears pointed straight up, alert and awaiting any word.

The final folder in the stack was a bit different from the first, coming over from the crime scene crew in Grove City. While not as thorough or as legible as Earl's, it gave the high points in bulleted fashion, outlining that the intruder had gained entry through the rear garage door. Marks on the wood casing were indicative of a crowbar being used, though one had not been found on the scene.

The shards found in the garage were not glass as Greene and Gilchrist had previously thought, instead being heavy plastic consistent with a taillight.

Pausing for a moment, Reed raised his attention to the window before him. He aimed his gaze on nothing in particular, the cars parked out in the lot swirling into an amoeba of random colors as his focus glazed over. He tried to imagine someone entering through the garage, to determine how a taillight could have been destroyed in the process, though nothing came to him.

Shifting back to the file, he read through the last page of the report quickly, noting that it appeared nobody had entered the actual house.

Reed felt a flag go off in the back of his mind, noting that if connected, it was the second time in as many days the perpetrator had been inside a house with unfettered access and had not taken a thing.

Whatever was motivating these actions, it was certainly not wanton greed.

Placing the file back with the other two, Reed shoved the stack aside and moved to the computer. A simple shift of the mouse brought the monitor to life, a series of icons arranged vertically along the left side of the screen.

Moving straight for the CPD database, Reed entered his name and badge number, going into the file depository and opening the search function. He entered Iaconelli and Bishop as the investigating officers and set the engine to running, less than 10 seconds passing before a result was spit back at him.

Well over 1,000 cases featuring one or both of them.

Feeling his stomach clench, Reed glanced down to Billie, her dark eyes staring back up at him. He held the gaze a moment, working down the growing distaste in his mouth, before going back to the screen and clearing both names.

Moving the cursor on the search form from investigating officers to a general search, Reed typed in Dennis Weston.

A few moments later, more than three times the previous result sprang up before him.

"Dammit," Reed said, leaning back once more. Warmth crept across his features as he stared at the screen. He ran a hand over his face and wiped the ensuing residue across the leg of his jeans before going back and typing all three names into their corresponding fields.

The number shrunk, but not near as much as Reed would have liked, still totaling more than 200 in total.

There was no way they could possibly hope to go through so many cases by hand. Even grabbing every available person in the precinct, it would take an inordinate amount of time. Already the clock in the wake of the first shooting was close to 36 hours and counting.

More time was something he simply didn't have.

"Okay, now what?" he whispered, Billie blinking her lidless eyes at him, remaining silent.

The two were still locked in the pose, Reed thinking, Billie awaiting direction, when Reed's cell phone sounded on the desk beside him. Loud and sharp, it snapped both their attention toward it, Reed letting it ring twice before glancing at the number on it, a local call that was not saved into his contacts.

"Reed Mattox."

"Detective, this is Cassidy Glenn."

A crease formed between Reed's eyebrows as he glanced over to his computer screen, noting the time in the corner. It was too soon for her to already be checking in, meaning something new must have arisen.

"What's happened?" Reed asked.

"There was a hit on Diedra Weston's Audi," Glenn said. "Get this, it was parked outside the dry cleaners shop that she went to yesterday afternoon."

Reed's eyes opened wide at the statement, a puff of air passing over his lips. "The killer climbed into her car in a busy parking lot, rode with her to her house, then drove it back to the same spot?"

"Yes," Glenn said, "which also means he probably left his parked there the entire time."

Again a look of surprise came over Reed's features. "Wow. Any surveillance cameras?"

"I don't know yet," Glenn said. "I'm on my way now. You want in?"

Chapter Twenty-Nine

The drive back across town, Reed's second in less than six hours, took twice as long as the original trip. Hoping to avoid the mess of the downtown workday letting out, he stuck to the northern half of the outer belt, instead running into the afternoon rush from Ohio State and the omnipresent orange construction barrels that seemed to always dot the central Ohio landscape.

By the time he arrived his mood had dipped from urgent to sour, his facial expression relaying as much. The corners of his mouth were turned down in a slight frown, his brow pinched as he pulled up to the New Albany Town Plaza.

How or why the small assemblage of businesses had awarded themselves the moniker *plaza* Reed wasn't sure, the entire expanse covering seven storefronts. Arranged in a horseshoe formation, two businesses comprised either end, a trio forming the back portion. In the center of the arrangement were a dozen rows of parking spots, spotlights positioned every 20 yards or so throughout.

The entire left end of the parking lot, a full four of the twelve rows, was cordoned off by local law enforcement, a handful of cars and enough police tape to mummify a body stretched out around the scene.

Per usual in such matters, especially during daylight hours, even more so in locations such as New Albany, a healthy swath of onlookers was pressed tight on all sides, looking to see what the commotion was about.

Seeing them standing there, Reed could only imagine as to the speculation that was running rampant, an adult version of the childhood game Telephone. Within the hour the entire town would be convinced that a police shootout had taken place in the streets, the entirety of the Plaza painted red with blood.

The thought drew a sharp shake of the head from Reed as he parked as close as he could and killed the engine, not bothering to negotiate the thick tangle of people any further. Instead he clipped Billie to the short lead and let her clear a path, knowing she would do a far better job than his unmarked sedan could ever hope to.

She did not disappoint.

At full height she rose right to his waist, her inky black form a rarity for a Belgian Malinois. Combined, the effect was to incite a reaction in whoever saw her at a glance, people stepping back, recoiling in fear, before realizing she was there to help and switching over to abject curiosity.

Fortunately for Reed, by the time that realization occurred he was already well past them.

Reed found Glenn standing in the center of the portion of the lot that had been cleared, only a single car parked inside the area demarcated by bright yellow plastic tape fluttering in the breeze. Her arms were folded across her chest as she stood in conversation with one of the men Reed had seen inside the Weston living room, a white paper suit unzipped, the top half hanging free around his waist.

Approaching from the side, Reed made sure he and Billie were both visible as they approached, waiting a few feet back for Glenn to motion them in. Once she did they stepped forward, the group forming a loose triangle, their backs to the crowd, voices low.

"Wade, this is Detective Mattox, he was at the Weston house with me this morning," Glenn said, careful not to gesture or make any movements that could be interpreted, or more aptly misinterpreted, by the gawkers nearby. "Reed, Wade Porter, head of the crime scene unit here in New Albany."

Taking a cue from Glenn, Reed nodded slightly. "Porter."

"Mattox," Porter replied.

Turning to the side, Glenn motioned to the car nearby. "We received a call from a local patrol an hour ago that spotted the car parked here."

Following her movement, Reed looked over at the Audi S3, a four door model with windows tinted well beyond what he thought admissible by the law, the exterior waxed to a mirrored shine.

It wasn't hard to figure out how the patrol had noticed it, the car an obvious sore thumb, even in a town such as New Albany.

"Cameras?" Reed asked, shifting his focus up to the light poles overhead.

"The Plaza has a small security office," Glenn said, "but they only monitor things during working hours. I had the guard go back and run things, he said the car was present when the cameras went live this morning."

"Shit," Reed muttered, looking past the lights to the lot around them. "So he gained access to her car, rode to her house with her, then returned it overnight before the cameras came back on."

"Looks that way," Glenn said, nodding.

Beside her Porter stood with his hands hooked into the belt of his suit, saying nothing. Three days of heavy growth covered the bottom half of his face, making it impossible to read any expression as he listened, nothing but his eyes moving.

"What about yesterday?" Reed asked. "Were they able to get a look at him as he climbed into her car?"

"I asked them to go back and look," Glen said. "They'll let us know as soon as they do."

"Assuming they were even parked out here," Porter added, his first words of the conversation. The sound of his voice drew the attention of both Reed and Glenn toward him, surprise on their faces.

"Meaning?" Glenn asked.

"Meaning you guys aren't from here," Porter said, "but believe me when I tell you, this place gets busy on the weekends. This little lot were standing in here doesn't begin to cover it."

The familiar clench appeared in Reed's stomach, his solar plexus drawing tight. Beside him he could sense a similar reaction in Glenn, her visage pinching inward.

"So where do they park?" Glenn asked.

"On the street," Porter said, both shoulders rising in a shrug. "Or in the overflow parking out back."

Rotating her head at the neck, Glenn glanced over at Reed, the look even more pronounced on her features. "Are there cameras back there?"

"I don't know," Porter said, "but I doubt it. It's basically just a big concrete pad backing up to an empty lot. Doesn't even have parking spots painted on it."

"Great," Glenn muttered, raising a hand and running it back through the side of her hair. "Were you able to get anything from the house this morning?"

"Nothing so far," Porter said. "Pretty surprising really, damn near everything in the house belongs to one of the Westons. Place like that, you'd figure there'd be a housekeeper, a chef, somebody else, but we didn't find anything except from the deputies that showed up and untied her last night."

"Son of a bitch," Glenn spat, once more running her hand back through her hair. She rotated in place and looked out at the crowd, again realizing they were watching her every move, before lowering her hand and trying to play it cool.

"Odds of you finding anything in the car we can use?" she asked.

"Don't know," Porter said, offering another shrug. "He was pretty careful at the house, but a car is different. Almost impossible to climb in and out, be seated for that long, and not leave behind a hair or something."

Reed nodded, having heard the same explanation a time or two from Earl.

He remained silent a moment, mulling over what Porter had just said about the house. He allowed his gaze to gloss over, his mind piecing together the care that was taken, the effort to make sure nothing was left behind.

"What are you thinking?" Glenn asked, the question drawing Reed from his trance.

Without answering he shifted to Porter and asked, "Tell me, did you happen to just come straight from the Weston house?"

Chapter Thirty

The crime scene van was a plain white paneled model, the same kind that Earl drove, the same as every other unit in the greater Columbus area. Reed couldn't help but smirk as he saw it sitting just outside the yellow police tape, an eyesore in the picturesque community. He imagined that somewhere there was an entire fleet of matching vehicles, all stretched out, ready to be deployed at a moment's notice.

The rear door wrenched open with a harsh shriek of rusted metal, loud enough to bring winces from Reed and Glenn both as Porter pushed it open. Diving in head first, he pressed his hands onto the rubber mat in the back of the van, climbing forward on all fours before reaching a particular grey plastic bin and dragging it back toward the bumper.

One foot at a time he retreated to the ground before pulling the box over against the front of his thighs and unclasping the hasp. Reed watched in silence as he opened the top, a bevy of sealed plastic bags inside, and began to rifle through.

Less than a minute later he found what he was looking for at the bottom of the container.

The bag was one of the larger inside the bin, over a foot in length. Made of clear plastic, a white label was affixed to the outside, writing in black marker strewn across it.

Inside was a coil of rope of indeterminate length, all spooled up tight. Constructed of a trio of braided strands, it was solid white in color, just a few slight smudges of red present.

"Okay, you know I can't let you take this, or even really let it out of my own hands," Porter said. The words and the expression on his face both showed he was uneasy with what he was doing, his gaze flicking past Reed, tracking for anybody that might be nearby.

"I know," Reed said, "and trust me, I'm not trying to mess up the chain of custody. If there's anything viable on there, we're going to need it to build a case."

Maintaining the integrity of evidence was one of the first things they had been taught at the academy, a maxim that was hammered home to the point of annoyance every chance the department got thereafter.

"I actually don't even need to get within two feet of it, I just need her to get a few good hits of it," Reed said, nudging the top of his head toward Billie.

The look of uncertainty remained on Porter's face. "I don't know. Like I said, this guy is careful. I doubt it will work."

"Doesn't matter how careful he is," Reed said, "he can't hide from her."

There was more he could have added, a veritable wealth of knowledge he had accumulated in the previous 10 months about the power of his partner's senses. Instead he let it go with a small smile, watching as Porter peeled open the top flap of the evidence bag and extended it to Billie.

On cue, the dog leaned forward and dipped her muzzle just above it, taking in great long pulls. She stood completely still a long moment, only the sides of her nostrils moving, before stepping back and looking up at Reed.

She had it. She was ready.

"What is this for again?" Glenn asked, watching the entire thing play out, a look on her face much closer to Porter's than Reed's.

"She's going to tell us where he went after he dropped her car off," Reed said. "If nothing else, we'll know if there's anything we can hope to get off the security cameras. Maybe we'll even get lucky and he dropped something along the way."

He didn't wait for a response, sensing the building energy in Billie, anxious to get going.

"Search," he commanded, the word coming out sharp and loud, Glenn and Porter both flinching slightly.

The word was still in the air as Billie shot forward. She began to swing side to side in a sweeping motion, her feet moving quickly, her nose pointed toward the ground. She drew in one long breath after another, tugging for more leeway from her partner.

Under optimal circumstances Reed would have her on the long leash, allowing her a full eight feet of length, anchoring it to his belt, or even better, would have let her run free. Given the confines of the plaza though, and the sheer congestion of people and cars around, he couldn't do that. Instead he did his best to stay in lockstep with her, allowing her to draw him forward.

Covering a path more than six feet wide, Billie pushed forward through the cordoned off area, searching like a canine metal detector. She pressed forward for more than half the length of the lot, showing no signs of recognition until she was just a few feet from the car.

Reed knew it the moment she picked up the scent, a visible charge passing through her body. No longer did she swing her attention from side to side, instead focusing on a single point before her. With her nose lowered inches from the ground, her body moved into a coiled stance, pulling straight ahead, moving diagonally away from the Audi in a direct line.

"She got something?" Glenn said, her voice much closer than Reed realized.

Turning over his shoulder, Reed offered only a smile, not wanting to distract Billie, not risking the sound of his voice interrupting her search.

He could hear Glenn's shoes hit against the asphalt as she jogged to catch up, falling in beside him. Together the odd trio continued across the open swath of concrete, moving for the corner of the lot.

"Clear those people away," Reed hissed, keeping his voice low. "Looks like we're going around back."

With a nod Glenn jogged out in front of them, pulling her credentials from her hip. She waved them over head and entreated people to move back, Reed watching her movements but unable to hear her words, the sounds swallowed up by the ambient noise of the crowd.

Bending at the waist, Reed passed beneath the outer edge of the cordoned off area, Billie pulling him straight ahead. On either side of him the crowd was peeled back, people staring slack jawed at what they were seeing, as if he was a modern day Moses walking through the Red Sea.

Ahead of him he could see Glenn continuing to make sure folks stayed back, the crowd thinning.

By the time they made the edge of the Plaza, most everybody was in their wake. Reed could feel their stares on his back as Billie continued to move on, her entire being singularly focused on the scent in her nostrils. She used it to propel them both forward, walking around the edge of the end unit in the Plaza.

The backside of the strip mall was exactly as Porter had warned, nothing more than an open expanse of concrete. There were no markings of any kind painted on the ground, no curbs or ties to demarcate the movement of traffic.

A little more than half of the space was full as they made the corner, Billie hitting it at a trot. She pushed straight past the first three rows and onto the fourth, moving past a pair of trucks and an SUV.

Further still she pushed before pulling up abruptly.

At least 20 feet of open ground separated them from the nearest automobile.

"What?" Glenn asked, coming up alongside them. She was panting slightly from the combined effects of the impromptu jog and pushing the crowd back, her hair whipping around her face. "What happened?"

Reed waited before answering, watching as Billie moved side to side, hoping to pick it up again.

After a moment she lowered her backside to the ground, staring up at him.

"This is where he was parked," Reed said. "Trail runs out here."

"You're sure?" Glenn asked.

"Positive," Reed said. "He was parked around back so his car was off-camera. Dropped hers back when he knew it wouldn't be noticed, came and retrieved his."

"Dammit," Glenn muttered, pressing her fists into her hips, the bottom of her suit jacket bunching around her wrists.

"Careful," Reed said, echoing the word Porter had used just moments before.

An angry snort rolled from Glenn as she walked a few steps past Billie. She aimed her attention at the ground and extended a toe in front of her, swinging it back and forth.

"Anything?" Reed asked.

"Nope," Glenn responded, venom beginning to appear in her voice.

"We'll have to mark this off and have Wade come take a look anyway."

"Yeah," Glenn said, raising her face toward the sky. She closed her eyes and remained in place a moment. "Have I mentioned yet that this guy is really starting to piss me off?"

Chapter Thirty-One

Big had referred to it as the Blood Tingle, that feeling that always came right before things started, that permeated the entire body. It was as inevitable as the outcome itself, nature's way of sharpening the nerves, of bringing everything into clear focus.

For The Kid, the preferred term was the Scalp Itch. He could certainly see where Big had come up with Blood Tingle, though for him the feeling wasn't quite as systemic. His hands, his feet, even his internal organs, weren't affected. They remained completely even, as steely as his resolve, impervious to the outside world.

He could be changing his oil or checking his email or kidnapping Diedra Weston, his interworking didn't care.

Where he always felt it was along his scalp. It began right at the nape of his neck, traveling up and outward, following his hair line, passing along his ears and over the crown of his head. From there it converged right along his brow, the entire top part of his skull itching, feeling as if it might catch fire at any moment.

When that arrived, The Kid knew game time was imminent. He knew that he was just moments away from doing something that mattered, that required every system in his body working in concert.

The Scalp Itch had not yet taken full hold, but it was just starting. The Kid could feel it arising along his hair line, just above his shoulders. It lingered in slight bursts, the sensation much the same as a foot or hand that had fallen asleep, the nerve endings writhing in anticipation.

Just as fast it dissipated, his body going through a practice run, much the same as he was.

The right corner of The Kid's mouth twitched as he felt tingling rise and ebb, his back pressed against the dimpled stucco of the freestanding garage just outside the home of his next target. In front of him hung a heavy canopy of vines, their leaves brittle, already turned brown but not yet fallen for the winter.

Tucked behind them, he knew he was invisible to anybody that didn't know to look for him, whether they are standing at the kitchen window less than 10 feet away or even strolling along the walkway just beyond arm's reach.

Of all the targets thus far, this was the easiest. The schedule that was kept made gaining access painfully simple, so much so that it almost removed any amount of fun for The Kid.

The arrogance the target carried made it so that security at the home was nowhere what it should be for anybody, let alone someone in their position. It was the third time The Kid had been on the property, the spot he was now tucked away in such an obvious hide that it showed the lack of awareness the target employed.

This was the final scouting run for The Kid, a result more of his growing boredom with watching the camera than the actual need to be onsite. He didn't expect to discover a single thing differing from the previous trips he'd made, not one detail that he hadn't spent the entire afternoon observing.

His presence was born from his need to be *doing* something. He had never been known for his ability to sit still, a trait Big had always tried to caution him about, saying it might one day be his undoing.

Whether or not that would ever come to pass The Kid wasn't sure, but he was reasonably certain this would not be that day. Especially not with tomorrow so close, with the culmination of everything he'd been working for inching steadily onward.

The end was near. So very near.
For him, and for Big.

Chapter Thirty-Two

Reed had a headache. Two trips between the extreme opposite corners of the Columbus metro area meant he and Billie had spent the better part of four hours in the car on the day, most of it fighting a heavy slog of stop-and-go movement. He could tell by the incessant fussing in the backseat that Billie was becoming of the same mind as he, both of them anxious to be out of the metal confines of the sedan.

Adding to the pounding in his head was the directive from Grimes to stop by his office as soon as he could get there. The clock on the front dash said it was only a few minutes after 6:00, well within the time frame Grimes was normally still in the building, but he could tell by the strained tone that it was a mandate and not a request.

He needed to get to the precinct, and he needed to be quick about it.

A dozen different thoughts ran through Reed's mind as he finished the loop around the outer belt of the city and wound through the side streets of Franklinton, skirting the edge of The Bottoms en route to the 8th.

At the top of the list was everything that was happening with Weston, from the extreme care that was taken by the killer not to leave behind a single fiber of anything useful to the odd fact that he had let Diedra Weston live. Adding to it was the realization at the lot, that just like with his own case, the killer had taken a chance by securing a car, but had been successful in leaving them absolutely nothing to go on from it.

The thought brought a sour taste to Reed's mouth as he thought back to his own case, the heightening tension from the fact that two of his colleagues, arguably the two people outside of Grimes and Jackie that he worked with the most, were both still in the hospital. That meant that every last person in the station was feeling the strain, all looking to him to get things figured out.

Underscoring it even more, try as Reed might to keep it suppressed, was his own history with the loss of a partner threatening to bubble up at any moment. Thus far he had managed to keep thoughts of Riley at a minimum, the lone exception being his conversation with Bishop, but he knew they were never far from the surface, waiting to consume him.

The light in Grimes's office burned bright in the first floor corner of the 8th as Reed pulled up, eschewing the parking lot for the visitor stalls out front. He slid to a stop using the same spot he had just two nights before after first leaving the hospital, already the event seeming like a lifetime ago.

Beside it was parked a plain black sedan with government plates that Reed had never seen before, though a sense of déjà vu settled in upon viewing it, feeling like he had seen many similar to it in the years prior. For a moment he sat behind the wheel and stared before shaking his head clear of the thought and climbing out.

Forgoing the use of any lead, Reed let Billie out of the back, the two of them going for the front door in unison. Together they moved straight past the bullpen of the lower level and into the executive suite of the precinct, finding Grimes's office door open, light spilling into the hall-way, an unfamiliar voice accompanying it.

Putting himself between Billie and the door, Reed tapped lightly on the frame twice, a thin noise sounding out, just enough to draw Grimes's attention toward him. He raised his chin upward once to let the captain know he was present before taking a step back, ready to retreat to the bench in the hallway until the meeting that was going on was concluded.

"Detective," Grimes called, stopping Reed less than a step back from the door, "you guys can come on in."

Glancing down to Billie, Reed patted the outside of his thigh once before stepping into the office. Grimes made no effort to stand as he entered, instead flicking his gaze over to the chairs across from his desk, Reed following the lead.

Seated across from Grimes was a middle-aged man with blue-black hair and a heavy five o'clock shadow, a small cleft in his chin. He stood as Reed entered, stopping even with the bridge of Reed's nose.

He was a few inches wider than Reed and wearing a suit without the jacket, his tie loosened and his cuffs rolled halfway up his forearms.

"Dan Gilmore, FBI," the man said, shoving a hand in Reed's direction, making it very clear from his stance and introduction that Reed was supposed to be impressed.

"Detective Reed Maddox, my partner Billie."

Gilmore flashed a quick glance to Billie before returning his gaze, a hint of an eye roll passing over his features.

Less than 10 seconds into their encounter Reed could already feel his animosity for the man rising, from the unnecessary bombast of his voice to the aggressive handshake to his quick dismissal of his partner. He also recalled the sedan parked out in front of the building, remembering why the automobile had seemed so familiar, realizing it was because he *had* seen so many like it over the years.

And just as with the owners of nearly every last one of them, he found himself already disliking this one.

Bypassing the second chair in front of Grimes's desk, Reed leaned himself against the side table in the room, folding his arms across his chest. He made a point not to look at Gilmore, instead focusing on the captain and asking, "You wanted to see me?"

"Actually, I did," Gilmore said, jumping in before Grimes had a chance to speak.

The move pulled the glares of both Reed and Grimes over at the same time, neither saying anything.

"I wanted to know why this precinct, namely you, was digging through the files of Dennis Weston earlier today."

Warmth traveled the length of Reed's spine, threatening to manifest as sweat at any moment. Reed could feel his face flush slightly as he stared at Gilmore, making no effort to respond before switching his gaze over to Grimes.

The captain held it for a moment, seeming to debate the proper response, before nodding just slightly.

"I am working with the state BCI on his murder last night."

"Why?" Gilmore snapped.

Again Reed could feel his body temperature rise. "What business is that of the FBI's? Franklin Medical is a state facility, outside the BOP."

Reed didn't want to have to point out this entire matter was outside the FBI's jurisdiction, leaving it just short of that, far enough along to make his point.

Across from him the jab seemed to land, the skin tightening a bit around Gilmore's eyes.

"You didn't answer my question," Gilmore responded.

"Nor you mine," Reed replied.

Not once in his discussions with Glenn had any mention of the FBI been made. The BCI had been handed the case free and clear, no requirement for cooperation, no requests for a joint investigation.

On certain matters such as interstate trafficking or terrorism, the FBI was handed automatic control, though nothing of that sort seemed at play. A home invasion and murder were terrible, but no more than thousands of other such incidents that occurred everyday around the country.

"Captain, I expected a little more cooperation than this," Gilmore said, turning his face toward Grimes but keeping his gaze on Reed. "The FBI and CPD have always had a good working relationship, it would be a shame to see that end now."

"A relationship that has been fostered on mutual respect and communication," Grimes said, his voice even, the implication clear.

It was enough to pull Gilmore's gaze from Reed to the captain, the scowl on his face growing more pronounced. He remained that way before finally nodding twice, pursing his lips before him.

"Okay," he finally said, "I can see this is going to be some kind of home turf thing, the two of you ganging up on the outsider."

He paused there a moment, trying to drive home his point, before saying, "Two patients that were recently released from Franklin Medical are on our watch list. We have concerns that one of them might have committed this crime."

"You let two people on your watch list be released from custody?" Grimes asked.

"And why hasn't this information been shared with the lead investigator?" Reed asked, reasonably certain that Glenn had not been apprised of anything of the sort.

The look on Gilmore's face grew a bit more pronounced as he looked between each of them before standing. He shoved his hands into the front pockets of his slacks and continued to glare, Reed and Grimes both meeting the stare.

"Look," he said, lowering his voice a bit, "I came here as a professional courtesy. Tread lightly on the Weston case."

He paused there, his mouth half open, the impression clear there was more he wanted to say. Just as fast he closed it, nodding at Grimes. "Captain."

Without another word he turned on a heel and exited the office, not acknowledging Reed or Billie as he left. A moment later the front door could be heard swinging open and slamming shut, the sound echoing through the nearly empty precinct.

Once the sound faded away, Reed drifted over to the chair Gilmore had been using and lowered himself into it. He could feel the sweat that had arisen in the small of his back causing his shirt to cling to his skin, feel droplets along his brow.

"What the hell was that all about?"

Grimes stared at him a moment before shaking his head just slightly. "I can't be sure, but I think he was here to try and strong arm us."

"You realize he was lying out his ass about two recently released inmates and all that, right?"

"Of course," Grimes said. "You should have heard him in here blowing smoke before you arrived."

Reed grunted in response, though said nothing. The demeanor change in the man had been obvious when Reed shut him down right off the bat, causing him to reverse course out of the gate.

Still, that left a great many questions and very few answers.

"Thoughts?" Reed asked.

"Bah," Grimes said, waving a hand at the door, letting his expression relay what he thought of the man. "Why were you looking in the files of Dennis Weston?"

"BCI and I believe his death and the shootings of Iaconelli and Bishop are connected," Reed said. "Both were of a very personal nature, both aimed at police personnel. At neither scene was any forensic evidence left, though a witness each time heard him use the word *payback*."

"So our suppositions this morning were correct?" Grimes asked.

"To the letter," Reed said, nodding just slightly.

Grimes paused a moment, mulling the new information. His chin receded back into his neck, the folds of skin piling up high as he did so, his standard position when processing new information.

"Leads?" Grimes asked.

"Nothing from the scenes," Reed said, "but I think I was just handed a new one."

Pulling his eyebrows in tight, Grimes stared at Reed a moment before understanding set in.

"Just be careful. Asshole or not, the FBI doesn't take well to outsiders poking through their dirty laundry."

Chapter Thirty-Three

Glenn went through the same emotional progression Reed had upon hearing of the visit from Gilmore. Her first reaction was surprise, followed in order by confusion, defensiveness, and finally anger. She lingered a bit longer on each of the stages, a fact aided considerably by her not being in the same room with the man, but ultimately ended in the exact same place.

Seated in the front seat of his car, parked in the front lot of the Mercy West hospital, Reed listened intently as she parsed her way through it. He had left nothing out of his description, telling her the entire interaction, what little of it there was to relay.

"And that's it?" Glenn asked, the first real follow up question she had fired his way since ending a long string of garbled mumblings.

"Pretty much," Reed said. "Captain and I both got the impression he thought walking in, waving his creds and telling me to stand down was going to do it. When that didn't work he tried to flex a bit, then left."

"Hmm," Glenn said, the word coming out in a short, angry grunt. "And when you say flex?"

"I mean he tried to scare us away," Reed said. The insinuation was clear during the meeting, though with all the other vitriol Reed was

DUSTIN STEVENS

working with at the time, he hadn't given it quite as much due as he should have.

Only after the fact, while driving away, had he really zeroed in on that being the purpose of the stop.

"But why?" Glenn said. "This isn't the Feebs case. If they wanted it, we would have happily handed it over."

Now, having seen the strong likelihood of a connection between his case and hers, Reed wouldn't give it away for anything, especially to a prick like Gilmore.

Twenty-four hours earlier though, he would have tossed it their way without a second glance.

"I agree," Reed said, "and when I pressed him on that, he got skittish. Wasn't two minutes later he jumped up and ran out."

"Just like that?"

"Just like that," Reed said. "Kind of surprised Grimes and me both, but, whatever."

"Yeah," Glenn said, shoving out another breath.

Reed could hear some of the acrimony in her voice fleeing, though it was still clearly present around the edges. He himself was still hovering somewhere close to a similar state, remaining silent.

Outside, the front lights of the hospital were all on for the night, the emblem perched high above blazing like a macabre Christmas tree topper. A reflection of it refracted off the front hood of the car, giving the interior an unnatural glow.

In the backseat Billie sat on her haunches, filling the space between the two front bucket seats. Reed could see her in his rearview mirror, her focus on him.

No doubt she had sensed the physiological change in him that occurred the moment he encountered Gilmore, her presence letting him know she was close if needed.

"You get anything this afternoon?" Reed asked.

Another loud sigh, this one a bit more intense than the previous, sounded out. "No, just a whole lot more of the same. Local traffic cameras were about as useless as the ones from the Plaza. A couple of

174

them picked up Weston's Audi driving away, but the damn windows on the thing were so tinted we couldn't see anything in the backseat."

Reed nodded in the darkness, having thought that exact thing the first time he saw the car parked outside the dry cleaners shop.

"I also swung back with Mrs. Weston," Glenn said. "Yesterday afternoon, the place was overflowing with people. She had to park out back."

She paused there, not needing to go any further. Their best hope at seeing anything on camera was when the killer had gained access to her car. Her being parked out back meant that it all occurred out of view from anybody.

"Any word from Wade on the car yet?" Reed asked, already having a strong supposition but having to ask the question anyway.

"Not yet," Glenn said. "I think the house and the car back-to-back put them a little behind. As you probably noticed, New Albany isn't the kind of community where things like this seem to occur in bunches."

A smirk rocked Reed's head back against the seat behind him, the sound filling the interior of his car. "Not a lot of crime in Stepford, huh?"

"How about you?" Glenn asked, bypassing the question. "What's your plan?"

Any trace of mirth faded from Reed's features as he looked up again at the front façade of the hospital before him.

"I'm going to pop in here and check on my guys, then I'm going to pay someone a visit, see if I can't figure out the real reason Dan Gilmore came calling tonight. That work?"

"Keep me posted."

Chapter Thirty-Four

The bottle was cradled in a way that bordered on reverence, the look on Derrick Chamberlain's face just south of awe. It was balanced in his left palm, the glass stem of the neck resting against his wrist as the fingertips of his right hand gently traced over the label.

"Johnny Walker Blue," he whispered. "Wow. Thank you."

"Um, should I give you two a moment?" Reed asked, allowing his face and his tone to relay the heightened discomfort he was beginning to feel.

The sensation was one that had settled in long before observing the weird amount of deference paid to the bottle of whiskey, starting the moment he left Mercy West a half hour before. It started deep within, the same as it did every time he had to make this particular visit, feeling like butterflies in the pit of his stomach that slowly morphed into a tangle of writhing snakes.

The transition began in earnest when he stopped off to purchase the alcohol that was being so lovingly caressed across from him, reached a fevered pitch as he stood at the front door of the quaint house on a bucolic street in Hilliard and explained to Chamberlain's grandmother for at least the 15th time who he was and why he needed to speak with her grandson.

Somehow, the feeling had managed to grow even stronger as he descended the stairs from the first floor of the home, an ode to all things grandmotherly, an overwhelming amalgam of scents and warm colors, into the basement. Different in every way from the scene above, it was a mecca to arrested development, the kind of thing that seemed more fitting in the basement of a frat house than the dwelling he was actually in.

Reed had made enough pilgrimages into the basement in the name of work to know that one half was a converted living space, replete with a king sized water bed and kitchenette. The other was left open, an 80 inch television, towering speakers, and matching subwoofers filling most of the space. A couple of leather recliners were parked before the television, the only other seating options besides the desk chair in front of the enormous computer system arranged along the back wall.

"Jay Double-U Bee," he said, sounding out the three initials for the alcohol phonetically. "Damn, you must really need something big."

Derrick Chamberlain and Riley had been matched up as neighbors in their freshman dorm, never a more unlikely friendship having developed in the world. The strength of that bond endured through graduation and even a full decade beyond, clear until Riley's untimely demise less than a year before.

Insistent upon being called Deek at all times, it was in the course of that friendship that Reed had first encountered him.

Graduating with a degree in computer science, Deek had eschewed more than a half dozen corporate job offers, instead going into business for himself as a cyber-sleuth. Word was he made enough to own the house they were now in free and clear, every other one on the block as well if he so chose.

Instead he opted to spend no less than 10 hours a day locked in first-person video games, the reason for the vast entertainment system spread beside them.

Subsisting almost entirely on Red Bull and Fruit Rollups, his body had the appearance of a palm tree, a waif thin frame tasked with holding up a large head with even bigger hair.

"Maybe," Reed said, scrunching the right side of his face slightly, "potentially."

The answer did nothing to dampen the enthusiasm on Deek's face as he looked at the bottle another moment before begrudgingly setting it aside.

When Riley had first enlisted her friend's help a half-dozen years before, she had explained to Reed there were only two ironclad rules when coming to him. First was to never arrive empty handed. He was a self-employed businessman and working with computers was how he paid the bills.

Honest wages for honest work and all that.

Second was if they wanted a really good job done fast, don't ever let that payment be in cash.

At the time Reed had no idea what she was referring to, only later figuring things out. Some trips it was something as simple as a six pack, others a full handle of Jack Daniels. The severity of the ask tended to dictate the size of the payment.

Given what Reed found himself in need of at the moment, Johnny Walker Blue seemed fitting.

"How *potentially* are we talking?" Deek asked.

"FBI," Reed said, using his toe to rotate the recliner he sat in a few inches to get a better view of Deek's reaction.

If he was bothered in the slightest by what had just been said, he didn't show it.

"Working with or against them?" Deek asked.

Reed paused a moment, considering the question.

"I only ask because it will dictate how well I need to cover my trail," Deek said, waving a hand before him.

The movement, the flippant delivery of the statement, brought a smile to Reed's face. "Neither, I think. They aren't covering the case with us, but some jackass in a suit came sniffing around this evening and tried to shoo me away."

"You've never struck me as one to be shooed," Deek said. He leaned forward at the waist and extended a bony leg in front of him, grasping the elastic bands of his wool sock and tugging it upward.

"I'm not," Reed said, "nor is my captain, which is why I'm now here."

"Captain," Deek said, his voice a touch detached as he pulled on the opposite sock before setting his feet flat on the floor. "Grimy?"

"Grimes."

"Right," Deek said, nodding slightly. "Yeah, he doesn't seem like one to be pushed aside either."

This time Reed settled with a simple head shake, not bothering to vocalize a response.

"Is this official or off-the-books?" Deek asked.

"It's official," Reed said, "in that he knows I'm here, as does the BCI, who I'm sharing the case with. As far as the Feds are concerned though, this conversation never took place."

At that Deek twisted his head at the neck to look at the bottle on the floor beside him, nodding slightly. "And hence, the good stuff."

"There it is," Reed said. A small part of him hated that his motivations were so blatant before the larger part won out, reasoning that was only the case because he hadn't much tried to hide them.

There was no reason to. He knew Deek wouldn't care either way.

"So what do you need?" Deek asked, slapping both palms down on his thighs, the sound of skin-on-skin contact buffeted only by a pair of print boxer shorts.

In quick order Reed went through the initial incident with Iaconelli and Bishop, followed it up with everything that had occurred with the Westons in the previous day.

Not once while he spoke did Deek take down a note of any kind, his face twisted up slightly in thought, absorbing every word.

Reed knew better than to bother commenting on it, trusting that everything was being recorded in Deek's own way.

"So you need to see their overlaps?" Deek said. "Simple enough."

Again Reed's face scrunched slightly to the side, his features contorted as he raised a hand on edge and wagged it. "Well, sort of. That's the first part of it, anyway."

A moment passed as Deek sat in silence before nodding his head back a few inches.

"The second part being this FBI pinhead and how he intersects with all this?"

"There it is," Reed repeated, jabbing a finger out in front of himself for emphasis.

A side-by-side of the detectives and Weston would be simple enough. He had been able to get a decent start on that already, having been pulled off only because of the discovery of Diedra Weston's car and the daunting number of cases that the initial run returned.

"If I were to guess Gilmore's age I'd put him at 40ish, meaning all of these parties have a pretty substantial track record to go through. Might want to start with the most recent and work your way back from there."

Again Deek remained silent a moment, his eyes pinched up slightly as he stared above Reed's head, his lips moving imperceptibly.

"That should be doable," he finally whispered, his gaze still locked on some indeterminate point in the distance. "Rush job?"

"Do we ever see any other kind?"

Chapter Thirty-Five

The first tiny sliver of daylight was just beginning to peek out over the horizon as The Kid pulled to a stop. The front brakes on his car squealed slightly as he shifted into park and turned off the ignition, the ticking of the engine the only sound. Remaining behind the wheel, he sat for a moment, making a point of avoiding the rearview mirror.

There was nothing there he wanted or needed to see right now.

Instead, he kept his focus aimed on an indeterminate point in the distance, his eyes pinched just slightly against the first stray golden shafts of light shooting straight up across the morning sky to the east.

When he'd initially put the agenda together, had planned things out, it had seemed so simple. The list was premade for him, the methods of their dispatch as well. All he had to do was follow the template already laid out, paint by the numbers, stay inside the lines, and everything would be alright.

The first step was easy, almost too much so. It had given The Kid the false assumption that they would all go in a similar manner, that no problems would be faced. He hadn't realized it at the time, but it had softened him, caused him to lower his guard just a bit.

The second was somewhat more difficult, though not in the execution. Gaining access to Didi Weston, subduing her and her husband, those things had been no problem at all. The problem there was in the finish, in having to watch the life pressed from Dennis Weston one agonizing breath at a time, at seeing the anguish his wife endured as it happened.

The Kid had seen death before. One doesn't grow up near The Bottoms, doesn't pedal in his chosen profession, without having at least some tangential experience with it.

These were the first times that he had been an active participant though, let alone the sole perpetrator. A week before, he had never fired a weapon at another human being, let alone done so with the intent of ending life.

A day before he had never forced someone to watch the death of another.

The third step, he hadn't been ready for. Not for the fight that ensued or the sheer horror of the aftermath. Just picturing it caused The Kid's eyes to slide shut, for the skin of his cheeks to pull slightly, the salt from his dried tears having drawn them taught.

Without even glancing down he could feel the burning sensation of the skin scraped free from his knuckles, could sense the cleaning solution on his arms after scrubbing the blood away so many times.

This was not how it was supposed to go. It was not supposed to have been so difficult.

He was not supposed to be having second thoughts.

Pushing a long breath out through his nose, The Kid opened his eyes. He focused on the sun continuing to push itself up above the horizon, bringing with it the first sunny day the area had seen in weeks.

Watching it, seeing it nudge steadily upward, The Kid let go of the debacle from the night before. He ignored the searing pain the sun caused on the back of his retinas, keeping his gaze aimed on the tangerine orb as it climbed.

Someplace deep within, his fears abated.

The sun was out, as sure a sign as ever could be for such a day.

Reaching for the driver's side door, The Kid pushed it open, stepping out into the cool morning air.

He had preparations to make.
And then it was time to go visit Big.

Chapter Thirty-Six

When he and Riley first transitioned from the uniformed division over to detectives, Reed had figured he would get used to the grind. After a year or two, he would gain the ability to turn his mind off at the end of the day, to leave things behind and detach, go enjoy a ballgame and a beer each night.

At the very least be able to get a full night's sleep.

The ensuing years had proven how wrong that supposition had been. If anything, the opposite was true, Reed finding it more and more difficult to turn things off with each case he worked. Instead of gaining distance he was clinging too tightly, spending his evenings at the kitchen table scouring through case files, lying awake on his bed at night and staring at the ceiling, his active mind refusing to let him rest.

While being in such a state was beginning to take its toll on his body, the previous 10 months having stripped a dozen pounds from him, it did also present the occasional small benefit, such as when Deek texted him at 5:00 a.m. to say he had something.

Phone parked on the nightstand beside his bed, Reed rolled over and checked the message the moment it came in. He didn't bother to comment on the time, instead pushing straight to asking if he could come directly over. When the response came back in the affirmative a moment later, Reed had gotten up to fill Billie's bowl and let her out the back door before jumping in the shower, the same routine they went through most mornings, if not an hour or two earlier.

Twenty minutes later they found themselves on the road toward Hilliard, Reed pushing the engine hard, enjoying the roadways free of traffic, already dreading the scads of drivers that would soon be joining them. Dispatch was mercifully silent as they went, Reed keeping the radio off, the two of them making it back to Deek's in right at half an hour.

Under the early morning light the house looked a bit different from the night before, though only to add color to the basic ranch home. What had before appeared to be shades of grey turned out to be light blue, the shutters painted dark burgundy.

Small fall arrangements that Reed hadn't noticed the previous evening were arranged in each of the window sills, pumpkins and gourds with swaths of bright faux leaves woven throughout.

Billie made no fuss as he left the car, enjoying a few extra minutes of rest curled up on the back seat. Like every good Marine she had fully bought into the maxim of grabbing rest wherever she could, her dark form spread the length of the car, barely cracking open an eyelid as he departed.

The sun was just rising at his back as Reed stepped out, the orange light hitting everything, adding to the autumn scene. With practiced hands, he lifted his badge over his head and allowed the chain it was affixed to rest against his neck, the small silver implement slapping lightly against his chest.

For as much as he hated wearing the thing, especially at such an unholy hour, he knew it would shave at least five minutes off the ensuing conversation.

Stepping up onto the small front porch, he knocked twice before taking a step back. The bulb above the door still burned bright from the night before and the din of morning news found his ears as he stood and waited, a full minute passing before the sound of slippers sliding over a tile floor could be heard.

The distinctive sound of three separate locks disengaging rang out before the doorknob turned, the weather stripping encasing the frame holding the dark red gate in place a moment before finally giving way.

On the opposite side of the door stood Mrs. Chamberlain, still in her bathrobe and slippers. Bright red curlers held her silver hair in small loops around her head, a mug of coffee with a picture of Garfield on it gripped in her hand.

"Can I help you?" she asked, her face folded up against the morning sun, lines etched across much of her skin.

"Good morning," Reed said, putting on his best cheerful voice, "Detective Reed Mattox, CPD. I'm here because Deek is helping me with a case and asked me to stop by."

In times past Reed would have let Riley handle the entire interaction, knowing they would be hugging and ushered inside in seconds. Since her demise, he had found the going a bit tougher, his own approach honed to always mention he was with the police and Deek was helping them.

It seemed appealing to her sense of familial pride was the surest way to get past the gatekeeper.

Actually, in his experience, it might even be the only way.

"Oh yes, yes," she said, stepping to the side and waving him in, "I remember now, of course. He was just telling me about it yesterday at lunch."

The fact that Reed had not met with Deek until a full 10 hours after lunchtime was not lost on him, though he made no mention of it as he stepped inside. He merely continued to smile and nod, slipping past her on the front foyer and going straight through the side door into the basement.

With each step down the artificial sound of video game violence grew a little louder, Reed picking up the cackle of machine gun fire followed by an explosion of some sort. Rolling his eyes upward he shook his head as he made his way down the last few steps, coming into view of the enormous television all lit up.

In the center of the screen was the outstretched tip of an M-16, the front of it and the view of the player moving in unison, simulating a first-person approach. Around the periphery of the screen was a dilapidated town looking like a cross between the Old West and modern

Afghanistan, interlopers wearing head kerchiefs and shades of brown popping to and fro.

"Some people like to read the newspaper in the morning," Reed said, coming to a stop behind the chair he'd used the night before. He kept his hands pushed into the front pockets of his sweatshirt and added, "Maybe watch Good Morning America and drink some coffee."

In front of him the screen froze, the gun stopping at an angle, people along the outer edge coming to a halt mid-step. The springs on the second recliner wheezed as Deek slammed the foot rest down and leaned forward, turning to regard Reed over his shoulder.

"True, but that stuff's for people waking up. I haven't been to bed yet."

"Okay," Reed countered, "so watch some Letterman or something."

A look of equal parts surprise and disgust crossed his face. "You know he retired, like, months ago, right?"

Reed had no idea. Most of his nights were spent on duty, the rest doing anything but watching late night television. "Oh, right."

"Right," Deek said, raising his eyebrows enough to let it be known he didn't believe the excuse Reed was trying to concoct. Rather than wait to hear whatever that might be he stood, looping around the front of his recliner and heading toward his workstation.

"Man, I have to be honest," he said, disappearing from view behind his bank of monitors, "this was one of the tougher requests I've had in a while. Turns out the FBI must have beefed up their firewalls or something."

Something about the way the statement was phrased, Reed knew he was being prompted to inquire, setting Deek up to explain how he had managed to deliver anyway.

Somehow, it had become one of the hallmarks of their interaction.

"But you still got in?" Reed asked.

"I did," Deek said. "Just saying, it took some doing."

Taking a few steps forward, Reed rested his hand along the back of the recliner Deek had just been using. From that angle he was able to see past the corner of the workstation, Deek's visage illuminated by the screens. "And?"

Deek remained silent a moment, his attention on the monitors, before turning to stare at Reed. "Eleven."

Reed waited for more explanation to come. When none did he prompted, "Eleven?"

"Yep," Deek said, rotating his desk chair to look over at Reed. His elbows rested on his thighs, his hands hanging down between his knees. "Your detectives and Weston, they had tons of crossover. Turns out more inmates from your precinct end up in Franklin County Medical than anywhere else in the metro area."

Never before had Reed considered the numbers, though it made sense. Franklin Medical was for prisoners that were in need of major medical attention, whether it be physical or mental. He didn't have a difficult time imagining that a great many people from The Bottoms suffered some form of mental health need.

It was even easier to surmise their affinity for violence, many carrying that tendency with them into incarceration.

They liked to fight, and that usually came at a price.

"Your boy Gilmore though," Deek said, "that's where things got interesting."

Reed bristled slightly at the insinuation Gilmore was or would ever be his boy, though he let it go. Instead he raised his right hand, flicking his fingers back toward himself, motioning for Deek to continue.

"The details are pretty sketchy," Deek said, "and if you hadn't tipped me off about what to look for, there's no way I would have found it."

"Meaning?" Reed asked.

"Meaning the man was never mentioned by name. The closest it ever got was his initials, *always* entered by Dennis Weston himself."

For a moment Reed stood, processing the information. His face squinted up as he tried to make sense of it, superimposing the new information over what he already knew.

"The warden of the facility was going into individual patient files?"

"Looks that way to me," Deek said, raising his hands wide to either side, "and I could be wrong here, but it would appear the two had some sort of referral program going on."

"Referral..." Reed said, drawing the word out as he thought on it a moment. "As in..."

"As in every time Weston entered D.G. into the system, that particular inmate got out less than a month later."

Reflexively, Reed's eyes bulged at the information. His focus zeroed in on Deek, who bore a self-satisfied smile on his face.

"You're kidding me."

"All eleven of them."

The revelation came as a sharp blow to Reed, vastly expanding the scope of every previous working theory he'd had. He raised both hands to his face and rubbed twice, feeling the warmth from his palms against his cheeks.

"Gilmore had himself a damn informant farm system going over there."

"Sure looks that way," Deek said.

"Which is why he showed up and tried to scare me off," Reed added, thinking out loud. "He's probably doing this off the books and didn't want anybody stumbling across it."

Opposite him Deek remained silent a moment before raising a hand and scratching at the stubble on the underside of his chin. "Huh, I'd forgotten about that. Makes sense though."

Already Reed's mind was racing in a dozen different directions. The information had effectively shifted the trajectory of two investigations, meaning that he and Glenn were about to have a very uncomfortable conversation with a federal agent.

"Anything else?" Reed asked.

A look resembling hurt passed over Deek's face as he again spread his hands wide. "In the last eight hours? No, that's all."

A half-smile formed on Reed's face as he shook his head. "Not what I meant at all. That's damn good work. Just wanted to make sure you weren't holding back any last bombshells before I really started trying to form a plan of attack here."

"That's all," Deek repeated.

A moment passed as Reed stood rooted in place, trying to best wrestle the information into a cohesive order in his mind. "You have the 11 names?"

"Right here," Deek said, reaching out to the side and picking up a thin stack of printouts. He extended the papers to Reed, who stepped forward and accepted them, glancing through once before lowering them by his side.

"Thank you, again. I appreciate this."

A wan smile tugged the left corner of Deek's mouth up as he glanced over toward his living quarters. "Thank you for the bottle of J-Dub Blue. About this time tonight, I'll be appreciating that as well."

The dual nature of the statement was not lost on Reed, relaying both appreciation and the fact that if any further assistance was required, it should be requested sooner rather than later.

"You enjoy that," Reed said, raising the papers to his brow and turning toward the stairs.

Halfway there a thought occurred to him, something that he had forgotten about until lying awake in bed overnight, his mind trying to put together every loose end that remained.

"One last thing," he said, taking another step back and leaning against the banister on the staircase. "If someone had a Facebook account, would it be possible to see who had accessed it?"

Deek's bushy mop of hair rose from behind the screens as he stood, a look of confusion on his face. "What do you mean?"

"I mean..." Reed said, pausing to parse out the best way to ask the question. "If someone had posted they were going on vacation, would it be possible to tell who might have seen that message?"

How the killer had known the Hendrix's were going to be out of town was the only thing from the theft of their car that still remained, a detail that seemed benign at this point, but Reed still wanted to figure out.

"No," Deek said. "That's public information. If you gave me a machine or even an account, I could tell if they had looked at a certain person, but not the other way around."

Reed paused a moment, a slight frown tugging at his lips, before raising the pages in farewell. "Thanks again for this. I appreciate it."

Chapter Thirty-Seven

Adrenaline surged through Reed to the point of almost being detrimental. He could feel it coursing through his body, sending his pulse upward, his heart pounding. Sweat coated his skin, warmth permeating him, causing him to lean forward behind the steering wheel and peel away his hooded sweatshirt.

What Deek had uncovered was either masterful or an abomination, depending on the stance Reed wanted to take. Looking at it solely from the standpoint of a detective, it was a stroke of pure luck, the kind of thing that could unlock multiple cases within the hour.

At the same time, if what the evidence seemed to intimate was true, it meant that a highly unethical, or even illegal, enterprise was being conducted between a state prison facility and a local FBI agent.

The thought brought an acrid taste to Reed's mouth as he remembered the day before, the smug man sitting in Grimes's office, trying to assert his presence without overstepping too many boundaries. As he played the image back again and again in his mind, Reed's body temperature only continued to rise, going upward in direct correlation to the venom within.

In the backseat Billie had picked up on the change the moment he stepped out of the Chamberlain house. No longer was she content stretched out on the backseat, her body upright, pacing the cramped confines.

Reed could feel the car swaying from her movement as he wound toward the precinct, thinking nothing of it, knowing he would be doing the same exact thing if given the chance.

At a quarter before 6:00 in the morning, the parking lot to the precinct was virtually deserted. For the third time in as many days Reed didn't bother with the staff lot, going for a visitor stall out front. It was still more than two hours before the building officially opened for the day, meaning with any luck he would be long gone before a concerned citizen happened to show up in need of assistance.

Grabbing up the printouts off the passenger seat, Reed climbed out, leaving Billie free to roam at his side. She fell in a foot from his hip as he ascended the two short steps and passed through the front door. Inside, most of the building was still dark, shrouded in shadows, save a single light just barely visible beyond the frosted glass of the executive suite.

"No way," Reed muttered, slapping his thigh once to let Billie know of the redirect and heading toward the light. A moment later he passed through the door and knocked on the frame of Grimes's office, the rest of the wing void of life.

"Do you ever leave this place?" Reed asked, taking a step forward.

Seated behind his desk was Grimes, his uniform fresh, but everything else looking like it had been through the wringer many times over. Dark circles underscored each of his eyes and his cheeks sagged on either side of his face.

If Reed were to guess he would project it had been days since the man slept, though he wouldn't say a full week was out of the question.

"I could ask the same of you," Grimes said, his voice even more graveled than usual, coming out as little more than a grunt.

"I'm the guy you assigned to track down whoever shot two of our detectives," Reed said by way of an explanation, taking another couple of steps forward. "What's your excuse?"

"Two of our detectives got shot," Grimes said, not a moment of pause, not a hint of self-reverence in his tone.

For a moment Reed felt his lips part, the words to respond evading him. He held the stance for a moment before stepping forward and dumping himself in the seat across from Grimes, not waiting for an invitation.

He held the printouts up in his hand and said, "I just came from my computer expert's house."

"Do I even want to know how much Mr. Chamberlain cost us this time?" Grimes asked.

"No," Reed said, "because I covered it. But even if I didn't, it would have been worth it."

The left eyebrow of Grimes arched upward, an expectant look on his face.

In quick order Reed rattled off everything that had been found, beginning with the commonalities between the detectives and Weston and finishing with the hand notations of Gilmore's initials in 11 different files. As he spoke, the frown on Grimes's face grew incrementally deeper, almost reaching his jaw line on either side by the time Reed finished.

"Who are the 11 people?" Grimes asked.

"I don't know yet," Reed replied. "That's why I'm here. Figured I would run all of them, see what they were picked up for originally, how our guys figured in. From there, I'll give BCI a call, see where it goes."

"Hmm," Grimes said, nodding. "You haven't talked to Investigator Glenn yet?"

"No," Reed said. "Figured I'd wait another 10 minutes until 6:00 and then start calling."

Grimes paused a moment, seeming to consider the statement, before nodding a second time. "Goes without saying, you need any clearance or anything in your search, you just have to ask."

Reed opened his mouth to respond before pausing. He tilted his head and glanced out the window, the sun just a smudge on the horizon.

"You know there's a good chance we're going to end up pissing the FBI off on this."

"Sounds like Agent Gilmore has it coming," Grimes said.

"I agree, but just the same, if you know anybody that could ease the landing a little bit over there..."

As Gilmore had alluded to the day before, the two agencies did enjoy a fairly good working relationship. What Reed was holding would no doubt dent that a bit, but there was no reason to let one itinerant asshole bring it down completely.

It all depended on how things were handled.

"I'll make a few calls," Grimes said. "Can't promise anything, but I'll wake some folks up, get them to clear the way."

"Appreciate it," Reed said.

Grimes nodded. "Just the same, if I can't find anybody, you know what still needs to be done."

Chapter Thirty-Eight

Reed didn't make it all the way until 6:00. At three minutes before the hour he phoned Glenn, not in the least bit surprised when she answered after only a single ring. Completely ignoring all apologies or salutations, he launched straight into what Deek had been able to pull.

Twenty-four minutes later she was seated by his side, two of only five people in the entire building, Billie sitting vigil between them on the floor. Her hair was still wet from the shower, the collar on her suit coat flipped up in the back, as she drug over the same chair Grimes had used the morning before and sat less than a foot from Reed, both having prime viewing of the screen.

"Okay, what have you found so far?" she asked, alternating her gaze between the screen and the twin stacks of printouts in front of Reed.

"These here are ones I've already looked into," Reed said, dropping his fingertips atop the closest pile and sliding it her direction.

She snatched up the pages the moment his hand was lifted away, pulling all six pages, just over half of the total, onto her lap and rifling through them.

"So all 11 of these originated with your guys," she said, reasoning through things out loud.

"Yes," Reed said, "the arresting officers in all 11 were Ike and

Bishop. From there, whether it was directly after sentencing or after bouncing through the system for a while, they ended up over at Franklin Medical under Weston."

"And eventually they all were released within a month of Dan Gilmore's initials showing up in the file."

"Also notice that his name is the last thing in every one of them," Reed said, looking over from the CPD database on his screen to the pile in her lap. "Once he got involved, the docs became completely hands off. No more check-ins, no more follow ups."

Shuffling through them, Glenn checked the veracity of the statement before lowering the pages in front of her and staring out through the window before them. At half past 6:00 the sun was still not fully above the horizon, the earlier orange hue giving way to an orb the color of cornmeal. In the lot, a pair of middle-aged women met up behind their respective cars and walked toward the building, purses hitched up on their shoulders, lunch sacks in their hands.

"Also note, there's no real rhyme or reason to the timing of their release," Reed said, pulling up the next person in line and grabbing a pen to begin making notations.

"What do you mean?" Glenn asked, pulling herself back into the moment, turning to face him.

"Some of the guys were close to their parole date," Reed said, "but some of them still had a ways to go. Look at this guy here."

Extending the bottom of the pen toward the screen, Reed tapped at the line indicating the initial sentencing. "He was inside for multiple counts of GTA, was supposed to serve another four-plus. Suddenly Agent Gilmore shows up with his magic wand, and..."

"Out he walks a free man," Glenn said.

Like himself, he could sense a certain urgency rolling off of Glenn. Her words were clipped, her movements sharp as she went through the forms.

Reed knew the feeling extremely well, having been operating under it since leaving Grimes's office less than an hour before. There was so much information to be obtained, all of it within reach, he just needed to force his mind to move fast enough to absorb it all.

For two long days he had been following procedure, going through his paces, putting everything together that he needed to. Despite that, not once had he felt like he was really that close to anything resembling a breakthrough.

This was different. This had all the earmarks of pointing him in the right direction, for the first time being able to shift from reactive to proactive.

Oftentimes, that was what made all the difference in an investigation.

Pushing his attention back to the screen, Reed made a couple of notations. Using the free space along the right column, he wrote down the crime the man was convicted of, the sentence that was handed down, how much time remained on it, and the date of the infraction.

There were scads more information he could fall back on if he needed to but for the time being he was content to hammer on the major categories, hoping some sort of pattern would emerge.

It took less than 10 minutes for him to go through the remainder of the list. When he was finished they fanned them out over the top of the desk, standing shoulder to shoulder, Glenn with her arms crossed, Reed with his hands thrust into the front pockets of his jeans.

"Okay," Glenn said, opening things up, "right off, we've got five drug dealers – three for meth, one each for heroin and cocaine – and three armed robbers."

"We've also got solo offenders for grand theft auto, sex trafficking, and gun running."

"All charges that would make use of a crew, most likely committing more than a single offense," Glenn said.

Reed nodded. "Which makes sense. As Deek put it, Gilmore was using Franklin Medical as his own private informant farm league."

He paused and glanced over to Glenn, "It's a baseball thing, like a minor league system."

"The Clippers play five miles from here," Glenn snapped. "I know what a farm team is."

Under any other circumstances Reed would have apologized, this time choosing to let it go. Instead he focused in on the pages before him, staring at the blue ink scrawled across them in his own handwriting, trying to make things fit.

"It doesn't make sense though," he said. "If someone sprang you early from incarceration, would you target them? Or worse yet, would you target the officers that arrested you and the warden that oversaw you?"

He glanced across to see Glenn open her mouth to respond before pausing and matching his look. "Good point. Why would they go after them at all? They had to know that after they became informants they were in the state and federal system. If anything started happening, that would be first place people looked."

This time it was Reed's turn to respond by opening his mouth before pausing. He remained that way, processing what was on the sheets in front of him, recalling as many of the files on the screen as he could.

"Not if you were dead."

The statement seemed to originate from somewhere deep inside of Reed, his subconscious blurting it out before his active mind even had a chance to fully process it yet. As the words escaped him he could sense Glenn turning to stare beside him, almost feel Billie doing the same from the floor.

Inches from his ear Glenn said something, though the words failed to register as Reed lowered himself back into his chair and began clicking back through the files.

"This one," he said, reaching over and tapping a sheet on the far edge of the desk.

"This one," he added, moving to one a bit closer.

"And these two," he finished, shoving over a pair of printouts closest to him.

Standing on the opposite corner, Glenn shuffled all other papers together and set them aside, leaving just four sheets in a row before them.

"These four died not long after being released," Reed said.

He leaned forward and ran his gaze over each in order, stopping on the last one. His heart rate spiked as he stared at it, all moisture fleeing his mouth.

"Son of a bitch," he whispered.

Beside him Glenn pressed in tight, her hip flush with his as she read the same thing he was staring at.

"Marco Sanz, died October 23, 2014. Exactly one year ago today."

Her voice was no more than a whisper, the words just barely penetrating Reed's psyche.

"Was pulled over by Iaconelli and Bishop for driving with a busted taillight, found to be wanted for questioning in connection with nine different car thefts."

The words hit Reed in the stomach, driving the wind from his lungs. He rose to full height and ran his hand back over his scalp, his short hair feeling like bristles against his palm.

"The first crime scene the other night," Reed said, "it was staged. Somebody lured them in to make a point, to take them down just the way they had Sanz."

"And giving Weston a choice," Glenn said, pushing back from the paper and matching his stance, just a few feet separating them. "Just the way Sanz was probably presented with a choice – turn informant or stay inside another five years."

Reed nodded, moving through the progression. Whoever was doing this had already taken out the arresting officer and the overseeing warden. "We have to get to Gilmore. If this is the anniversary, whoever is doing this has been setting things up for today."

"He's next in line," Glenn said.

"I just hope we're not already too late," a voice said from behind them.

Both Reed and Glenn turned at the same time to find Grimes standing less than 10 feet away. In the commotion of the previous few moments neither had heard him approach, had any idea how long he'd been standing there.

"What's going on?" Reed asked.

"I made a few calls after our meeting," Grimes said, the frown on his face every bit as pronounced as it had been in their previous encounter.

"Agent Gilmore was expected to be in for an early briefing this morning. As of this time, nobody has seen or heard from him."

Chapter Thirty-Nine

For the first time since moving to the 8th and collecting his own department-issue sedan, Reed had someone riding shotgun. It made the small confines of the front seat feel cramped, the few things he normally kept on the passenger side stowed in the middle console between them.

Not to be left out, Billie pushed her muzzle up close as well, her hot breath landing on Reed's bare forearm.

"Dammit," Glenn spat, venom dripping from the word. She kept her arms folded tight over her torso, her chin drawn back into her neck, before shooting out her right hand and smacking the dash. "Dammit dammit dammit."

The sound of her palm slapping against hardened plastic echoed through the car. Inside the cramped space it sounded like gunfire, three quick bursts.

On cue a low growl rolled from Billie, her body pushing forward another inch.

"Down," Reed snapped, the growl stopping mid-stream, Billie retreating back to her seat. There she rested on her haunches, her head fully visible in the rearview mirror, attention focused on Reed.

The interaction gave Glenn pause, her hand just a few inches above the dash, poised to smash down again. Her mouth hung open half an inch, surprise on her face, before she too fell back in her seat.

"Sorry."

Reed brushed past the apology with a quick shake of his head, glancing between the road and the GPS mounted above the radio. Outside, the morning traffic was well into the early throes of rush hour, cars lined up at every light, the freeway beyond moving at just a crawl.

"She just doesn't know you that well," Reed said. "And she gets her cues from me, which isn't helping."

He could see Glenn turn in his periphery. "But you aren't saying a word."

"No, but she also reads my body language, can tell when I'm amped up or pissed off." He rolled his head to the side to glance at Glenn and added, "Trust me, she knows I'm every bit as angry as you right now."

Glenn's eyebrows tracked a bit higher as if she might comment before turning back to face the street. "I'm just...can you believe they actually said *we give our agents a certain level of autonomy, they don't have to be accountable to us 24 hours a day?*"

Reed's past brushes with the FBI were blessedly limited, though based on stories he'd heard from other guys on the force, that sort of approach wasn't terribly unheard of. Even if every single person at the branch office was scared shitless for Gilmore and they were sending a full search party out to retrieve him, they'd never stoop so low as to let a local detective and a state investigator know it.

Damned sure wouldn't invite them in on anything.

Despite that, this time Reed had the impression that their response had nothing to do with a jurisdictional pissing match. While condescending as hell in the delivery, what they had said wasn't incorrect. Their agents most likely did have a great deal of autonomy.

That's what had allowed Gilmore to set up his side venture with Weston in the first place.

"You want to try him again?" Reed asked.

Working in silence, Glenn took out her cell phone and scrolled to the most recent listing in her call log, a number Grimes had secured for them from one of his contacts. Three seconds later she lowered the phone back into place, the grimace on her face even more pronounced.

"Straight to voicemail."

"Great," Reed muttered, checking the screen on his GPS, pushing as fast as the mid-morning slog would allow. More than once he had wanted to turn on the sirens, had even discussed it with Glenn, but the fact was they had no reason to believe something was afoul beside someone not answering their calls.

There were any of a number of different explanations for it. The man could have gone out to watch Monday Night Football the previous evening and had a couple too many beers. He could be entertaining a lady friend. He might simply not want to answer a call from an unknown number, Reed very much the same way.

Knowing so little, they were forced to fall in with the rest of the working world, pushing straight in from Franklinton toward German Village.

In total the drive took 28 minutes, roughly 20 longer than it should have. Upon reaching their destination they found a mid-sized row house on a side street, the exterior dark brown stucco, wide wood trim encasing the doors and windows. A free standing garage stood 10 feet from the main house, the two connected by a small breezeway.

Like most every home in the small enclave on the south-central part of the city, the home was neat, with a wrought iron fence and gate running along the front walk.

Unlike most of the others, though, there were no pumpkins lining the front porch, no fall decorations affixed to the windows. Given the dark color scheme and the lack of visible signs of life, the place looked ominous, even foreboding, despite the early morning sunshine.

Pulling up to the curb, Reed pushed the gear shift into park, the car barely ceasing to move as Glenn jerked open the passenger door. Bolting through the gap between the seats, Billie was out behind her a moment later, a black blur that Reed didn't even attempt to slow down.

Instead he jerked open his own door and jogged around the front hood of the car, meeting them both in front of the gate. Twice he tapped at the butt of his gun as he went, not wanting to draw on a busy street, a handful of school children waiting for the bus on the corner.

"Billie and I will take the front door," Reed said. "You watch the garage in case he or anybody else comes out the side."

Glenn peeled away without a word, following a stone pathway through a tiny front lawn that was void of grass, the ground covered in a heavy layer of gravel. Low-slung bushes lined the front fence and the house.

Reed gave her 20 seconds to get into position, seeing her take up a post on the far corner of the house with a vantage of the entire side of the property. Matching him, she stood with one hand just a few inches from her weapon, like an old west outlaw prepared for a duel.

Stepping up the three short steps to the front door, Reed balled his hand into a fist and pounded against the heavy implement. The outside of it felt wet against his palm, the sound echoing through the house, as he paused a moment before pounding twice more.

"Agent Gilmore! This is Detective Reed Mattox, you in there?"

Dozens of times before he'd stood in similar situations, on the outside of a door waiting for someone to answer. Without fail, whenever someone was approaching the house would let him know, creaking slightly, giving away the sound of footsteps, always prefacing their approach.

Just as surely, the homes let him know when there was nobody moving about inside.

"There's nothing doing at all in there," Reed said, turning his head a few inches so Glenn could hear him. "Do we have anything approaching probable cause right now?"

Breaching the home of a federal agent would be a quagmire that would probably get them both fired, would certainly torch relations between all the represented agencies for the foreseeable future.

Still, given what Reed had discovered that morning, what he had seen at the hospital in the preceding days, he didn't much care.

"Hold on," Glenn said, freezing Reed in place. His chest tightened slightly as he lowered himself down a step, his focus on the corner of the house, waiting for Glenn to reappear.

A moment later she did so, her weapon out, gripped in both hands before her.

"We've got signs of forced entry on the side door. I'm going in."

Reed's first instinct was to reach for his gun as well, the weapon sliding free of the holster on his hip. In an instant he assumed the same position as Glenn, his right hand curled around the handle, his finger riding along the outer edge of the trigger guard. His left he kept cupped beneath it for support, both extended in front of him, his elbows locked, muzzle aimed toward the ground.

"Wait!" he yelled, the concentrated adrenaline in his system pushing the word out much louder than intended. No doubt every passerby on the street had heard him, a fact Reed could not care less about as he bounded down from the steps.

The stone path was uneven underfoot as he covered the short distance in four long strides, Billie out in front of him. He made the corner to see Glenn by the door, her weight on her right foot, her left six inches in front of it, a textbook stance before breaching.

"What?" she asked, her face twisted up in anticipation, annoyance. "I've got signs here."

"I wasn't telling you to wait for me," Reed said, moving into position behind her. "Breach and step aside."

She began to respond before flicking her gaze to Billie between them, frenetic energy rolling off of her in waves. She bounced in place on all four paws, every coiled muscle in her body seeming to writhe.

"On three..." Glenn said, making no further objection, offering just a small nod.

Turning her focus back to the door, she rocked on her heel once, preparing to spring her body forward as she took a deep breath.

"One...two..."

With each word she rocked back a bit more, preparing her slight frame for movement.

"Three!"

Her heel made contact between the handle and the jamb, the thin wood casing providing barely any resistance before splintering off. The sound of it filled Reed's ears as he watched the door swing open, the interior of the house dark, no signs of life visible.

"Clear!"

Chapter Forty

The reaction was as if Billie had gained the ability to teleport. One moment she was standing in the breezeway, splitting the difference between Reed and Glenn. The next she was gone, disappearing into the depths of the house, the sound of her shoulder slamming against the edge of the door the only sign of her passing.

The sight of it gave Glenn pause, her body frozen just outside the door, waiting long enough for Reed to sprint past her into the house.

Sending Billie in first every time was far and away the worst part of having her for a partner. It wasn't the act of her clearing a scene itself, at that there was nobody better. She could move much faster than any human could, her expert smell ferreting out things that Reed would only hope to guess at.

The part that he despised more than anything was having her exposed for those few moments upon entry. There was just no way of knowing what lay behind a closed door, whether it be a booby trap or a psychopath with a weapon, determined to start firing at the first sign of movement.

Reed was fortunate that both of his parents were fairly young and in good health. Losing Riley, his partner, his best friend, was far and away the worst thing he had ever been faced with. Three long months had passed before he felt up to regular interaction with the world again after it happened, another four before he was fully okay with shifting between the graveyard and daytime shifts.

Ten months had now passed, and not a single day passed when there wasn't something, anything, that either reminded him of her or that he wished he could call and share with her.

Using all of that as concentrated fuel, Reed pushed himself through the side door, sprinting through a small mudroom, a washer and dryer along the wall, a drying rack set up alongside it. Following the sound of Billie's feet on hardwood floors, he moved through a Spartan kitchen, stainless steel appliances lining the countertops.

Behind him he heard a second set of footsteps, Glenn's square heels clicking against the ground. The smell of sawdust he noticed upon entry had faded, concentrated to the one small area around the door, bits of wood debris still hanging in the air. In their stead was a hint of Chinese food, the smell peaking by the sink and receding as he moved forward.

Reed was one step beyond the kitchen, just a few inches inside a dining room featuring only a square table and a pair of Ikea chairs, when Billie exploded into barking. Deep and baying, the bellows reverberated through the house.

Forgoing his search, Reed sprinted straight through the dining room and into a narrow hallway, abandoning his shooter's stance so he could run unabated. Concern for his partner, urgency over what might be found, and unadulterated adrenaline propelled him forward, his running shoes squeaking on the floor as he went.

Twenty feet after leaving the kitchen, the hallway gave way to a living room. The ceiling opened into a high vault overhead, the room stretching the full two stories of the rest of the home in height. Around the outside of it was a matching set of brown leather furniture, a flat screen on one wall, a home stereo system on the other.

None of those things even registered with Reed.

Instead he noticed the sharp coppery scent of blood in the room, the smell so intense it seemed to hang like a cloud over everything, threatening to permeate his hair and clothes. He picked up on Billie trotting a quick line back and forth across the middle of the floor, her toenails clattering against bare wood, her gaze aimed upward.

"Oh, sweet mother of God," Glenn said from behind him, her breath coming in ragged gasps. She remained there a moment, just a few feet from Reed, before turning to the side and beginning to heave, the sound of her retching finding Reed's ears.

Had there been anything of substance in his system, Reed might have done the same. Had the sight before him not evoked a similar response, he may have turned and tried to push her back down the hallway, careful to preserve the integrity of the crime scene, not wanting her vomit to contaminate potential evidence.

Reed did nothing of the sort, though. Remaining rooted in place he stood and stared at the man that just 24 hours prior had come to the 8th and tried to scare Reed away, to make his presence known, to evoke fear without saying as much.

A single rope was extended up from the foot of the sofa, the texture of it rough, the surface a light tan in color. It rose at a 45 degree angle over 15 feet before being draped through the inside of a wrought iron chandelier and coming straight down, ending abruptly in a noose.

At the bottom of the noose, his body rotating just slightly, was Dan Gilmore. Still dressed in the same tie and dress shirt Reed had seen him in the day before, his shoes were off, his sleeves rolled to mid-forearm.

While awful, none of that was what had shocked Reed, had caused Glenn to lose everything in her system from the previous two days.

Hanging from the front pocket of Gilmore's shirt was the entirety of his tongue, the top edge looking like it had been sawed away with a serrated knife. Blood had dried over his chin and the front of his shirt so thick and dark they were almost black, the first few flies beginning to buzz about.

A wide band of blood spatter was present on the floor around Gilmore's body, the droplets dried and hard, Reed knowing it was only a matter of time before they began to mildew.

"Down," Reed said, shaking himself awake, transitioning from stunned first responder to detective.

On command Billie fell silent, coming to a stop by his feet. Together they continued to stare at the scene before them, both giving Glenn the dignity of not turning to look her way, waiting until she came forward and joined them, standing three across.

"Think maybe the FBI should extend a little less autonomy to some of their agents?" Glenn whispered.

Beside her, Reed nodded. "The man was a first class egomaniac, but he didn't deserve this."

He paused, again sweeping his gaze over the scene before them. "Hell, nobody does."

Chapter Forty-One

The small metal pellet rattled back and forth inside the aluminum can as The Kid shook it, holding it at waist height and flicking his wrist back and forth. He moved it no more than a handful of times, his head on a swivel, watching for anybody that might be nearby. Mid-morning on a Tuesday, he didn't expect anyone to be out, the groundskeeper having given up for the winter ahead, allowing the grass to grow a little shaggier, leaves to begin piling up.

Still, he had to be at least quasi-careful. Even if what he was doing was a far cry from the things he'd done the last couple of nights, it was still a crime.

Using the toe of his shoe, The Kid pushed aside the small pile of grass clippings and dead leaves that had piled up at the foot of the headstone. Cut from plain grey granite, it just barely came to The Kid's knee, the edges rough and unpolished, same for the back.

Only the front had been buffed to a mirrored shine, the name Marco Sanz chiseled into it, the deep-set letters painted black to stand out against the slate backdrop. Beneath them were the dates July 13, 1986 – October 23, 2014 using the same typeset and color scheme.

Nothing else adorned the stone. No written epitaph, no pictures of angel wings or hands folded in prayer. Just a name and two dates.

All that The Kid could afford.

At the bottom of the stone was a small smear of black, time and weather having stripped much of it away. Dropping to a knee, The Kid held the spray paint out in front of him and in large block letters wrote a single word.

BIG.

The year before he had used a Sharpie marker, even gone as far as to write "MISS YOU BIG" in the same oversized script he now used, but the ink had barely survived the year on the polished stone.

There was no way that would happen this time.

"Hey, Big," The Kid whispered, ignoring the smell of spray paint and fumes that filled his nose. He told himself that was the reason his eyes watered as he stared at the front of the stone, reaching out and running his fingertips over the name carved into it.

In his 25 years, The Kid had come to find that few words were more misappropriated in the English language than *brother*. He'd heard people refer to guys they played on a sports team with, went to school with, served in the military alongside, as brothers. Witnessed people of the same race use it.

Marco Sanz had been none of those things to The Kid.

He had been so much more.

"How you been?" The Kid whispered, bringing a hand to his face. He pressed his thumb and forefinger down over his eyes, feeling the damp-ness against his skin, before lowering them and pinching the end of his nose, more moisture meeting his grip.

"I know it's been a little while since I came out to see you, but I've been busy, you know? Doing everything I promised you I would."

The Kid could feel the wet earth seeping up through the knee of his jeans as he leaned forward, propping his elbow on his opposite leg. Just a few feet from the headstone he allowed tears to drip silently down his cheeks, staring at the last vestige of the only real family he had ever had.

"And it's going so well," The Kid said. "All that time, all that research, it's been perfect. You'd be so proud."

He paused, just the slightest hint of a flicker pulling at the right corner of his mouth.

"I almost got 'em all too. The detectives, the warden, even that FBI agent you hated so much. Made sure they got what was coming to 'em."

All mirth fled from his features, replaced by a stony visage. Red veins permeated the whites of his eyes like spider webs as he stared at the headstone, the corded muscles of his neck twitching slightly.

"Just got the one more," he said. "Of everybody, got to make sure he gets his."

Chapter Forty-Two

"What in *the hell* made you two twits think you could enter the home of an FBI agent?!"

Twin veins bulged on either side of Supervisory Special Agent Devon Cohn's forehead, snaking down from his strawberry blonde hair that was cut short and pushed to the side. With them came an unhealthy rise in blood pressure, painting his features bright red, his ruddy cheeks appearing like they might pop at any moment.

Because the man had just lost an agent, Reed was trying to give him the benefit of the doubt, reasoning that everybody had their own way of dealing with grief. The antics, and the ongoing outburst, though, were both working to shorten the amount of leeway he was willing to extend considerably.

"Mr. Cohn," Glenn said, taking the lead, "we did notify your office this morning that we had credible evidence that Mr. Gilmore could be in danger."

"First of all," Cohn snapped, cutting her off, "Dan Gilmore and I are both *agents*, thank you.

"And second, you were both told that our agents have a certain amount of leeway, but you thought it would be a good idea to come here and breach his home anyway?"

With each word his voice seemed to grow louder, the man starting to believe in his own bravado. Behind him a trio of criminalists from the Columbus field office of the FBI was at work on the scene, Gilmore's body having been lowered to the floor, but nothing else touched.

Adorned in blue paper suits with FBI stamped across the back in yellow letters six inches tall, each pretended not to notice as Cohn bandied on, casting sideways glances his way, their expressions neutral.

Reed found their restraint admirable, far outpacing his own.

"And to bring a dog in here, too?!" Cohn yelled. He waved a hand to Billie as he yelled, his voice rising to the point of hysterics. "How stupid can you people be to let a damn mutt near a crime scene?"

"*Detective*," Reed said, watching the criminalists work, seeing both Cohn and Glenn swing their attention toward him in his periphery.

"I'm sorry, you say something?" Cohn asked, leaning forward at the waist, incredulity that Reed dare interrupt him on his features.

"Yes, *agent*," Reed said, sliding his gaze from the crime scene crew to the man across from him. "She is a detective, and you will refer to her as such."

Somehow Cohn's face managed to grow a shade deeper in color, his chest swelling as he drew in a breath of air, ready to push forward again.

He didn't get the chance.

"We entered the house because, like Investigator Glenn said, we had rock solid evidence that the man was in danger. We warned your office and we tried to contact him. When neither worked, *we* showed the level of concern *you* should have and came to check on him."

With each word Reed seemed to gain steam, the shock of finding Gilmore's body receding from within, replaced with growing acrimony for whoever it was that was targeting law enforcement agents.

For the self-important prick that was now reading them the riot act for doing their job.

It wasn't hard to see where Gilmore took his cues from.

"We got here and the Investigator saw signs of forced entry," Reed said. "We entered, and my partner cleared the scene, alerting us to your agent's body."

Five feet away, all three of the techs working the scene had stopped what they were doing, openly staring at Reed, listening to every word.

"If we had done as your office instructed, he would still be hanging here right now and who knows how long it would be before you guys saw fit to get off your dead asses and come check on him."

Reed knew the remark was a bit foul, the kind of thing no commanding officer ever wanted or needed to hear, but he was far past caring. The man had insulted him, his cohort, and his partner. He was making a scene solely for the sake of doing so, leveling his emotions at the closest targets.

It was unfortunate what had happened, but it damned sure wasn't their fault.

"And just to be clear," Reed said, "if given the chance to go back half an hour and do it again, I'd do it again."

He thought about asking Glenn if she would as well, knowing there was strength in numbers, wanting to present a united front against the man. Just as fast he dismissed it though, wanting to preserve her position as the good cop in their duo, knowing he had done the work to put Cohn on his heels and Glenn could now pick through the wreckage for whatever they needed.

She didn't disappoint.

"Agent Cohn, do you have access to Agent Gilmore's informants?" Glenn asked.

A moment passed as Cohn simply stared at Reed, his jaw hanging slack. His face passed through five different shades of color in order, receding from bright red to chalky white in record time.

"No," he finally managed, shifting his attention over to Glenn. "Dan had a pretty extensive network. We didn't keep close tabs on them, trusting that he would take care of it."

After the last word he drew in a deep breath and pulled himself up an inch higher, rotating at the waist to look at the techs behind him. On cue they began to move again, abandoning their curiosity and falling back to the task at hand.

"Not that I would be sharing them with you anyway," he said, turning back to face forward. "This is an FBI agent; we will be conducting the investigation."

"So you've never heard the name Marco Sanz?" Glenn asked, ignoring the last statement from Cohn.

"No, who is he?"

"Was," Reed said, keeping his voice even, just a bit of an edge present. "He died, a year ago today."

This time Cohn opted to completely ignore Reed, keeping his focus squarely on Glenn. "And you guys think this is related?"

"You don't?" Reed asked, raising his voice a bit, refusing to be ignored.

"I don't think I'm in any position to say what is related right now without doing a full investigation," Cohn said, his attention still on Glenn.

"Meanwhile, law enforcement personnel are falling under attack every single day," Reed said. "Tell me something *agent*, what happens if Gilmore isn't the last one?"

This time it was too much for Cohn to keep his attention aimed forward. He clenched his teeth together and turned toward Reed, open hostility visible.

"Like I said, I'm not going to speculate about anything until after we've done an investigation."

His voice resonated from deep in his diaphragm, dropping several octaves, a desk jockey's best attempt at sounding tough.

If not for the fact that he was entrenched in the role of bad cop, Reed would have laughed out loud.

"Which, unfortunately for the three of you, starts right now," Cohn said. "So, thank you for calling this in, we'll take it from here."

Reed didn't realize his hands were balled into fists until he felt his fingernails dig into his palms. He clenched them tight another moment, feeling Billie pressed into his thigh, an unspoken message that she was there, awaiting his word, ready to strike.

"That's it?" Glenn asked. "You have no interest in hearing what we've found, in seeing how your case and ours fit together?"

Cohn kept his attention on Reed another moment before shifting over to Glenn. He held a hand toward her, his fingers outstretched wide, and said, "Look, I am sorry for what happened to the detectives and the warden, but they are not my concern. Agent Gilmore was my guy, that's where my attention will be.

"If in the course of our investigation I find something that connects these cases, I'll be in touch."

Two distinct trains of thought fought for top billing in Reed's mind, neither of them especially good. The first was to keep both hands balled into tight fists and use them to pummel Cohn into a bloody pulp. There might be a bit more spatter on the floor when he was done, but he would feel infinitely better and most likely be doing the world a great service in the process.

The second was, no matter what Cohn's investigation found, even if it included a flashing neon sign pointing to someone with pictures of all three incidents stapled to their chest, there was no way they were ever getting a call from Cohn.

"Okay," Glenn said beside him, her voice relaying she had reached the exact same conclusion. "Just keep us posted."

Chapter Forty-Three

Despite the enormous mass of human and canine crammed into the small interior of the car, nobody made a sound. All three sat quiet and brooding, those in the front seat both deep in thought, Billie behind them staring straight ahead, waiting for some cue on how to respond.

From the moment they arrived at Gilmore's to the point when they were unceremoniously punted from the case by Cohn just barely eclipsed an hour and a half, it still very much morning, landing squarely in the lull between rush hour and lunch time. The streets were largely barren as Reed angled them back toward the precinct, again avoiding the freeways for a couple of major boulevards, making only the occasional stop for changing lights.

As he drove he kept his hands gripped tight at 10:00 and 2:00, not in any way related to driver safety but so he had something tangible to squeeze in his fists. He could feel the warmth passing through his palms into the rubber steering wheel cover, every few minutes rotating them back toward himself, small shards balling up and falling down. Several dozen covered the thighs of his jeans as he drove, though he didn't bother brushing them away.

"Back there," Glenn said, her head aimed out the passenger window, her voice belying the demeanor they both seemed to have, "were you really as pissed off as you seemed, or was that just to clear the way for me?"

"Yes," Reed responded. He shot the word out quickly, reflexively, before pausing and lowering his voice. "I've seen a lot of men like him before, guys that think they can get their way by being a blowhard. I knew that if we were ever going to get anything useful, I had to take the wind out of his sails."

The answer caused Glenn to turn her head a few inches toward him, focus now aimed directly out through the front windshield. "You guys get a lot of crossover work with the FBI?"

Another moment passed as Reed considered the best way to respond. He didn't want to lie to her, had no reason to, but he didn't want to put her on the defensive either.

"My last partner was a woman," Reed said quietly, hoping that would be enough.

It took a few seconds for the point to be received, Reed knowing the moment it was, seeing her lips part, her jaw going slack in understanding.

"All that blustery grandstanding, you just think he was trying to scare me?" she asked.

The last thing Reed wanted to do was get into a deep philosophical discussion about women in the law enforcement field. It was something he had been forced to observe more times than he could count with Riley, something that she seemed to accept far better than he ever could.

"Chivalry may be dead, but misogyny sure as hell isn't."

He left it at that as they crossed over the border into Franklinton, a green sign pockmarked with bullet holes welcoming them to the suburb. Below it was a proclamation of the current population, though the numbers had been obscured by a heavy dusting of orange spray paint.

"I'm a big girl, you know," Glenn said. Her voice was quiet, but there was a clear challenge in the phrasing of the sentence, in the tone that underscored it. "Been doing this a long time."

Jabs of trepidation, of concern that he had overstepped, of annoyance that they were even having the conversation, all smacked Reed in the solar plexus. It tightened on his lungs, brought a renewed flush of warmth to his skin, as he drove forward.

"I know all that," Reed said. "That wasn't me trying to ride in on a white horse, that was as much self-serving as anything. I was already pissed, and he wasn't giving us much to work with."

He could feel her gaze on his skin, saw her hair swing past as she turned to stare at him. He kept his focus on the road ahead, only glancing over after a moment, meeting her gaze before shifting back to the road.

Apparently, it was enough to quell whatever questions she had inside.

"Sorry," she muttered. "Still a little pissed off myself."

She extended a hand toward the dash, just as she had on the drive over, her fingers trembling as she restrained herself from smacking the hard plastic again. After a moment she curled her hand into a fist and pulled it into her lap, cupping it with her opposite hand.

"And it did work," she whispered. "I just...I get so damn tired of this shit. All of it. Territorial pissing matches, assholes trying to slam their dicks on the table, the whole damn system tripping us up, like they're trying to help the criminals instead of us."

A hint of déjà vu passed over Reed for a moment, this too a conversation he and Riley had had many times before.

Sadly, just as they always had before, he knew this one too would end with no clear answers.

"Just so we're on the same page," Reed said, bypassing her previous statement entirely, more pressing matter on his mind, "neither of us have any intention of handing this off to the FBI, right?"

Chapter Forty-Four

Reed had to admit they made for an odd looking trio. Him out to one side, a 30-something man in running shoes and an unzipped hooded sweatshirt. Opposite him Investigator Cassidy Glenn, wearing a black pantsuit, a v-neck pullover under it, her long hair swinging free behind her. Between them Billie, her head and ears both erect, total height rising well past Glenn's hip.

The unique nature of the group didn't seem to be lost on anybody else either, the few detectives that were present in the bullpen watching them as they passed, few making any attempt to hide their curiosity.

When Reed had first moved over, he had endured the usual round of banter that accompanied new assignments. It had been a bit easier on him, Iaconelli and Bishop withstanding, once word got out about what had happened to Riley, though it still did nothing to stop the glances.

Six weeks later it had all begun in earnest again when he became the entirety of the K-9 Unit for the 8th. Not only was he down a partner, he was choosing to replace her with what appeared to be a solid black wolf.

Never had he even paused to consider the comments that must have been made around the water cooler, though it wasn't hard to figure there were plenty lobbed his direction.

Even though a total of 10 months had now passed, he was still the new guy in the unit. The sudden appearance of a woman, in addition to Billie, would surely have the gossip mill working overtime in a matter of minutes.

Not that he gave a damn about that either.

Still riding his anger spike from the encounter with Cohn, the pre-existing adrenaline surge from seeing Gilmore strung up in his own home, Reed had tunnel vision. His hands clenched and released by his side as he moved a step ahead of the others and led them back through the maze of desks to his in the corner, dropping himself unceremoniously into the seat.

Still piled in a loose stack were the printouts Deek had made for them that morning, Marco Sanz sitting right on top. Reaching out, Reed slid it over in front of the keyboard, glancing at the thin information on the page, his own handmade notes in the margin.

Glenn and Billie both took up spots beside him, all three arranged in the same positions as before, while Reed called his computer to life, the CPD database already open on screen and staring back at them.

Alternating his gaze between the page and the keyboard, Reed entered the file number for Sanz and put the engine to searching, twisting the monitor to the side so Glenn would have a better view.

The legs of her chair scraped against the tile floor, bumping into Billie's shoulder, causing the massive animal to scramble up onto her feet as Glenn moved in a bit closer.

"Sorry, Billie," she mumbled, her focus on the screen. Lines formed around her eyes as she squinted, her face illuminated by the monitor.

"Alright," Reed said, reading aloud, "Marco Sanz, born July 13, 1986, died one year ago today, making him 28-years-old."

Using the mouse, he scrolled down lower in the file, a chronology appearing in bullet point form, the screen a sea of black and white entries.

"Wow, this guy got started early," Reed said, a sardonic lilt to his voice. "First brush with authorities came at age 11 for vagrancy. Soon thereafter came vandalism, petty theft, trespassing. That was all before high school."

He paused there for a moment to make sure Glenn had caught up before pushing further down the screen.

"Then he really picked things up," Glenn said. "Did his first stint in juvie for assaulting a teacher, six months later was back for breaking into a house and trying to steal a pair of sneakers."

"Smart," Reed said, shaking his head as he moved the mouse a bit lower.

"And finally at age 27 he did eight months of a three year sentence for grand theft auto," Glenn said.

A small grunt was Reed's only response as he continued moving downward, past the official cover sheet and into the associated files. He buzzed quickly past all of the juvenile offenses, pausing at each new header to make sure it wasn't the case he was looking for before moving on.

Resting her forearms on the edge of the desk, Glenn watched the pages scroll by, her attention on the screen. "It seem odd to you that somebody that amassed that kind of sheet by 17 suddenly went clean for 10 years before getting nailed for boosting cars?"

It was not the first such file Reed had looked through, though even he had to admit the gap in offenses seemed especially long.

"Two things," he said, continuing to move through the sheets. Most of them looked like they had been scanned and entered manually, the fonts and handwriting on almost all a little different, the clarity at varying levels.

"Either he went away and got an education, became better at his craft."

"Ah," Glenn said, "the old prison-as-higher-learning argument."

To that Reed nodded, having heard the theory rehashed so many times it was almost cliché in law enforcement circles. It was a train of thought especially popular with politicians and newspapers, people that had a vested interest in trying to cut funding or tell a compelling human interest story.

In Reed's own mind, if someone truly wanted the information, the world today could provide it whether they went to prison or not. The internet, and a hundred other resources, was out there detailing everything from hotwiring an engine to assembling an IED using household cleaning products.

To him, the biggest thing prison did was harden people. It took the most extreme tendencies within them, the jagged edges, the parts that society wasn't supposed to see, and it amplified them. It caused people to become meaner, angrier, more resentful.

Once that happened to a person, the fact that they might have gotten a few extra tips in their trade was largely irrelevant.

"That," Reed said, "or someone took him under their wing, started running interference for him."

Silence fell for a moment as Glenn considered the idea, eventually pushing her lips out slightly and nodding. "Could explain why Gilmore wanted him as an informant, using a small fish as bait for the bigger prize."

Again Reed grunted in agreement, finally finding the most recent of the arrest records. On sight he recognized the slanted writing of Martin Bishop, the transcript detailing a pretty non-descript traffic stop for driving with a busted taillight. When they ran the plate on him they discovered a warrant for questioning in connection with a string of automobile thefts in the area, all targeting high-end rides, the total value at nearly half a million dollars.

Once he was finished reading through, Reed paused an extra moment to make sure Glenn was caught up before pushing down again, the next item in order a copy of the warrant that had been issued and over five pages of supporting documentation.

"You see what I'm seeing there?" Reed asked, bypassing the dense paragraphs of text and instead focusing on the half dozen thick black bars stretched horizontally in various places across the screen.

"Why the hell are the names of his suspected co-conspirators redacted?" Glenn muttered, the combination of disdain and bitterness the exact same mix of emotions Reed felt.

"And who did it?" Reed asked.

"Looks legit though," Glenn said. "He was wanted for questioning as a possible participant in nine different car thefts stretched over a 14 month period."

"Our guys picked him up, brought him in, turned him over to the Robbery unit downtown," Reed said, picking up where she left off, pushing the screen lower so they could both see. "They leaned on him for a while, he wouldn't give up anybody, so they took it to a grand jury and threw him in the clink to await trial."

"While he was there, got the holy hell beat out of him, transferred from Corrections to Medical," Glenn said.

The narrative broke there, a series of digitized photographs rising on the screen. Three in total, they each showed a 20-something man with light brown skin. Based on last name, Reed guessed him to be Latino, though a mixed race of Caucasian and African-American was also possible.

In all three photos, a thick white bandaged encased the top half of his head, his left eye encircled by a band of blue bruising. The bridge of his nose was bent slightly to the side, his bottom lip puffy and split.

"Damn," Glenn read, Reed pushing the screen down past the images. "Broken nose, fractured orbital bone, severe concussion."

"Three broken knuckles," Reed added, "so he definitely fought back."

"Still..." Glenn said, letting her voice fall away. "Damn."

Rolling the silver ball atop the computer mouse, Reed pushed the file lower still, past the photos and assorted medical reports, down to the final discharge from Franklin Medical.

Like the prior file, large swaths of it had been redacted, including any mention of Dan Gilmore or the final handwritten assessments from Dennis Weston.

Pausing there, Reed stared at the screen, allowing a loud sigh to be heard.

"Remind me again how you found out about the connection between Weston and Gilmore?" Glenn asked. "I'm guessing your files on all of these guys looking something like this."

Releasing his grip on the mouse, Reed ran a hand back over his scalp before scratching at the nape of his neck. "I didn't run them. I have a...let's just call him something of a tech wizard that helps me out with this stuff from time to time."

The comment pulled Glenn's attention toward him, a crease appearing between her eyebrows. "Oh-kay?"

The only acknowledgement Reed made was to lift the right corner of his mouth slightly before lowering it and his hand back into place. "I'm not sure where he dug, but my guess would be he either pulled originals from Franklin Medical or he went to the FBI themselves."

The crease disappeared as Glenn's eyebrows rose high on her forehead. "No shit?"

"Like I said - tech wizard."

Reed left it at that as he turned back to the computer, again using the mouse to scroll down the page. "Okay, so he was released on October 3rd of last year..."

"And less than three weeks later he was dead," Glenn said, watching as the official release forms faded from sight, the next thing in order coming up.

It too was a written police report, this one from Hilltop, jurisdiction of the 19th Precinct, no more than 10 miles from where they now sat. It contained a detailed workup and full description of everything that was found at the scene, Reed giving it a quick onceover, recognizing the name for the filing officer as Kyle Dawkins, a guy he knew by sight and reputation, but hadn't had a lot of personal interaction with.

Seeing and dismissing it in a moment, Reed moved on down the screen. All breath was pulled from his chest, sweat again appearing on his skin as he stared past the report to the images beneath it. Beside him he heard Glenn inhale sharply before raising the back of her fist to her mouth and turning away, her hair creating a slight breeze as it swung past Reed's shoulder.

Remaining completely motionless, Reed stared a moment at the screen before minimizing the program from sight. He sat for several more thereafter, drawing in deep breaths, willing his heart rate to slow down.

He'd already seen Dan Gilmore hung, his tongue removed from his throat that morning.

He didn't need to see Marco Sanz, too.

Chapter Forty-Five

Reed hadn't noticed it upstairs in the bullpen, though in the close confines of Grimes's office he could plainly detect the scent of blood. It clung to his and Glenn's clothing, to Billie's thick hair, the molecules penetrating their pores as they stood in the living room of Dan Gilmore's home.

Seated across from them it was possible Grimes picked up on it, the frown on his face a bit deeper set than usual.

"I hear you guys had quite an enjoyable interaction with the FBI this morning," he opened.

The comment drew a slight wince from Reed, recalling the spat with Cohn, his own behavior throughout. He knew Grimes well enough to know his captain would have his back as much as possible, but that still didn't mean he was free to exploit such loyalty.

"Yeah," Reed said, drawing the word out an extra syllable or two. "That's on me, Captain."

"No," Glenn said, extending a hand toward him, "that's on the FBI. The guy was stomping around and yelling, basically just trying to make a scene. Reed shut him down cold, tried to get something productive out of the man."

Grimes remained silent a moment, fixing his gaze on Glenn before shifting his hound dog eyes to Reed. "Did it work?"

"Just enough for him to tell us they would be conducting an investigation and they didn't need our help."

Another moment passed as Grimes remained in the same position. With his fingers laced atop his stomach, he tapped the pads of his thumbs together, clearly mulling something.

"And he didn't even want to hear what you'd uncovered up to that point?"

"Not one word," Reed said.

Again Grimes retreated into his usual pose before raising a hand and running it over the length of his face. "Christ," he muttered, passing the hand atop his features once more before returning it to position on his midsection.

"So, Marco Sanz," Grimes said. "Before this morning, I'd never heard of him."

"Nor should you have," Reed said. "He was arrested on a basic traffic stop before your time, found to be wanted in connection to GTA, passed along to Robbery.

"Before somebody associated with him decided to shoot Ike and Bishop, there was absolutely no reason for you to have ever crossed paths with him."

"Somebody associated?" Grimes asked. "As in, not him?"

"No," Glenn said. "He died a year ago today. We had a strong supposition that everything happening was tied to that, but now we know for sure."

She fell silent, twisting her head slightly to see past Grimes, to look out the window at the parking lot. The midday sun refracted off the tops of dozens of cars, a handful of solo pedestrians traveling to and from the building interspersed between them.

Grimes waited a moment for her to continue and when no sound came he shifted his focus over to Reed.

"Dan Gilmore was killed in the same exact way as Marco Sanz," Reed said. "Hung with a thick rope from a light fixture, his tongue removed and stuffed in his front pocket."

A low grunt rolled from Grimes. "Standard retaliation in gang circles for someone believed to be a snitch."

"Right," Reed said, "but we found nothing in his file to indicate gang affiliation."

"Who was he running with?" Grimes asked. "I doubt he amassed that many car thefts by himself."

"Don't know," Reed said, "all other names have been redacted from his file."

The frown deepened again, stretching into an inverted crescent over four inches in length. "You're kidding me."

"Most of the notes from his Franklin Medical file too," Reed said, "including all mention of Dan Gilmore."

"Yet somehow the killer knew all about it," Grimes countered.

Reed paused there a moment, pondering the statement. He had not yet even considered the notion of somebody on the force being involved, especially with all the targets being law enforcement themselves.

Still, as much as he hated to admit it, he couldn't completely rule out the possibility.

"You really think this could have been one of ours?" Reed asked.

"No," Grimes said. "More likely, Sanz told whoever this is about it when he got out. Just saying, we can't completely rule anything out."

"Hmm," Reed said, nodding. He glanced over to Glenn, her head still cocked slightly to the side, no doubt wrestling to push the conglomerated images of Gilmore and Sanz from her mind.

After her display of digestive pyrotechnics in Gilmore's living room, he was willing to give her all the time she needed.

"At this point, I'm inclined to think the killer is done," Reed said. "They've gotten the officers that arrested him, the warden that oversaw him, the agent that turned him, which ultimately got him killed."

"And planned it so it all culminated on the anniversary of his death," Glenn added, her voice just a touch detached as she turned back to face the conversation.

"Right," Reed said. "So hopefully they're finished, but that also means no new leads or information. Whatever happens from this point forward is on us."

The words were not meant as a challenge, though Reed recognized they sounded as such. They hung in the room for several moments, nobody saying anything, before Grimes asked, "So where does this leave you?"

"First stop is the court," Reed said. "I'd like to get a transcript of his initial trial. He was in Franklin Medical at the time, but hopefully somebody that worked with him will be mentioned."

Grimes nodded, remaining silent.

"We should also put someone on his gravesite," Glenn said. "If today was important enough to plan all this around, bears to reason they'll show up to pay their respects at some point."

The notion was something Reed had not considered, being so focused on their side of the investigation. Her reasoning did make sense though, their only hope that the killer hadn't already been by, the day fast approaching noon.

"Greene and Gilchrist said they're happy to do whatever," Reed said. "McMichaels and Jacobs are always up for some overtime."

"I'll take care of it," Grimes said.

Reed wasn't sure if he was referring to signing off on the overtime or making sure somebody got out to the cemetery, but didn't bother inquiring further.

If Grimes said it was covered, it was.

"After that?" Grimes asked.

Glancing over to Glenn, Reed drew in a long breath through his nose. He held it there, his lungs expanded as wide as possible, before releasing it slowly.

"If the file reveals nothing, we track down the officers that found Sanz's body last year," Reed said. He paused again, playing back Sanz's file in his mind, forcing himself to slow down, to process, not to skip past anything important.

"And maybe in the meantime I'll give Deek a call, see if he can't get around some of those redactions we saw all over the original reports."

Chapter Forty-Six

There were five different courthouses that comprised the Franklin County judicial system. Spaced equidistant around the city, one each was assigned to the respective corners of the map – Worthington, Gahanna, Bexley, and Grove City – with the fifth placed downtown. Each court had its own geographic region to cover, designations that had started as five equal orbs and been gerrymandered a bit over time to accommodate for case load.

Twenty months prior, the case of *Franklin Co. v. Sanz* had been handled in the Grove City branch. The clerk had explained to Reed over the phone that while the official court holding was public record and could be read through Westlaw, Nexus Lexus, or a number of other such sites, the full official file had to be accessed in person.

Hanging up without objection, Reed, Glenn, and Billie had loaded back into his sedan, leaving hers still parked in the front visitor stall and heading south. Again he fought the urge to run the siren or lights, longing for the time it would save, knowing that the privilege of using such things had to wait until absolutely necessary.

For whatever reason, Reed couldn't deny the feeling that such a time was coming, but it still was most certainly not upon them yet.

The lunch crowd made the roads a bit busier than they had been driving back from Gilmore's, though most of the traffic was heading back in toward the city as opposed to away from it. Pushing hard they were able to make the trek in just over 15 minutes, much of it spent in silence, Glenn with the case file open on her lap, offering only the occasional comment on something she found.

In the backseat Billie had resumed pacing, her usual stance when starting to get antsy, excess energy beginning to build up. Unlike most days, when Reed would be sure to let her out for a few runs, the occasional trip to relieve herself, thus far she had been cooped up much of the morning.

Like them, she had no doubt gotten an adrenaline spike from the scene at Gilmore's, Reed only able to guess at how much luck she was having in getting it to dissipate.

The Grove City branch of the Franklin County court system announced itself with a freestanding sign constructed of gold letters on a black background. Rising three feet in height and stretched twice that in length, it stood on the front lawn, landscaped with its own mulch bed and several fall mums in a menagerie of colors.

Behind it rose the courthouse itself, a throwback to the '50s style of architecture, made entirely of light colored brick. Rising three stories tall, it was wide enough to make the building still seem squat, three even rows of windows lining the front. The first floor was deep-set into the ground, giving cause for a front staircase that rose eight feet before serving as entry onto the second floor.

The front lawn of the courthouse was cut short, fresh ruts displaying that regular maintenance was still underway despite the calendar. A pair of young men in slacks and ties walked diagonally across it as Reed pulled around to the side of the building and eased into the visitor lot, taking the third available diagonal stall facing the building.

"She said the clerk's office is around back," Reed said as they exited, Billie again pushing her way out right behind him, refusing to be left behind. Reed made no effort to stop her as she went, merely reaching behind his seat and taking up the short lead and affixing it to her collar.

Twenty minutes after leaving the 8th Precinct, the trio passed through a door into the bottom level of the building, a small bell ringing overhead, announcing their presence. As it did so, a short, diminutive woman with hair bottle-dyed the color of cranberry juice stood from her desk and walked forward to the front counter.

She held a hand up to cover her mouth as she went, waiting until she swallowed before saying, "Sorry about that, you just caught me having lunch."

"Sorry to interrupt," Reed said, waving a hand in her direction. "This is Investigator Cassidy Glenn, I'm Detective Reed Mattox, we spoke on the phone a few moments ago."

The woman stared blankly at him a moment before the proverbial light bulb went off above her head, her mouth and eyes all three widening into congruent circles. "Oh, yes!" she said, almost yelling, raising a finger toward the ceiling. "You wanted to take a look at the *Sands* case."

"*Sanz*," Reed corrected. "S-A-N-Z."

The woman's face fell as she realized her mistake, rotating at the waist to glance back at her desk, the pile of fast food growing cold behind her. "Oh," she said. "Apparently I pulled the wrong file. And here I thought I would be helpful and save us all some time."

"That's okay," Glenn said, "we didn't mean to interrupt. We're happy to go dig for ourselves."

The woman glanced to both of them, her uncertainty obvious, before again turning to look at her lunch. "Are you sure? I'm happy to go find it."

"Not a problem," Reed said.

"Just point us in the right direction," Glenn added.

"Well, come on back," the woman said, waving an arm at them, all three circling around the counter as she led them past her desk and a couple of small offices to a short stairwell.

She paused at the top of it and extended a finger, saying, "Forgive me if I don't make the trip, too. My knee isn't what it used to be."

"Not a problem," Reed repeated. "What are we looking for down there?"

"Just follow the signs," she said, "everything is arranged by date."

Nodding his thanks, Reed descended the stairs first, Billie's feet clattering against the polished tile, fighting for purchase. The sharp decline of the stairs caused her to gain momentum as she went, her bulk almost slamming into Reed's knees from behind, depositing her in the basement and forcing her to jog forward to slow her descent.

Behind them Glenn came one step at a time, her heavy shoes knocking against the floor.

"That was graceful," she said, pausing at the foot of the stairwell and surveying the room around them.

"She can't be a lady all the time," Reed replied, taking in the spread as well.

The basement level of the building looked to be one large warehouse, the entire space open, no walls or dividers of any kind. Standard metal shelving units filled most of the area, each one loaded with brown file boxes. Separated into two columns, they stretched out straight before them, a walkway six feet in width dividing them.

Elongated light bulbs were affixed to the ceiling in even rows, casting a bright white light over everything.

"So, he was sentenced in February of 2013, right?" Glenn asked.

Flicking his gaze to the ceiling, Reed did the math backwards in his head, starting with Sanz's death and going from there. "Yes. He was already inside at the time, but that's when he was officially sentenced."

"Okay," Glenn said, raising a hand before her and pointing to the white cards affixed to the end of each shelving unit. "It looks like these start in 2005 and work their way forward, so we need to look down on the far end there."

Dropping Billie's lead to the floor, Reed let her drag it behind her as they moved forward, walking quickly through the rows until they found 2013. Starting on the right side of the aisle, they moved about halfway down the length of the row before finding the cases for February, more than 50 boxes filling 10 shelves in total.

"Damn," Reed muttered, "all this for one month?"

"And this is just one branch of the County court system," Glenn said.

"Never let it be said the taxpayers aren't getting their money's worth," Reed said, going to the opposite end of the February files and beginning to work his way back toward Glenn.

Scrolling the names scribbled in blue marker along the side of the boxes, they both worked in silence for the better part of five minutes before Glenn found what they were looking for, snatching a box off the bottom shelf and dragging it out, the weight of it smacking against the tile floor, sending an echo through the cavernous room.

"*Franklin Co. v. Sanz.* Let's take a look and see what we've got."

Lowering herself to her knees, Glenn rested her backside on her heels and shoved the top of the box to the side, a plume of dust rising in its wake. On the opposite side Reed dropped to the floor, crossing his legs in front of him, Billie posted up just past his right shoulder, her muzzle a few inches away.

Reaching in, Glenn pulled out the first folder, a dark brown jacket with metal clips at the top. The name and date of the case were scribbled across the front in black marker. Without opening or glancing inside she handed it across to Reed, going in for a matching one, each side settling in to read.

The file in Reed's hand was the evidentiary submissions for the case, a half dozen grainy photographs and a few more sworn affidavits and depositions. Their sources ranged from owners of the cars to police officers working the cases, the veracity of them also tracing the full gamut of reliability.

"Anything good?" Glenn asked, the first either one of them had spoken since sitting down.

"Evidence," Reed said. "Not much of substance. You?"

"Court transcript," Glenn said. "With him already incarcerated, the whole thing reads like a whitewashing."

Reed nodded, expecting nothing less based on many of the reports he'd just glanced through. As best he could tell, nearly every statement that hadn't originated with a law enforcement officer boiled down to an angry car owner wanting somebody to pay for what had happened, the particulars not being that important.

Much as he hated to admit it, a couple of the official reports from the officers kind of read that way as well.

Placing the file to the side, Reed went in for the next file in order, this one much thinner than either of the first two. Flipping open the top cover, he found a single piece of paper affixed to the inside of the left flap, the word Witness List at the top in block letters.

Two columns were typed on the page, one each for the prosecution and defense. Under the prosecution more than a dozen names were listed, almost all of them matching names he'd seen in the previous folder. These he passed over and dismissed in quick order before settling his gaze on the side of the page demarcated for the defense.

There weren't enough names to call it a list, just three in total. The name at the top was Maria Sanz. Though Reed had absolutely no information about her beyond those two words he reasoned this was most likely a mother, the same person that most often turned up at the top of defense witness lists, the idea to put a crying mother or spouse on the stand and have them extol their moral upstanding.

As Sanz was only in his 20s at the time, Reed figured the top name was his mother, the next in line, Sonya Johnston, to be his girlfriend.

That left only a single name unaccounted for.

"Can you scroll through that transcript and see what you find for Anthony Wittek?"

Chapter Forty-Seven

Nobody had bothered climbing into the car. Still parked along the side of the courthouse, Reed leaned against the front hood, one arm crossed over his stomach, the other holding his phone out in front of him. Two feet away Glenn stood with one leg cocked to the side, her hands shoved into her front pockets.

Both pretended to ignore the gusts of chilly breeze that blew across their bodies, tugging at their clothes, pushing Glenn's hair out behind her.

Nearby Billie paced on the lawn of the courthouse, her nose lowered to the ground, in search of a spot to do her business while never being more than a few quick bounds away.

"Cried?" Grimes asked, his voice carrying out over the speaker on his Reed's phone. Even through the distortion of the phone, it was obvious there was some disbelief present.

"Three different times," Glenn said. "We just read it straight from the transcript."

A low, shrill whistle sounded out over the line, Reed looking up to Glenn and nodding in agreement.

From the sound of things in the file, his initial reaction to the witness list had been spot on. There were the expected statements from Sanz's mother and girlfriend, both proclaiming him to be a veritable saint, the kind of person the community could use more of. Neither had said anything of any real value though, never once moving past sweeping platitudes, their testimony noticeably thin on anything of substance.

Anthony Wittek had been a different case altogether.

From what they could glean from the statements, Marco Sanz had been a friend that became a big brother figure to the younger Wittek. The questioning glossed over how the two had met, instead focusing on how Sanz had mentored Wittek, had taken him under his wing when nobody else would.

Repeatedly throughout his testimony he had referred to Sanz as Big, using the term interchangeably with his real first name, the entire affair interspersed with several episodes of breaking down. More than once he had begged for his friend to be released, saying he was no longer cut out for prison life.

Without any video footage it was tough to determine how sincere the performance might have been, the transcript in places reading close to a bad television show. Listening to Glenn go through it, Reed could almost picture this young man sitting on the stand, trying to force out a few weak tears, reading from a script.

At the same time, he had been around the culture of young men, especially those in criminal enterprises, enough to know that crying and asking for leniency were extreme breaches. There was a reason the mothers and girlfriends were usually the only ones to show up at trial, the friends and associates popping up days later during visiting hours to remind those inside to keep their mouth shut.

The sound of keys clattering could be heard on the other end of the line as Grimes entered the name into his computer. "Anthony Wittek has two priors, one for receipt of stolen property, another for hacking into the system of a home security company.

"Probation for the first, did a couple months on the second, released early due to overcrowding."

Reed made a face, shaking his head at the back end of the report.

"Known whereabouts?"

"Last address is from two years ago, during his final scheduled meeting with his parole officer. He could still be there, but I doubt it."

Reed flicked his gaze up to Glenn, thinking the same thing.

"Anything in the system since?"

"Not even a parking ticket," Grimes said.

Shaking her head, Glenn turned toward the street, shaking her head, watching traffic flow by.

Reed couldn't help but agree with her stance. If this was their guy, and all signs seemed to indicate it was, or that he was at least connected, there was precisely zero chance that he was still hanging out at his last known address. He had almost certainly fallen off the grid the minute his required check-in period had expired, going underground to begin planning.

The acts that had been committed in the previous days took a level of detail that would not arise from nowhere, would have to be born from something like extreme loyalty. The actions of Anthony Wittek during trial certainly seemed to indicate as much.

"Okay," Reed said, "thanks, Captain."

"What's your next step?" Grimes asked.

Letting the phone sag a couple of inches, Reed looked to Glenn. The two stayed locked in a gaze for a moment before Reed raised the speaker again and said, "I'm going to talk to Deek, see if he was able to pull any other names and if he can find us a current address for Wittek."

As he spoke, Reed slapped at the thigh of his leg, grabbing Billie's attention, pulling her back toward them.

"Okay," Grimes said. "Keep me in the loop."

Chapter Forty-Eight

Reed wasn't sure exactly where they were headed, but he pushed the car north anyway. He reasoned that most likely, based on where Sanz had originally been pulled over, he had lived at least somewhat close to Franklinton. That also meant there was a decent likelihood that Wittek, or whoever else, might be nearby as well.

Beyond that, even if they weren't, at least he would be that much closer to the precinct, to Deek, even to Glenn's office.

The only thing he did know for sure was that Grove City held little more benefit for them, the town center fading in his rearview mirror as he circled onto the freeway.

This time he let Glenn hold the phone, the implement gripped between her thumb and fingers, a full inch over her palm. She kept it raised above her thigh, her wrist acting as a support, the timer on the screen counting upward for zero.

The line rang three times before being answered, the voice on the other end sounding somewhere between a stoned surfer and someone being awoken from the dead.

"Detective," Deek said, adding nothing more.

"Hey, Deek," Reed said, "I've got you on speakerphone right now with Investigator Cassidy Glenn from the BCI."

"Huh," Deek said, a hint of surprise in his voice. "What happened to the pooch?"

Unable to stop it, Reed felt the right corner of his mouth curl into a smile. He glanced over to Glenn to see a similar smirk, her eyebrows raised a bit as she glanced to Reed.

He could only imagine what her reaction would be if she actually met Deek, especially if said encounter took place in his den of iniquity.

"Billie's here, too," Reed said, "but she won't be adding much to the conversation. Just wanted you to know who you were talking to."

"Ah," Deek said, Reed envisioning him rocking his head back, his mouth falling open. "Gotcha."

"So what were you able to find from those files?" Reed asked. "Any of those names come without a thick black line drawn through them?"

The sound of bare feet on a hard surface was the first response, followed by the plastic wheels of a desk chair rolling across the same. Next in order came fingers slapping against a keyboard, Deek waiting almost a full minute before responding.

"Fair warning, considering you've given me about an hour so far, I've only been able to get through the first part of the file. I'm guessing whatever you're into here is some pretty heavy shit because the security was extra tight, even by FBI standards."

Reed again glanced to Glenn, the investigator meeting his gaze, drawing her mouth into a line.

"Only one name," Deek said, "though it came up a dozen times or so. File doesn't give much detail on the guy, and I figured you had plenty of access to his standard police jacket without me poking around in there too, so I didn't do too much digging."

His jaw set, Reed nodded. Deek was correct in that they had plenty of access to files once they had a name, it was just getting past the redactions that was tough.

"What's the name?" Reed asked.

"Raul Vazquez," Deek said. "From the way this thing reads, they were thick as thieves, no pun intended."

Glenn made a face at the poor joke and asked, "Does it say how he and Sanz were connected?"

"Sounds like they were partners in this car theft enterprise they had going," Deek said, "or at least whoever was leaning on Sanz thought they were."

"And Sanz never gave him up?" Reed asked.

"Never said a word," Deek replied.

He paused there, a long break punctuated by more movement of the chair, by another series of clattering on the keyboard. "Looks like he's the reason Gilmore offered Sanz a deal, too."

Reed felt his eyebrows rise as he continued pushing north up the freeway, leaning heavy on the gas to get around a pair of semi-trucks before moving back into the outside lane, their exit fast approaching.

"Gilmore was interested in Vazquez?" Reed asked.

"Interested?" Deek asked. "Guy had a major hard-on for him. Enough surveillance in the file to write a book. He just didn't have an in."

Reed glanced over to the passenger seat, Glenn's face twisted up, shock and concern on her features.

"What?" Reed asked.

"He has access to Gilmore's files?"

"Seriously?" Deek asked, jumping in before Reed had a chance to respond.

"She didn't mean anything by it," Reed said, raising his voice slightly for effect. "She just doesn't know you the way I do."

"Uh-huh," Deek said, skepticism obvious.

Reflexively, a half-smile formed on Reed's lips as he looked to Glenn and mouthed, *I'll tell you later.*

Keeping his attention aimed her way, Reed glanced sideways at the road a couple of times, a square green sign just off the shoulder announcing Franklinton approaching in two miles.

"You ever heard of Raul Vazquez?" Reed asked.

"No," Glenn said, "but I don't work in robbery at all. You?"

"No," Reed said, giving a tight shake of his head. "Deek, any chance you can get an address for him?"

More banging on the keyboard was the only response as Deek went to work, Reed and Glenn both leaning toward the phone.

"You thinking of going over there?" Glenn asked.

"Don't see how we can't," Reed said. "His name was mentioned as the business partner of a dead man that seems to have ignited a string of killings."

"The FBI will be pissed. Could torpedo their investigation."

"Do we care?" Reed asked. "They're already pissed and the investigating agent is dead."

"Good points," Glenn conceded, her right shoulder rising slightly in a shrug.

"Alright," Deek said, "there's an address here in Gilmore's notes that he was watching pretty tight. If I were a betting man, I'd say this is your place."

"Where?" Reed asked.

"Hilltop," Deek said, "not too far from your new stomping grounds. You want me to send it over?"

"Please," Reed said. "And try to stay out of that bottle for the rest of the afternoon and keep your phone handy if you could."

A moment passed before Deek said, "I could do that, for a small fee."

Again the half-smile appeared on Reed's face. "Whatever you want."

He raised a hand and slashed it across his throat, signaling for Glenn to end the call. She did so without another word being exchanged between the two sides, dropping the phone flat against her leg and staring expectantly at Reed.

"I'll explain later," Reed said, sensing a questioning look on his skin. "Can you go down the call menu and get Grimes on the line?"

She did as asked, again propping the phone up on her leg. This time the line rang only once before being picked up, the captain's graveled voice sounding a bit deeper than their previous conversation.

"Was he able to help?"

"Who'd you put on watch over at Sanz's gravesite?" Reed asked, moving straight past the opening question.

"McMichaels and Jacobs, why?"

"Can you get Greene and Gilchrist up and have them join us?" Reed asked. "We're going to roll up on Sanz's business partner, not sure what to expect."

Silence met their ears for a moment before Grimes asked, "Should I be sending over a SWAT unit instead?"

Reed glanced to Glenn, having considered the same thing himself. "Not right now. We don't know what we're going into, showing up with that kind of muscle might incite something we're not prepared for."

It was apparent by the chorus of noises Grimes made that he wasn't entirely onboard with the request, did not like the open-ended nature of it at all, but to his credit he said nothing. "Okay. You have an address?"

"I'll send it straight to them," Reed said. He paused and glanced to Glenn, flipping on his blinker as he eased his foot up off the gas and drifted onto the off-ramp leading toward Franklinton.

"Also, can you get on the horn with the 19th and tell them we'll be dropping into their jurisdiction for a few minutes?"

Chapter Forty-Nine

With a ball cap pulled low and a pair of non-prescription glasses he'd picked up at a drug store for six bucks, The Kid was virtually invisible. He sat at the counter lining the front window of the coffee shop, a dog-eared paperback in front of him, a tall cup of steaming black coffee by his side.

Scrawled on the side of it in black pen was a name that was decidedly not his, the ink standing out against the white paper background.

Sitting with his shoulders hunched, the toes of his shoes just grazing the ground as his feet dangled from the lowest rung on the stool he sat on, he positioned himself so it appeared to anybody nearby like he was engrossed in his novel. He had torn away the front cover, hoping to dissuade anybody that might see and recognize it, causing them to remember him or even worse attempt to engage him in conversation. Every so often he was careful to turn the page, just another college student in the area killing time.

The ruse was easy enough for The Kid to pull off, he himself that very thing not too long ago. Of course that was before he had traded in his books for something a little more lucrative, joining the crew, finally making valuable use of his myriad skills.

It was there that he had first met Big, a happenstance encounter that over time became so much more.

The memory of the event still brought a smile to his face, a day that was more than four years prior.

Watching the streets was something The Kid had done from an early age, the solitary piece of advice he'd ever received from his father that was worth hanging on to. He'd always told him he never knew when he would need a quick cash infusion, none being better or more reliable than those on four wheels that rolled by every day.

Bored one evening, in dire need of rent money, even more in need of something to do, The Kid had decided to test the notion. He'd spotted a low-slung Cadillac with custom rims and tinted windows two weeks before, noticing it parked outside the same house every evening without fail.

At first it was just wanton curiosity, but as the days passed a pattern emerged. Every afternoon at 5:00 the man that lived at the house would leave for work. Less than an hour later, the Cadillac would arrive and stay until midnight.

Shortly thereafter, the man of the house would return.

Twenty-one years old, a struggling part-time college student, part-time whatever else he could get into, The Kid saw an opportunity.

What he didn't see was Big casing the same car.

Looking back on it, The Kid was fortunate things went the way they did. Anybody else would have put a bullet in him without thinking twice, finding his lack of skill, his audacity for encroaching on their turf, a direct affront.

At the very least, he would have caught a beating.

For whatever reason, though, Big had taken a liking to him. Had sat and watched the entire clumsy affair from across the street, was laughing as he pulled up alongside The Kid running down the middle of the street and told him to get in, the intertwined sounds of a handgun barking and the Cadillac's alarm wailing in their wake.

From that moment on, he had been brought into the crew. He'd had to start as an underling, just as everyone did, but under Big's arm he was protected. He was taught the requisite lessons he needed to know, was given the chance to put his own talents on display.

Idly turning a page in his book from right to left, The Kid flicked his gaze up to the duo standing on the corner outside the coffee shop. He watched as they stood and drank from cups just like the one beside him, both laughing, oblivious to the cool afternoon air.

Only one of them was his target, the last of his list. After that he would finally be free to move on, knowing he had put Big to rest for good, could move on himself with a clear conscience.

To where that might be he wasn't yet sure, having not allowed himself to fully revel in the notion until everything was completed. Once it was, he would grab what little he had and slip off into the night, not stopping until he found some place or someone he loved and not a moment before.

Leaning back from the counter, The Kid raised his drink to his lips and took a long pull. He ignored the bitter taste of the coffee and used his heightened position to watch as his target climbed into the passenger side of the car, still laughing, a smile affixed to his features.

A moment later the car disappeared from sight, The Kid returning himself into position, his forearms resting against the front edge of the counter.

Today, this day, had been a long time coming. Everything he'd prepared, all the work he'd done, the vow he'd made, was almost concluded.

He had just one more stop to make.

Chapter Fifty

The blue and white cruiser was sitting on the curb as Reed pulled up. It was parked straddling the driveway, blocking any cars from coming or going, either bumper sticking out by more than a foot on both ends.

Reed's first thought upon approaching and surveying the house was that it wouldn't matter anyway, getting the same vibe he had when rolling to a stop outside of Dan Gilmore's place.

The house was two stories tall, the outside covered in grey vinyl siding, shutters painted black. An awning bisected the two stories, protruding from the front of the house, vertical beams supporting it, shading a concrete porch. Large green spots of mold dotted the shingles on the roof, gutters overflowing with leaves.

Alongside the house was an oversized garage, twin doors both standing closed. Each was made of wood and peeling badly, a row of windows painted over across the top of them.

Much like the house, leaves were piled up in the gutters and along the front of the doors.

No cars sat in the driveway. No lights were on in any of the windows.

Greene and Gilchrist both climbed out upon seeing them, each already dressed for the night ahead, wearing their long sleeved uniforms, solid black from head to foot. Greene stood along the driver's side door as Gilchrist circled around to join him, both putting the car between themselves and the house.

Leaving just a couple of feet between their rear bumper and his front fender, Reed killed the engine and left the keys in the ignition, a burst of brisk air hitting him as he exited the car. He paused a moment once hitting the street, waiting for Billie to spill out behind him, Glenn climbing out on the opposite side.

"Thanks for coming," Reed said, closing the door behind Billie. Twice he tapped at the base of his weapon as he walked toward the officers, casting a long gaze at the house before turning back to the men before him.

"What have we got?" Greene asked, not acknowledging the thanks.

"Officers," Reed said, extending a hand to his side, "Investigator Cassidy Glenn, BCI."

He moved his hand in the opposite direction and said, "Officers Derek Greene and Adam Gilchrist, CPD."

The two sides nodded at each other, neither offering a verbal greeting.

"Investigator Glenn was given the lead on the Warden Weston case. Since the two overlapped, we've been working together on this."

Gilchrist nodded at the explanation, Greene remaining silent.

"This here," Reed said, motioning toward the house with his chin, "is the residence on file for Raul Vazquez, a known car thief and someone that used to run with Marco Sanz."

"And Sanz is?" Greene asked.

"The reason law enforcement personnel are being targeted all over town," Glenn said.

Gilchrist's eyebrows went up a fraction of an inch, his eyes widening in equal proportion. "As in, plural?"

"Including our guys, four in the last couple days," Reed said.

"And Vazquez did them all?" Greene asked.

"Doubtful," Reed said, "though not impossible. We think the killer is a guy who spoke at Sanz's trial named Anthony Wittek. Before Sanz death, they both ran on a crew that was headed by Vazquez."

"So we don't know where Wittek is right now?" Greene asked, connecting the dots in Reed's statement.

"No," Reed replied. "We've got Deek digging, but in the meantime, we figured we'd stop in here and poke around. Might be able to get a bead on Wittek, might find something else we hadn't considered yet."

At that both officers turned to look at the house, neither commenting on the plan. They remained that way a moment before Gilchrist said, "We've been here about 10 minutes. Haven't seen any signs of life."

Matching their gaze, Reed nodded slightly. He wasn't surprised, still not expecting to find anybody home, knowing they had to go through the process just the same.

Driving over, he'd had no idea what to expect. In the back of his mind he'd pictured an abandoned warehouse somewhere, roll-top doors on either end, a crew of men with welding torches going to town on a half dozen cars at a time.

In reality, the place looked closer to someplace a group of college kids would live. At one point it had probably been a home for a medium-to-large family, the front lawn well kept, the siding clean and neat.

Those days had long since passed though, the new tenants clearly caring little for aesthetics.

Aside from the garage, though, there was nothing to indicate that anything nefarious ever took place on the property.

"Okay," Reed said. "Investigator Glenn, Billie, and I will approach the front door. You guys remain here on the drive and keep a watch. If we have any reason to breech, you guys take the side door, we'll go in through the porch."

"Roger that," Greene said, Gilchrist nodding in agreement. Together they moved past Reed and circled around the back of his car, coming up through the yard and assuming a post at the end of the driveway.

Reed waited for them to get into position before glancing to Glenn and asking, "You ready?"

"I am," she said, "but I don't think it'll matter."

"I don't either," Reed said, "but that's what we thought at Gilmore's too."

The mention of his name caused a visible quiver as Glenn set her jaw, nodding for Reed to proceed.

Slapping at the thigh of his jeans, Reed started for the front door, Billie trotting out in front of them. They bypassed the concrete drive and went in a straight line across the front lawn, leaves crackling underfoot as they proceeded.

"I've got nothing in any of the windows," Glenn said, her gaze darting over the front of the house, watching for any signs of movement.

Reed heard her voice beside him, the words failing to register. Instead he kept his focus on Billie, watching as her body grew rigid. She extended her nose out straight ahead of her, letting him know she had picked up a scent, slowing her pace to one paw at a time.

Seeing her, Reed extended a hand, touching Glenn on the arm and motioning for her to stop. Reaching to his hip, he drew his weapon, rotating at the waist, making sure the officers had seen him, both doing the same.

"What's going on?" Glenn asked.

"I don't know yet," Reed said, "but watch your step. She'll let us know as soon as she does."

Sliding her Glock free from the holster on her hip, Glenn raised herself up onto her toes, turning her body sideways, crossing one foot over the other as the trio nudged toward the front door. A low growl emanated from deep within Billie as they moved forward, her entire body pulled taut, everything from the end of her tail to the tip of her nose extended in a straight line.

"It's getting stronger," Reed said, keeping his focus on her as she took the front steps one at a time.

Falling back into a single-file line, he followed after Billie in order, Glenn making up the rear.

It wasn't until he was halfway across the front patio that he too finally picked up what Billie had noticed, the smell assaulting his nostrils, turning his stomach.

"Guys!" he called, pressing his chin into his shoulder without turning to look at them. "Get ready to breach. We've got a body in here."

Chapter Fifty-One

Greene and Gilchrist flitted past the periphery of Reed's vision, both with weapons drawn, running straight up the driveway before disappearing around the side of the house. Both dressed entirely in black, they were little more than blurs as they scooted by, Greene in the lead, Gilchrist a step behind him.

"I'll bust the door, we'll handle it just like last time?" Reed asked, glancing over to Glenn.

Standing a few feet back from him, her body angled so she could see the front door and the driveway, she nodded. Already her mouth was drawn into little more than a dash across the bottom half of her face, her skin a bit pale.

Whether that was from the smell or any impending trepidation about what they might find, Reed wasn't sure.

"Billie, you ready?"

At the sound of her name, Billie looked up at him, her entire body still poised. She fixed her gaze on him for only a moment before moving back for the door, responding to his inquiry, one that was more rhetoric than anything.

Reed had seen her in action enough times to know the only thing that could possibly pull her back once she was on the trail of something was his command, and even then there was the occasional bit of reluctance.

"Greene?" Reed yelled, cocking his head a few inches to the side, raising his voice again to be heard.

"On your mark," Greene yelled, his voice taut, but not quite strained.

Assuming the same stance Glenn had that morning, Reed shifted his weight to his right foot, rocking back on it twice to gain a bit of momentum. On the third he pushed forward off the ball of his foot, using his left as a fulcrum and propelling himself at the door. As he went, he swung his right leg up in a fast half-arc, aiming for the narrow strip of wood between the knob and the door casing.

He didn't make direct contact with the spot he was hoping for, his momentum carrying him forward faster than expected, his foot not quite rising to parallel. Instead of connecting between the handle and the casing, he hit just a few inches below it.

Not that it mattered.

The door was a much cheaper design than the one at Gilmore's, the frame made from 1"x2"s, the thin pine tearing away in one long sheet. Instead of shards and sawdust there was only the screech of nails being pulled out, the clatter of a board 8' in length smacking against the floor.

A moment later the rubber bottom of Reed's shoe slapped against the linoleum of a small front foyer, heavy shag carpet coming up to within a few feet of the door. There he stood, one foot inside and the other still on the porch, his gun extended.

What had been merely an odor outside the door became an overwhelming stench, the smell engulfing him, causing his eyes to water, his breath to catch in the back of his throat. He drew in two deep gasps, fighting to clear his airway, before finally managing, "Clear!"

Billie's ribcage and tail brushed against his leg as she shot past him, disappearing into the house. A moment later he heard a second door being breached from somewhere in the back, the same sounds of a deadbolt tearing free, of wood splintering, finding his ears.

"Brace yourself," Reed whispered, as much for himself as for Glenn, and stepped inside.

Compared to the bright grey sky of the afternoon, the interior of the house was dim, a fact aided considerably by the chosen décor. Dark wood paneling lined the walls, the carpet a deep russet brown. In the front room, a couch and chair both sat empty, a matching set covered in black cloth, a coffee table between them. Piled high on it was an assortment of pizza boxes and beer bottles, ash trays and magazines.

In the corner sat an old box television, a fixture hanging down from the ceiling as the only light.

Along the back of the room a staircase ran up to the second floor, the same dark carpet and paneling making it almost impossible to differentiate from the rest of the space.

All in all, a scene from somewhere in the late '70s.

"Damn," Glenn muttered, the linoleum floor announcing her entry, her shoes clicking against the hard surface.

In front of her Reed nodded slightly, saying nothing, knowing exactly what she was referring to. If not for the sheer volume of adrenaline passing through him, of his concern for his partner still in the house, the smell would have been all he could concentrate on. With each step it grew stronger, threatening to be absorbed into his being, never to be relinquished.

On the opposite end of the living room Greene appeared, the shadow of Gilchrist behind him. "Kitchen's clear."

"Same for living room," Reed said. He glanced upstairs, listening to the sound of Billie bounding across the floor, before hearing her announce that the source of the smell had been found.

Loud and without restraint, it echoed down the stairs, one thunderous bellow after another.

"She's found Vazquez," Reed said, moving straight for the stairs and taking them two at a time, his heart rate increasing. Behind him he heard heavy footsteps following him, though whether they were from Greene or Glenn he couldn't be certain.

Hearing Billie's deep braying, free of any growling or malice, told him she was safe, but he still couldn't help but feel the same fear he'd had at Gilmore's rise within him. At the top of the stairs he forced himself to pause, to raise his weapon and check in both directions, making sure there wasn't something unforeseen waiting for him before moving toward the sound of her voice.

And the overwhelmingly potent smell.

The second floor of the house spread wide to both sides from the top of the stairs, a small bathroom directly in front it, bedrooms to either end. Ignoring the one on the left, Reed proceeded to the right, seeing Billie pacing in and out of the doorway, her attention aimed into the room.

Moving slow, flexing his knees into a crouch, Reed pressed a shoulder against the wall and approached the door, tilting his head to the side to see into the bedroom.

Upon doing so, the front of his gun dipped just a little, his throat constricting tight, stopping just short of an outright gag.

"Damn," he whispered, glancing back over his shoulder to see Greene in the hallway, Glenn peeking out around him, still a few steps down from the top.

"Down," Reed said, Billie falling quiet, the entire house silent as Reed stepped into the room. His eyes watered and his stomach curdled as he walked up beside her still standing rigid, lowering his left hand and touching the fur behind her ears. "Good girl."

On the bed were two people – or, more aptly - what remained of them. A male and a female, both lay without any visible clothing, only a sheet strewn over their torsos to cover their bodies.

More than a dozen bullet holes were interspersed between them, tearing small holes into the sheet, large smears of dried blood spread out from them in misshapen circles. Judging by the smell and the appearance of the blood, the two had both been there for some time, several handfuls of flies visible.

Beneath the sheet they appeared to be distorted, Reed guessing from the buildup of gases, their bodies already desiccating and beginning the decomposition process.

"Who's the girl?" Greene asked, stepping into the doorway.

Reed glanced over his shoulder to see him leaning against one side of it, Glenn filling the other. She looked just as she had that morning, as if she might vomit, one hand resting against the jamb for support.

Again he thought of asking her to go before contaminating the crime scene but opted against it, not wanting to create bad relations by embarrassing her in front of the other officers.

Clearly, they still had work to do before this was over.

"Don't know," Reed said. "My guess would be, to borrow a cliché, wrong place wrong time."

"Wittek came in," Glenn said, her voice a bit stronger than expected, "looking for Vazquez, found them both, emptied his gun in them."

Reed grunted, sweeping his gaze over the room. Past the initial sensory overload of the sight and smell, his mind transitioned, inventorying what needed to be done.

"Gilchrist?" he asked, turning back toward the door.

"Yeah?" the young officer responded from further back in the hallway, beyond Reed's sight.

"Can you call Grimes and tell him to get Earl and the 19th over here? It's their crime scene, but he'll be the one doing the work up."

"You got it," Gilchrist said. A moment later, the sound of his heavy footfalls could be heard as he descended the stairwell.

Reed turned back to face the macabre scene again and said, "I don't see any brass, but how much you want to bet they're the slugs that hit Ike and Bishop?"

"No bet," Greene said, "too easy. From the looks of things though, these folks have been here a while, a lot longer than Saturday night."

"True," Reed said. "There wouldn't be this smell until at least a couple days, the bloating and distortion even longer after that."

"Especially given how cool it is," Glenn added.

Reed nodded, continuing to take everything in. From what he could tell, the couple had either been asleep or in the throes of passion when Wittek entered. Neither had made a move to climb from the bed before the shooting started, both still in the middle of the mattress.

It also appeared that every bullet had found a target, no visible holes in the paneling above the bed or blood spatter on the wall.

"We also need to consider," Reed said, "that this one wasn't law enforcement. Could there be someone else targeted? An agenda even larger than we realized?"

Chapter Fifty-Two

Reed nodded to the cluster of officers standing on the front porch, each of the men giving him a wary glance before nodding in return. Previously housed in the 19th Precinct, Reed knew each of the men by sight, having worked in the same building with all four for at least a couple of years before moving over.

He knew the reasons for their aloofness were numerous, some that were legitimate, many more that were vested in the sorts of low-level pissing matches he liked to think the various precincts were no longer concerned with, but knew better than to believe. To them, while he had perhaps overstepped an unspoken boundary by uncovering a heinous crime in their jurisdiction, his problems extended back long before that.

After years of serving as beat cops, the same as the men on the porch, he and Riley had made the conscious decision to transition into being detectives. The move was made after long and careful debate, both wanting to make sure they could remain partners first and foremost, their secondary concern being about the escalating rates of crime in the area and how they thought they could best make an impact.

Not once were the topics of rank or pay ever considered.

Despite that, many of the fellow uniforms they worked with had taken it as a slight. Several started making comments, some even went as far as to cut off communication.

Whatever momentary reprieve he had gotten after the passing of Riley had been instantly revoked the moment he chose to change precincts, many in his wake feeling betrayed and deserted.

Judging by the begrudging acknowledgment on the front porch, many still harbored the same feelings, Reed not especially surprised, even less concerned. Instead he walked right past them and down the front steps, joining Greene, Gilchrist, and Glenn beside the blue-and-white cruiser still parked straddling the driveway.

By his side was Billie, the previous tension that propelled her onward having evaporated, her tail drooping a bit as she loped along beside him.

In addition to the cruiser and Reed's sedan were now a trio of additional blue-and-whites and Earl's white van, the collection of cars taking up most of the available space on the street. None of the vehicles had used their lights or sirens on approach, but that didn't keep the occasional onlooker from roaming past, pretending to be out for an afternoon stroll.

"Well, that was subtle," Glenn said, staring past Reed to the men on the porch.

"Yeah, well, that shit goes back a long ways," Reed said, not bothering to turn and look at them, knowing all four were at the least glancing over every few seconds, if not openly staring. "Not my biggest concern at the moment."

"What'd Earl have to say?" Greene asked, looking up at the bedroom window on the second floor, the curtain pulled back, shadows visible moving around on the opposite side.

Flicking his gaze to Glenn, Reed said, "You're going to love this. He ran the prints of our two victims through AFIS on his electronic pad and got hits for both.

"Raul Vazquez and none other than one Sonya Johnston."

Glenn's face fell blank for a moment, searching for the name, before recognition set in, her features snapping back to attention.

"Who's Sonya Johnston?" Gilchrist asked.

"Marco Sanz's girlfriend," Glenn said. "Even spoke at his trial."

"Probably showed up ready to take down his best friend's - his *big brother's* - killer, and found him in bed with his lady," Reed said.

"That'd do it," Gilchrist agreed, nodding once for emphasis.

Before further comment could be made, the theme song from *The Good, The Bad, and the Ugly*, sounded out, the low, mournful whistle resonating from Reed's hip.

For a moment the group stared in confusion before Reed raised a hand in apology and pulled it free, looking down at the screen. Holding it out in front of him, he accepted the call, switching the volume to speakerphone.

"Deek, I've got you out loud with Investigator Glenn and Officers Greene and Gilchrist."

"Alright," Deek said, a bit of a drawl sliding out with the word. Had he repeated it twice more Reed might have mistaken him for Wooderson from *Dazed and Confused*. "Anything good turn up at Vazquez's house?"

Reed glanced up at the others, his features grim, and said, "Depends on your definition of good. He was here, and so was his girlfriend, both with about half a dozen bullets in them."

In most circumstances, Reed would never dream of being so cavalier with the details of an investigation, especially with a civilian. Given the nature of the aid Deek was providing though, and the fact that his interaction with the outsider world was limited to his senile grandmother and zit-faced online gamers, he felt reasonably assured in doing so.

"Damn, man," Deek said, "sorry to hear that. Almost makes what I'm about to share that much worse."

Several quick looks were exchanged around the impromptu circle, Reed raising the phone a bit higher. "What were you able to find?"

"Well, you were right," Deek said, the omnipresent sound of background typing rolling out with his voice, "Anthony Wittek has become a ghost. No credit card activity, no library card activity, not a loan application or even a doctor's visit to speak of."

Reed waited, his gaze locked on the phone, knowing Deek would get to it soon enough.

"But I was able to find a single checking account that he opened almost a decade ago," Deek said. "The last deposit of any kind was more than two years ago, which from the looks of things was pretty hefty."

"Two years ago was before Sanz got pinched," Glenn said.

"Yep," Reed agreed. "Made a nice pile on their last batch of heists, been laying low ever since."

"I was curious though, figured this guy had to be paying the bills somehow," Deek said. "Every month he withdraws between $1,200 and $1,400 from the account. About half of that is in cash, all from one of three different ATM's in Hilliard."

He paused there, the keyboard falling quiet as well, and said, "Not too far from where you are, come to think of it."

"And the rest of it?" Reed asked, the words coming out a bit harsher than anticipated, though he did nothing to retract them.

"One check a month," Deek said. If he noticed or took exception to Reed's tone, he did nothing to indicate it. "Amount of $700, written out to Cash."

"Dammit," Glenn said, shifting her weight from one foot to the other, glancing down to Billie by her side.

"Not so fast," Deek said, raising his voice just a bit, letting them know he was still working toward something. "They were made out to cash, but they were all deposited by one Irma Bowdoin."

Rifling back through his memory, thinking over the files he'd pulled on his computer, the transcripts of Sanz's trial he'd seen, Reed tried to place the name.

Nothing came to him.

"Who is Irma Bowdoin?" Reed asked.

"Sounds like a 90-year-old woman," Gilchrist muttered, Glenn glancing his way and nodding in agreement.

"Close," Deek said, having heard the comment over the line. "She's 78, widowed, owns a house in Hilliard less than two miles from all three ATMs."

"Rent," Reed said. "He's paying her rent, making the check out to cash."

"Sure as hell looks that way," Deek said.

"Makes sense," Glenn said, shifting to face Reed. "Most ATMs nowadays have a hard cap on withdrawal amounts. That's too much for him to take out, so he writes her a check, makes it out to cash."

Reed processed the statements of both Deek and Glenn in order, fitting them against what he already knew. "Hey Deek, can you send me that address?"

"Will do."

"Thanks. Damn fine work."

Both sides signed off without farewell, Reed pocketing the phone and looking at Greene and Gilchrist each in turn.

"I don't suppose you boys are up for round two are you?"

"Hell yeah," Gilchrist said, his boyish features curling up into a smile before realizing the gravity of the situation and falling back into place.

Beside him Greene was a bit more stoic, meeting Reed's attention, his visage even.

"Like we told you outside Mercy West the other night, whatever you need, we're on it."

Chapter Fifty-Three

Deek was right. The home of Irma Bowdoin was less than five miles from the house of Raul Vazquez as the crow flew, meaning it took them just over six minutes for both cars to arrive. This time Reed opted to run with the front flashers on, choosing not to work the siren and alert Wittek in the off-chance he was there.

Once they made the final corner before Bowdoin's house he eliminated the lights too, shooting just past the driveway before sliding to a stop, Greene pushing their cruiser into the same position it had been at Vazquez's.

All four people and Billie spilled out in unison, moving forward across the lawn of the home without grouping up or pausing to state a game plan.

The house was a single level affair, red brick rising to waist height along the front before giving way to faded green siding. The door and shutters had all at one point been painted to match the brick, though they too had aged to a color far removed from its original intent.

A row of scraggly hedge bushes extending to knee height lined the front, a pair of small pumpkins sitting on the tiny concrete square in front of the door.

In the yard were a handful of maple and elm trees, none with trunks thicker than Reed's thigh. They did little to obscure the front of the house from view, though they had managed to cover most of the lawn with leaves of various colors.

A one car garage was connected along the right side of the home, screwed in tight against it, employing the same color scheme on a smaller level.

"We've got the driveway," Greene said, he and Gilchrist fanning out as Reed led Glenn and Billie across the front yard. Underfoot the leaves crackled with each step, the ground coverage too thick to avoid them, all three disregarding the sound as they went for the front door.

Reed hated the feeling of being exposed as they approached, as much for Glenn and Billie as for himself. The man they were seeking had already opened fire on two detectives, had killed two other law enforcement agents. He had to know at this point that his actions would land him at least in jail for the rest of his life, more likely on death row in Lucasville 80 miles south.

On one hand, it was entirely possible they were merely approaching the home of a senior citizen, nothing more than a little old lady watching her afternoon soaps. Maybe the check she got from Wittek every month was for something else, perhaps just living expenses from a distant relative or friend of the family.

If Marco Sanz had become like a brother to the extent of committing multiple murders, it wasn't unfeasible to believe he would exercise his own brand of altruism to help Bowdoin.

Despite that possibility, Reed couldn't take the chance of entering the home empty handed.

With his gun extended before him, Reed paused just a moment to glance back at Greene and Gilchrist, to make sure Glenn was in position, before raising his hand and knocking. Sweat caused his t-shirt to stick to his back and lined his upper lip, the cool air picking at it, a sensation crawling over his skin.

A moment passed with no response of any kind, Reed raising his hand again. This time he balled it into a fist and turned it sideways, slamming it hard into the door three times. Again he paused and waited, the unmistakable sounds of movement within the house finding his ears.

"Someone's coming," he whispered, positioning his weight evenly, turning his shoulders so as to make for a smaller target, his gun at the ready before him.

The cracked weather stripping gave out a weak gasp as the front door opened, a diminutive woman with short white hair formed into curls around her head standing before them. On her feet were plaid slippers with faux fur bunched around the ankles, a matching flannel housecoat enveloping her small frame.

Peering at him over the top edge of thick bifocals, she asked, "Yes?"

"Irma Bowdoin?" Reed asked, feeling his adrenaline ebb a tiny bit.

"Yes," she repeated, the middle vowel elongated just slightly.

"Ms. Bowdoin, my name is Detective Reed Mattox, this is Investigator Cassidy Glenn. We're looking for Anthony Wittek."

At the mention of Wittek's name the woman's face creased into a smile, her hands coming together before her. "Oh, Tony! He's such a good boy. Been renting from me for a couple years now, not the slightest bit of a problem."

Running his tongue out over his bottom lip, Reed glanced to Glenn. "Is he here now?"

"No," she said, "Tony doesn't live here. He lives next door. My husband and I built the place years ago for our son to move into, but when he didn't want it we started renting it out."

Feeling the adrenaline instantly spike again in his veins, Reed stepped back, looking quickly to either side, small houses much like the one he was standing in front of flanking them.

"Next door?" Reed said. "Would you might pointing out which one?"

For the first time since their arrival, a hint of suspicion played out on Bowdoin's features, the smile fading away. "What's this about? Is Tony in some kind of trouble?"

"We don't know," Glenn said, jumping in before Reed had a chance to respond. "His name was mentioned in a case we're working on, we just wanted to talk to him and see if knows anything that might help."

The excuse was thin, Reed knowing it the moment it came out. At this point they had everything they needed, were going to move regardless what Bowdoin's reaction was, but standing out front and arguing with an old woman was not something that ranked high on his list of things to do.

Unfolding her hands in front of her, Bowdoin crossed them over her stomach, hugging herself tight. She stayed that way before finally tossing the top of her head toward her left, in the direction of her garage.

"Over there," she said, "but like I said, Tony is a good boy. Whatever it is you think, I promise you're wrong."

Chapter Fifty-Four

Reed left Irma Bowdoin standing in her doorway. He hated to be rude to the woman, but even less did he want to stand on her front stoop and have a discussion about all the things her tenant had done in the last week. The list was long and nefarious, not the sort of thing that should be sprung on someone, especially with more stray onlookers beginning to pop up along the street by the minute.

They were about to get enough of a show as it was.

Hopping down off the concrete pad, Reed moved straight across the front yard, moving parallel to the road, his feet sinking into the leaves piled up and the soft ground beneath it. From the sound behind him, he could tell Glenn and Billie were both keeping pace, Greene and Gilchrist lowering their guns slightly, standing on the driveway and waiting for them.

"Next door," Reed said, thrusting his chin at the structure standing less than 10 feet beyond the edge of Bowdoin's garage.

To call it a house was a bit of a misnomer, the building much closer to a cottage, at best. There was no garage or even driveway leading up to it, only a serpentine path of round landscape stones across the front lawn stopping abruptly at the edge of the sidewalk.

Different in every way from the main house, it was made entirely of brick, square in shape, a door in the middle with a single window to either side.

No lights were visible behind either one, the blinds pulled, the home giving the clear impression that nobody was inside.

Greene and Gilchrist waited until Reed drew even with them before falling in beside the trio, the group moving five across toward the structure.

"What's the play?" Glenn asked, her voice bearing the strain Reed could sense in all of them.

"Knock and announce," Reed said, "then we're going in."

"Even if he's not home?" Gilchrist asked.

"Even if he's not home," Reed said.

The encounter with Bowdoin had only heightened the adrenaline within him, mixing with his growing animosity for Anthony Wittek, creating a very short fuse.

A psychopath, or even a sociopath, he could understand. He would never condone their actions, would never say he himself had been there, but he could at least get their motivations. They were singular in their goals, maniacal in their methods, unable to stop under their own power.

Wittek was different, the comments from Irma Bowdoin only confirming that. He had the capacity to act as a functional human being, a productive member of society. He was simply choosing not to, instead carrying out a vendetta on behalf of someone that was themselves a convicted criminal.

The thought brought a sour taste to Reed's mouth, his face twisting up as he marched straight to the front door and pounded on it with his flat palm, the sound carrying through the chilled air. There was no doubt every person on the block could hear it echoing out as he paused and pounded again, though he found himself incapable of caring.

This had dragged on long enough. No matter what wrong Wittek thought had been done to his friend, it was damned sure no reason for him to be out shooting police officers.

It was time he was stopped.

"Anthony Wittek! This is the Columbus Police Department! Open the door or we will be forced to come inside!"

The call was louder than necessary, louder than intended, Reed unable to stem the heightened vitriol roiling through him. Raising his hand once more he pounded three times against the door before stopping and taking a step back.

"Everybody ready?" he asked, his head aimed toward the ground, seeing Glenn and Greene in his periphery to either side, Billie just inches off his hip.

"Do it," Glenn muttered, the words still in the air as Reed rocketed forward and smashed the door in, his second in just over an hour.

The front gate was of a much heavier cut than Vazquez's had been, the deadbolt thick and sturdy. It tore through the door jamb, sending a shower of impromptu toothpicks to the floor, the sound of them cascading against tile audible.

"Clear!" Reed snapped, he and Billie hitting the door at the same time. Moving directly to the side, he kept his weapon raised, waiting as Greene and Glenn both entered, the trio fanning out through the home.

The interior floor plan read much the way the outside indicated, the right half of the building a combination living room and kitchen, the floor covered in white tile. The design and the color scheme made it seem bright and open, a contrast in every way to Vazquez's.

The furniture looked newer and fairly well appointed, most likely hand-me-downs from whenever the Bowdoins last upgraded next door. A loveseat and two arm chairs were arranged in a horseshoe shape, all light blue in color, a coffee table with a glass top between them.

In the kitchen was a small blonde wooden table, a pair of white chairs on either end.

The trio was still inching forward as Billie appeared from the opposite side of the house, making no sound. She stood in the kitchen before them, watching, her body rigid but without anywhere to aim her energy.

"It's empty," Reed whispered, lowering his gun just a few inches, following Greene as he moved into the left side of the house.

A short hallway extended straight away from the living room, the floor underfoot changing from tile to beige carpet. On the walls were a couple of landscape prints, small bedrooms extending out in either direction.

Going first, Greene moved to the right, toward the back of the house. Behind him Glenn moved to the left, Reed following her, finding a small bedroom with what looked to be a spare bed, the covers tucked down tight.

"In here," Greene called, pulling Reed and Glenn's gazes toward one another before moving across the hall.

In the back quadrant of the house was a second smaller bedroom, a portion of the area carved out for a bathroom. The light inside it was on, Reed glancing in to see a basic toilet-sink-shower assembly, a few toiletry items strewn about on a shelf positioned between the sink and the mirror above it.

Standing in the middle of the room was Greene, the closet door open in front of him. On the floor of it were a half-dozen gun cases of varying sizes and lengths, boxes of ammunition stacked in the corner.

Tacked on the wall above it were hundreds of photographs, most of them black-and-white with time stamps in the corner, looking like they had been printed from security camera footage.

The only pieces of furniture in the room were a bed and a desk, the bed unmade, the desk with a handful of papers strewn across the top of it.

Greene and Glenn took up spots in front of the closet, staring in at the back wall, as Reed went straight for the computer. Using a corner of the bed sheet to avoid leaving fingerprints, he lifted the top of it, the machine springing immediately to life, prompting him for a password.

Pulling his phone from his hip, Reed went to the most recent call in his log and hit send, dropping the phone on the bed beside him. The sound of it ringing filled the air as Reed leaned forward, his face just a few inches from the screen, and waited.

"My God," Glenn said. "Look at all these pictures of Gilmore. He must have been watching him for days."

"There's Ike and Bishop," Greene added.

The phone made it to the third ring before Deek answered, sounding the most alert Reed had ever heard.

"What's up?"

"I've got a laptop here," Reed said, "asking for a password. Any chance you can get in and see what's inside?"

"Is it online?" Deek asked.

"There's a thick white cord and a black power cord both connected to the back of it," Reed said. "That work?"

"That'll do it," Deek said. "You at the address I gave you?"

"Yeah."

"Give me a minute here," Deek said, his voice sounding distant as he went to work.

Pushing himself upright, Reed moved a few steps to the side, looking over Greene and Glenn's shoulder as they continued assessing the cluster of images on the wall.

"That's Dennis Weston and his wife, Diedra," Glenn said, stepping forward and motioning to a cluster in the top right corner.

"How about this here?" Greene asked. "He's a uniform, but not one of ours."

His attention was aimed downward, the combined bodies of him and Glenn blocking the pictures from view.

Reed waited a moment for them to part before glancing over to see a mouse on the screen begin to move under its own power, Deek having gotten access. He watched as the password screen dissolved before him, a bright blue desktop appearing, a series of icons scattered across it in a haphazard formation.

"What am I looking for?" Deek asked.

"Anything," Reed said, dropping to a knee and lowering himself in front of the screen. On it the cursor continued to move, going straight to the gray bar across the bottom.

"Alright," Deek said, "let's start with whatever he was doing before he shut down."

The cursor blinked twice before the icon at the bottom maximized to full-screen, an image frozen in place. Just like many on the wall it was black-and-white, appearing to be a closed circuit feed of some sort.

The picture was not live, but it didn't need to be.

"That's the same guy on the wall over there," Glenn said, she and Greene having both moved behind Reed without his realizing it.

"Still don't know who it is, though," Greene said.

Reed's tongue felt too sizes too large for his mouth as he stared at the image. His entire body prickled with sensation as heat rose to the surface, his gaze locked on the screen.

"I do."

Chapter Fifty-Five

The fact that Kyle Dawkins's home had a basement was a stroke of good fortune for The Kid. It made what could have been a logistical headache much simpler, not having to worry about overtaking him elsewhere, or even worse having to move him somewhere.

Had his only goal been something like the detectives, or even Vazquez before them, it would have been easy. He could have preyed on the innate hero complex that every cop seemed to possess, playing himself out to be in need, waiting for the man to come close enough before dispatching him.

Such a finale would have been too easy, though. It wouldn't have done Big justice, it would not have imparted the proper lesson to Dawkins.

The way he had handled the investigation of Big's murder, or rather not handled it, was appalling. The Kid knew who had killed him, had told the police exactly who it was.

It didn't matter. They didn't care about the death of Big. Just one more ex-con they wouldn't have to worry about, another car thief off the streets, out of their hair.

Couple of days of pretending to look at Vazquez, the whole acceptance of a weak alibi corroborated only by his mother, and that was that.

Case closed, not to be reopened.

For six months after the fact The Kid had stopped by the precinct at least twice a week, wanting only to know where things stood, why an arrest had not been made. With each visit it became more apparent that his presence was beginning to wear thin on them, The Kid noticing the grimaces and sideways glances, but not caring.

His loyalty was to Big. If becoming a nuisance himself was what it took to give him peace, he would do it.

Not until Dawkins finally told him to leave and never come back did he realize if anybody was to ever get closure, he would have to do it himself.

The memory of that day still brought a scowl to The Kid's face, a bitter taste to his mouth, as he stood in the basement of Dawkins's own home. Constructed of solid concrete block, the door at the top of the stairs was closed tight, the two small windows for the wells on the back half of the house blacked over.

The setup wasn't something terribly elaborate, Dawkins himself having given The Kid the original idea for it. For everything he had engineered in the preceding days it was almost a bit anticlimactic in appearance, though at this point what it represented was far more important than any message that could be relayed.

Standing in the center of the room was Detective Kyle Dawkins. A thick braid of rope was wrapped around either wrist and looped over one of the exposed ceiling joists, his arms raised high above his head, leaving him just enough length to balance on his toes. His upper body had been stripped bare, his slacks cut off above the knees.

Striping his entire body was a series of shallow cuts, none more than a couple inches in length, over two dozen in total. Every bit of him, from the hair plastered to his skull to his exposed feet, was soaking wet from the warm water The Kid continued to splash on his body, keeping the cuts open and seeping, preventing them from clotting.

Long red rivulets painted his skin, running south from each of the wounds, drops of faint red spatter covering the floor beneath him in a wide arc.

"Why...why are you doing this?" Dawkins asked. His voice came out weak and raspy, between pants, saliva and water dripping from his chin.

The Kid ignored the question, stepping forward and tracing the tip of his Buckmaster hunting knife against the outline of Dawkins's exposed bottom rib. The sharpened blade cut through the skin without opposition, pink flesh appearing for just a moment before bright red blood rushed in, filling the space and beginning to race down his torso.

The muscles in Dawkins's abdomen flexed as his body squeezed tight, a pained gasp escaping his lips. On the first few cuts he'd tried in vain to kick free before realizing he didn't have the freedom of movement to go anywhere of consequence.

Even his yelling had already subsided, reduced to nothing more than holding his breath before panting in agony, asking broken questions while trying to keep himself just above consciousness.

Hidden under the same black cotton mask he'd worn at the Weston's, The Kid said nothing, watching the dark blood run straight down until it touched the waistband of Dawkins's pants before dipping into the five gallon bucket of warm water beside him. Using a plain red plastic cup he had taken from the kitchen, he tossed the water high under his captive's armpit, letting it run down, washing over the new wound, purging it of any initial globules, pushing everything south.

"Why? Why?" Dawkins moaned, his head raised toward the ceiling, his eyes closed tight. "Take whatever you want. It's all upstairs."

The Kid remained silent, feeling his contempt rise for the man across from him.

Today was the third time he'd been inside Dawkins's home, each time longer than the one before. On this particular afternoon he had sat and waited over an hour for the detective to get off work, rushing straight home and going for the beer in the refrigerator, just as he always did.

If there was a single thing of value in the home, The Kid could have taken it any time he wanted.

For the man to even suggest such a thing was beyond insulting, displaying he still had no idea of the skill of his captor.

"Why?" Dawkins asked again, his eyes pressed into slits. "I've done nothing."

For a moment The Kid stood and stared at the man. He squeezed the Buckmaster tight in his hand, feeling his pulse race, his acrimony somehow growing even more pronounced.

"I know," he finally said, unable to control himself. "You did *nothing*, and that's why I'm here!"

His voice reverberated through the enclosed space, relaying everything that The Kid had felt for the past year. It pulled Dawkins's gaze toward him, his eyes fluttering open as he stared.

Knowing he finally had his attention, that his prey was pushing through into lucidity for what may be the last time, The Kid reached up and tugged the mask off of his head. The air in the basement felt cool against his exposed skin as he stepped forward, making sure Dawkins got a good look at him.

"Remember me?"

It took all the effort Dawkins could muster to focus on The Kid, his features blank for a moment before a flicker of recognition set in.

A cruel smile stretched across The Kid's face as he stared, seeing the look of knowing in the man's eyes. "Do you remember what you told me the last time I came to see you?"

He paused, waiting for an answer he knew was never coming.

"You told me my showing up all the time was like death by a thousand cuts. I was just keeping wounds open, not letting anything ever truly heal."

Standing just a few feet away, he made a show of sweeping his gaze the length of Dawkins, starting at his hands and moving to the floor before following it back up in the opposite direction.

"I'd say at this point we've got about 970 left to go, wouldn't you?"

Chapter Fifty-Six

Somehow the afternoon, the entire day for that matter, had slipped by without Reed realizing it. Between going to Vazquez's and Wittek's, hours had slid past, completely obliterated in an adrenaline-fueled haze.

The first notice Reed even paid to the advancing hour was the need for headlights as he drove toward the home of Kyle Dawkins. This time he went with lights and sirens both, a bevy of red brake lights erupting in front of him, vehicles peeling to the side to let him pass. In his rearview he could see Greene and Gilchrist, the two cars driving in tandem toward the address Grimes had given them, going into the CPD personnel files from his desk to provide the information.

Working in the western suburbs, Dawkins had taken a similar tact as Reed, though not resorting to quite such an extreme measure. Opting against living within the jurisdiction of his own precinct, or even in the dense urban confines provided by the outer belt, he had pushed a ways to the northwest, residing in Marysville.

The address indicated that his house was within city limits, Google Earth showing it was located on a residential street, neighbors close on either side.

Four previous phone calls had all gone unanswered, Glenn continuing to dial on a loop from the passenger seat. After each one went to voicemail, she swore softly before disconnecting and trying again, pressing the implement to her face.

Reed knew the feeling. There was no chance Dawkins was going to suddenly appear and answer, but she had to keep doing something, as much to keep her own psyche in check, to keep the combination of nerves and anticipation from becoming all-consuming.

If not for the fact that he was driving, he was sure he would be doing something similar, whether it be making repeated calls, checking his weapon, or any of a number of other things Glenn would find equally annoying.

In the backseat Billie seemed to feed off the collective nervous energy in the car, her pacing audible against the plastic seat cover beneath her.

This would be the fourth house that they had rolled up on in the previous 10 hours, though it felt distinctly different. This time they not only had a pretty good idea of who they were looking for and where he would be, they also had an opportunity to save a potential victim. Unlike the others, where they were called in after the fact, this would be a chance for them to get there in time, to protect one of their own.

To do what they couldn't do for Ike or Bishop, for the Westons, for Dan Gilmore.

Eighteen miles separated Hilliard from Marysville, Reed making slow progress before accessing the freeway and then picking up speed tremendously. By the time a basic green sign welcomed them to Marysville, 21 minutes had passed, enough for Reed's system to be supercharged with adrenaline, his heart rate spiked, veins bulging in his forearms, his entire back wet with sweat.

He kept the lights and siren on as he entered town, the bucolic streets ready for Halloween, carved pumpkins lining nearly every front step, plastic bags filled with leaves meant to resemble jack-o-lanterns dotting most of the lawns.

Overhead, curved light poles extended out from the sidewalk, illuminating the street in bright orange light.

The automated voice in the GPS system on the dash told Reed to take a right, followed by a left. It deposited him in a street running parallel to the main drag, a near copy of the previous two they'd been on, single family dwellings lining both sides, leaves piled high along the curbs.

"I'm guessing that's it," Glenn said, extending a finger in front of her and pressing the tip of it to the windshield. She held the pose a moment before pulling it back, a smudge visible on the windshield.

Ahead of them, Reed could see a loose tangle of cars arranged in a semi-circle in the road, all of them positioned to hem in a house on the right side. A handful of dark silhouettes could be seen moving about behind the pale blue cruisers, all of the men in uniform, their attention trained on the house.

Cutting the lights and siren, Reed pushed hard until just 20 yards away before slamming the brakes, sending Billie against the backs of the front seats, Glenn reaching out and bracing herself against the dash. The smell of charred rubber instantly found its way to their nostrils as Reed killed the engine, leaving the car parked at an angle on the street, and climbed out.

Emerging from the car, Reed could see at least 10 men positioned around the blockade, their focus now on him. He paused by the door just long enough to let Billie climb out before popping the trunk and jogging to the back. Moving fast, he peeled off his sweatshirt and tossed it into the well, taking up his Kevlar and looping the vest over his head.

"Here," he said, reaching back inside and emerging with a second vest, one that regulations required him to carry even though his partner was K-9. He held it out at arm's length for Glenn, waiting as she peeled off her suit jacket and threw it in atop his sweatshirt.

Greene and Gilchrist approached behind them, each already wearing their gear, their faces drawn tight.

"Detective Mattox?" a voice called, Reed slamming the trunk shut and stepping out from behind the car, his team assembled around him.

"Yes," Reed said, walking forward and meeting the outstretched hand of a man dressed all in black, his thick hair just starting to transition to silver.

"Sergeant Andrew Baines, Marysville PD. We got a message from your captain alerting us to a possible hostage situation and stating we were to establish a perimeter and await your arrival."

Reed nodded, looking past Baines to the house in question.

The home was two stories, painted light blue, with a solid white porch. Shrubs were evenly spaced in mulch beds along the front and a mailbox cover in the shape of a bass stood along the road.

"Either a hostage situation or a murder scene," Reed replied, "depending on if we arrived in time. Has the perimeter been set?"

A grimace passed over Baines's face as he registered what Reed had said, pausing a moment before nodding. "Yes. We have men positioned a block out in every direction."

"Good," Reed said, shifting himself to the side so he could see Baines and his team beside him.

He had had more than 20 minutes on the drive over to prepare how he wanted to handle things. Without having ever seen the location, or even having been to Marysville, it was impossible to form an exact plan, though he had spent enough time in the suburbs to know it would look something like the spread he was now staring at.

"What's on the backside of the house?" Reed asked.

"A small concrete patio, some trees. That's all," Baines said.

"Any signs of movement so far?"

"Not since we arrived," Baines replied.

Reed nodded, glancing over to the garage, a two car affair, both doors pulled down. A single light blazed in the living room window, though no shadows of any kind were visible.

"My guys and I will breach," Reed said. "We can't run the risk of alerting him and giving him time to dispatch Dawkins, so we're going straight in. Investigator Glenn, Detective Billie, and I in the back, Officers Greene and Gilchrist in the front.

"The second we go, you guys move and secure everything. Good?"

"Good that," Baines said, nodding. He turned and headed back to relay the plan to his team, disappearing without another word.

"Good?" Reed asked, sliding his gun from his hip and checking the slide before glancing up to Glenn, Greene, and Gilchrist grouped around him.

"Good that," Glenn responded.

Chapter Fifty-Seven

There were two distinctive blasts separated by less than a second. The Kid heard them in quick succession, the sounds finding his ears, passing through the closed door of the basement, overcoming the panting gasps of his prey.

His heart rate spiked, drawing his attention toward the top of the stairs, his body going rigid as he turned and stared.

Somehow they had found him.

In his desire, his need, to keep pressing forward these last few days, he had failed to give proper due to his back trail. There had been little need to think he should though, his actions meticulously planned, not a single fiber or clue left in his wake.

"Help...help..." Dawkins gasped, his voice no more than a dying sputter. Each time he spoke he lifted his face a few inches and tried to yell, the effort taking every bit of remaining energy he had, the sound just barely passing his lips.

"Shut it, *now*," The Kid hissed, pushing the words out between gritted teeth. He extended the blade toward Dawkins for effect, walking in a quick revolution of his victim, assessing his situation.

The very thing that had just minutes before been such a benefit to him was now an enormous hindrance. The requirement of complete silence, the need for privacy, now had him hemmed in. The only exits were through the door, where he knew at least two teams were waiting, or try and make it out through the tiny windows and up through the landscaping wells along the back of the house.

Located more than seven feet up off the ground, The Kid doubted he could even get up to them, let alone get his body through the narrow openings. In the slim chance he could, there were no doubt other officers surrounding the place, ready to pounce should he make a run for it.

He was foolish not to have brought his guns. In his desire to make Dawkins pay he had gone only with the knife, an energy that bordered on giddiness roiling through him as he had prepared and considered the pain he would soon inflict on the incompetent detective.

A moment passed as The Kid looked between the door and the windows, fear rising through his thorax, tasting like bile as it crawled up the back of his throat and gripped it tight. There it stayed, threatening to squeeze the air from him, before a new thought occurred, one he had not considered before, one that brought with it a feeling of deep rooted peace.

This entire thing was about Big.

The man had saved The Kid's life. Every day he had lived since their first calamitous meeting was one more than he deserved, one he owed to Big anyway.

If sacrificing any future days he might have was what it took to make sure they both were finally at peace, so be it.

In the center of the room, Dawkins continued to moan, trying to call out, his voice sounding like the feeble squawks of an infant bird.

"Just stop," The Kid said, no small amount of derision in his tone. "You're embarrassing yourself. They'll be down here soon enough."

Moving forward, he jabbed the tip of his blade out at Dawkins, drawing the meaty part of his thigh, a triangle-shaped gouge opening in the skin. Pulling it back, The Kid prodded him once, twice, more, fresh blood running out over pale skin, following the path of his leg hairs and dripping from his knee cap.

As badly as every part of him wanted to end Dawkins right then, jam his knife into his stomach and twist, to stand in front of him and watch the light fade from his eyes, he had to refrain a little longer. He had but one card yet to play, and he needed to make sure everything was in place before doing so.

This was his final chance to bring everything full circle, to finally put an exclamation point on his actions the last few days.

To make Big proud.

Chapter Fifty-Eight

"Anthony Wittek! We know you're down there!"

Reed had no real way of knowing that Wittek was there beyond the first few rungs of the shower curtain having been pulled free in the bathroom and the small smear of blood on the white porcelain tub. It was entirely possible that Dawkins had merely slipped and forgot to clean it up before stepping out, or even that he had injured himself and gone to seek treatment.

Possible, but not probable.

The more likely scenario was that Wittek had Dawkins in the basement, some hellish scene playing out behind the closed door on the side wall of the kitchen, a tiny crack of light peeking out at the bottom.

Behind him Glenn and both officers were grouped up tight, their weapons at the ready. Billie stood six inches from his knee, her fangs bared, the hairs on her back standing erect, giving her an extra two inches in height. A low growl started deep in her diaphragm and rolled out over her tongue, her face extended out in front of Reed, just a few inches from the door.

"Gilchrist, you jerk the door," Reed said. "There's no lock on it and it opens into the kitchen. Pull it wide, Billie will be the first one down. I'll follow right behind her.

"Baines and his men have the outside secure, so no need for anybody to wait as chasers. You see me go down, the more the merrier."

Greene and Glenn both grunted in response as Gilchrist moved to the side. If he had any qualms with being the one to pull the door and the last one down he didn't show it, his entire face flushed with heat, sweat apparent on his brow.

For what was likely the craziest day of his young career, Reed couldn't fault him at all for the way he'd handled himself.

"On three," Reed said. He glanced down to Billie, at her poised stance, and said, "One...two...*three! Clear!*"

Gilchrist turned the handle and jerked the door back, the flimsy particle board implement swinging open fast and smashing into the counter behind it, the wood splintering.

The moment the door opened into a gaping maw, light pouring into the kitchen, Billie bounded straight down, Reed watching her clear the first four steps in a single stride before sprinting down after her.

The stairs, plain blonde wood left unpainted or untreated, creaked under his weight as he turned sideways and moved straight down, hearing Billie snarling at the bottom, a young man cursing at her. Somehow his pulse managed to grow even faster as he reached the halfway point of the staircase, the entirety of the room coming into view.

A simple concrete block space, it looked to be used as little more than storage, a deep freeze and a couple of metal shelving units the only structures to speak of. A few piles of boxes and assorted outdoor decorations sat at random intervals.

All of that Reed saw and dismissed in a millisecond, his focus on Dawkins painted red in his own blood, the floor beneath him awash in bodily fluids.

Behind him stood who he presumed to be Anthony Wittek, one hand wrapped around Dawkins's torso, the other holding an oversized hunting knife. Every few seconds he swung it at Billie, her snarls continuing, her teeth gnashing as she danced backward and forward, always just beyond the reach of his weapon.

Red paw prints appeared beneath her feet as she went, moving closer and further away from Dawkins, dotting the bare concrete floor.

"Anthony Wittek! Put the knife down!" Reed said, feeling his stomach seize every time Billie moved in closer. "And step away from Detective Dawkins!"

Reed reached the bottom of the stairs and moved off to the right, creating space for the others behind him, the stairs continuing to moan as they reached the floor and fanned out. As a group they stood in a semicircle around the bloody centerpiece, Billie trotting in front of them, her displeasure reverberating through the room.

"You call that damned dog off," Wittek said, his eyes wide as he pointed the knife at Billie before drawing it up under Dawkins's chin, "or I'll kill him right now. You know damn well I will."

"I know you will," Reed said, "just like I know you killed Dennis Weston and Dan Gilmore, tried to kill Pete Iaconelli and Martin Bishop."

"You kill him, and there's no way you walk out of here alive," Glenn said from the opposite end of the spread, Wittek rotating a quarter turn behind Dawkins, jerking his attention toward her.

"There are four guns aimed at you and a detective that is dying to tear your arms off the second we give her the go-ahead," Glenn said.

"You put the knife down," Reed said, "we put our guns away, and everybody walks out of here."

"If not this gets real ugly, real fast," Glenn said.

On the last statement Wittek attempted to rotate before stopping. He clamped his eyes shut tight and gritted his teeth, saliva streaking down out of the corner of his mouth. "Shut up! Just the hell up! If any of you people had cared this much when Big was killed, none of this would have happened!"

Inching a little further out to the right, working to get a better angle on Wittek, to at the very least force him to continue rotating between he and Glenn, Reed said, "Big, as in Marco Sanz."

"Big as in my Big Brother!" Wittek screamed, tears forming in the corners of his eyes. "And don't you dare say his name! Don't you dare! He was nothing but an ex-con to you people, someone that wasn't even worth investigating, so don't act like you care now."

"So that's what this is all about?" Glenn asked. "Bringing to justice everybody that wronged your friend?"

"He was more than a friend!" Wittek yelled, his face a mix of sorrow and wrath. "And you people turned him. You used him, and when he got killed you turned your back on him!"

"If he was a big brother, I promise this is the last thing in the world he would want for you," Reed said. "Think about where you are, what you're doing. You really think Big would want you throwing your life away? Wasting it over something that was done to him a year ago?"

The look on Wittek's face revealed pure malice, the corners of his nose rising into a snarl. "Wasting it? Wasting it?"

Shifting his weight from one foot to the other, Reed allowed himself another two inches to the side. The bulk of Wittek's body was still tucked behind Dawkins, careful to keep himself wrapped tight, ignoring the blood and water that soaked the front of his clothes.

The previous emotion, the tears, the inner conflict, all melted away as Wittek turned to look at each person in the group.

"I think he'd be proud. The only wastes I see here are you people."

As a group, each person moved closer an inch, the shift in mood in the room palpable. They were down to their last few moments, the final shot they would have to stop Wittek before he took down Dawkins.

It was clear that the man had no intention of living. Even if he hadn't originally planned on becoming a martyr, the only reason he had let Dawkins live as long as he had was so he could have their attention, using the stage to air his grievances.

A flicker of movement on Dawkins caught Reed's eye, pulling his focus from Wittek to the man in front of him. For the first time since their arrival his face was open and clear, his attention on Reed. He held it a long moment before flicking his gaze straight up at the rope above him, his hands gripping it tightly, before shifting back down.

It took a moment for Reed to grasp what he was being told, to understand what Dawkins was trying to signal. Once it clicked into place, he nodded his head almost imperceptibly, no more than a fraction of an inch up and down.

Sound bled away as Wittek continued to talk, his face twisted up in hatred, spittle hanging from the end of his lip. In its place was the steady hammering of Reed's heart, pulsating through his ear drums, bathing his entire body in sweat.

He would get one chance.

He had to make it count.

His head held straight ahead, Dawkins kept his eyes aimed on a diagonal, his focus on Reed. He blinked once, holding it for a pause at the bottom. A second time he did the same.

Reed shifted his weight just slightly, rocking forward onto the balls of his feet, as Dawkins lowered his eyelids one last time. As he did so he squeezed the rope tight, using it to swing his body out to the side, for just a moment leaving the entirety of Wittek exposed, the knife held in front of him, a look of bewilderment on his face.

It was all the time Reed needed.

The first round struck Wittek in the chest, pushing him back a full step, creating precious separation. The second hit him three inches to the side, the pair encasing his heart, bright red blood sluicing down the front of his shirt.

The knife fell from his hand as he stumbled back another step, Dawkins momentum swinging the opposite direction, blocking Wittek from view.

"Go, go, go!" Reed yelled, rushing forward on Wittek. From the opposite side Glenn met up with him, both converging on their target as Greene and Gilchrist went straight for Dawkins.

In front of them Wittek wobbled in place a moment, his face slack-jawed as he stared down at the wounds on his chest. Twice he worked his mouth up and down, trying to find the words, no sound escaping him as he fell backwards, his body propped against the concrete block wall behind him.

Using the toe of his shoe, Reed kicked the knife across the floor, watching as red bubbles formed on Wittek's lips, his mouth still moving slightly, trying to say one last thing.

A handful of different retorts ran through Reed's mind as he watched the life seep from Wittek, some involving Big, some involving the detectives at Mercy West, a few more including the people that had lost their lives in the preceding days.

In the end, he chose to remain silent, letting Billie's barking be the final sound Wittek heard.

Chapter Fifty-Nine

The scene was much the same as it had been on Saturday.

By the time Reed finished up at the house and handed the scene over to the Marysville PD, Dawkins had already been transferred to Mercy West, taken via emergency squad, lights and sirens rolling the entire time it took them to load him up and disappear into the night. As the only trauma center on the west side of Columbus, it served as the hub for all major injuries in the area, running the full gamut from the gunshot wounds Iaconelli and Bishop sustained to the assorted injuries that Dawkins was suffering from.

Arriving more than an hour after Dawkins, word had again circulated through the law enforcement phone tree, bringing supporters out in droves. Many were still in uniform, even more than on Saturday night, the balance tipped toward solid black or blue instead of street clothes.

The assembled mass of darkened colors again engulfed much of the front lobby, everybody speaking in hushed tones, clumped into loose clusters that seemed to shift position every so often.

A noticeable difference was palpable in the room though, apparent the moment the front doors opened, becoming more obvious with each step forward. Whereas three days ago there was nothing but concern and speculation, grim faces all around, there was now a bit of optimism.

Another of their brethren had been attacked, but the perpetrator had been put down.

Reed had seen such a shift in temperament before, the result of being on the backend of an investigation instead of the front.

Coming straight from the crime scene, Reed and his makeshift team still wore obvious the effects of their day. Streaks of Dawkins blood was apparent on his forearms and across the front of his jeans, both knees stained in distorted circles where he had knelt down on the floor and tried to apply pressure to various wounds while waiting for the EMT's to arrive.

The markings were much harder to see against Greene and Gilchrist's black uniforms, though Reed knew they were there, perhaps even heavier than his own. Every so often the light overhead would catch them the right way, making the dark smears obvious, the backs of their hands dotted with faint pink circles.

For her part, the hair around Billie's paws was matted with blood, the tips of her nails stained, from spending so much time with her focus on Wittek, oblivious to the ground beneath her.

At a glance it appeared that Glenn was the cleanest of the bunch, a fact made so only because she was the one to sprint up from the basement in search of a cell phone signal. While the three others busied themselves with cutting down Dawkins, she had been the one to summon Baines, to call on the medics for immediate emergency transport.

The crowd parted slightly as they entered, a few of the faces familiar, including those from the steps outside Vazquez's house. Many of them nodded their approval at the group as they passed by, a couple going as far as to offer a thumbs up.

For a moment Reed almost smirked at the situation, thinking if the scene were from a movie the crowd would break into a cheesy clap, starting slow and building momentum, hailing them as conquering heroes. In reality, there was no way such a thing would ever happen. Not because they might not deserve it, but because to do so would discount the injuries sustained by their fellow officers.

As glad, or even relieved, as everyone in the room was about the apprehension, not one of them would ever lose sight of the fact that they were all targets whenever the wrong person decided on it.

Standing at the back of the crowd, taking up the same exact position he had on Saturday night, was Captain Grimes. He stood with his arms across his chest, his usual glower in place, speaking in low tones with McMichaels and Jacobs, a couple of other uniforms from the day patrol Reed knew only in passing as well.

As a group they fell silent as Reed and the others approached, the two sides coming together almost 10 strong.

"Detectives," Grimes said, "investigator, officers."

After each greeting he nodded slightly, receiving a nod or murmured hello in response.

For a moment Grimes stood silent, appraising the group. His gaze swept over each of them, including Billie, seeing their disheveled appearance, the markings of their most recent battle.

"Would you all excuse us for a moment," he said, glancing to McMichaels and the others he had been speaking with. He raised a hand and curled a finger back toward himself, motioning for Reed and the new arrivals to follow him. "There's something you all need to see."

Chapter Sixty

Grimes hadn't been specific about who he wanted to follow him, so the entire group moved as one mass down the hall, the clatter of their various utility belts, shoes, and toenails all making them sound like a veritable marching band as they walked the silent hospital halls.

Just like it had been the previous time Reed was in the place, half of the overhead lights had been extinguished for the evening, the mood somber and subdued. As they walked past a nurse's station, a pair of middle-aged women with heavy eyes and scattered hair looked up at them for only a moment before going back to their work, no doubt having seen a cavalcade of similar visitors in the preceding days.

Keeping a steady pace, Grimes remained a full 10 feet in front of the group, his uniform coat discarded, his white dress shirt the brightest thing in the hall as he led them to an end unit and peered in through an open door, knocking twice on the metal frame.

Reed could just barely hear a muffled response from inside the room before seeing Grimes turn to face them, standing on the far edge of the door and motioning for them to enter.

Arriving first, Reed did as instructed, walking into a darkened patient room, a single bed dominating the space. The usual assortment of accompanying monitors and trays were all lined up behind it, a bevy of lights and numbers providing the only illumination.

Lying on the bed, most of his body buried beneath heavy blankets, was Pete Iaconelli. Only his arms, shoulders, and head were visible above the coverings, his right arm in a sling, his left bandaged from his wrist to his elbow. A pair of IV lines hung from stainless steel poles beside him, Reed guessing one to be feeding him meds, the other fluids.

The man's face looked sallow under the green and yellow glow of the screen behind him, his thinning hair pressed back flat against his skull.

To Reed's surprise though, his eyes were open, tracking him as he entered.

"Hey, there," Reed said, keeping his voice low, walking around to the far side of the bed to allow room for the others behind him. "Good to see you awake."

Reed stopped just past the far bottom corner of the bed, less than a foot from Martin Bishop pulled up alongside his partner in a wheelchair. He extended a hand as he did so, "Glad to see you moving about now, too."

Bishop returned the handshake, squeezing a little tighter than Reed remembered him doing in the past. His gaze met Reed's for a moment before nodding, the slightest bit of moisture settling along the bottom of his eyes.

Releasing his grip, Reed reached out and patted the man on the shoulder, remembering their earlier conversation, knowing exactly what the man was trying to say, even if he didn't know how.

He'd been there himself. In some ways, was still there.

"They tell me you got the bastard," Iaconelli said, his voice little more than a gasp, just barely audible over the sound of the heart rate monitor behind him.

"Well, *we* did," Reed said, motioning to the others beside him. "Ike, Bishop, this is Investigator Cassidy Glenn with the BCI, she's been with us the last couple of days.

"Of course you know Officers Greene and Gilchrist, both of who really went above and beyond to make sure your shooter was found."

Upon introduction all three nodded, Iaconelli doing his best to respond, Bishop offering the same in response.

"And don't forget Billie," Glenn said, a few smiles appearing around the room as the dog's tail began to move slightly, her dark brown eyes looking up at the sound of her name.

"Oh no, we'd never forget Billie," Bishop said, drawing an instantaneous laugh from Reed, much louder and sharper than intended. At the sound of it Bishop and Grimes both chuckled too, even Greene cracked a smile.

A look of confusion passed over Glenn's face as she looked over, Reed waving her off for the time being, not particularly wanting to get into 10 months of back story and side comments that had been made since he and his partner arrived.

Not that it mattered much now anyway.

After the events of the last couple days, it was a fairly safe assumption that any lingering distrust was long since gone.

"Do we even want to know what it was all about?" Bishop asked. With his partner in such a state, he had taken on the speaking role for the group, a position he was clearly a bit uncomfortable with.

For a moment, Reed pondered the question. After everything that had occurred over the last couple of days, trying to explain how a random traffic stop they had executed almost two years before had now landed them in the hospital was more than he wanted to get into.

Was most likely a lot more than they wanted or needed to hear.

"Right now? No," Reed said, leaving it that, drawing a few mumbled comments of agreement from around the end of the bed.

Once the room had quieted, Bishop looked to each person and said, 'Really, all of you, thank you. I know catching the guy will never change what happened, will not suddenly make us better, but still..."

"Thank you," Iaconelli said, his voice a tiny bit stronger. "What you all did for us, for me, it won't be forgotten."

A moment of silence settled in, falling somewhere between awkward and uncertain, Reed glancing over to the room. For much of the last day he had been acting in the role as leader, but that was due entirely to the fact that he was the lead on the case.

Now that it was over, he had no desire to serve as the spokesman for the group, instead choosing to remain quiet, to wait out whatever might come next.

To his surprise, it was Iaconelli who broke the silence to speak again.

"Also, Captain," he said, "my partner and I were having a discussion before you guys arrived.

"In case it wasn't already clear enough, as soon as we're up and out of here, consider this our notice that we'll be retiring a couple months earlier than expected."

Chapter Sixty-One

It was after 10:00 by the time Reed pulled into the parking lot of the 8th Precinct. He didn't bother putting the sedan into a parking stall, instead easing to a stop in the middle of the driveway, the body of it sitting perpendicular to Glenn's car still in the first visitor stall.

"I guess maybe I should have parked out in the lot, huh?" she said, staring through the passenger window. In another couple of weeks there would already be a thin layer of frost clouding the windows, though for the time being the car looked to be in the same exact position it was when they left that morning.

"Naw," Reed said, "besides, after today, I imagine you can park any-damned-where you please around here and nobody will say a word."

An audible smirk rocked Glenn's head back an inch as she rotated to look at Reed, her cheeks bunched slightly in a half smile. "Yeah. What a day, huh?"

This time it was Reed's turn to smirk, bringing both hands to his face and rubbing them over his cheeks. "That might be an understatement. Never thought when we left this morning we'd end up kicking down half the doors in central Ohio today, did you?"

"No, I didn't," Glenn said. Her gaze drifted out through the front windshield a moment, her vision glazing over as she stared at nothing in particular.

She stayed that way a moment, saying nothing, before shaking her head, pulling herself back into the present.

"What a day," she repeated, thrusting a hand out toward Reed. "Detective, it was good working with you. You ever get the itch to work with a wider jurisdiction or bigger budget, let me know."

Reed's eyebrows rose slightly as he returned the handshake. "Oh yeah? You have some pull over there with HR?"

The right corner of Glenn's mouth nudged upward as she said, "Well, considering I *am* the investigative division, I think I could carve out a little bit of the budget for another investigator."

She turned in the front seat and extended a hand back to Billie, running her fingers through the thick hair between her ears. "And his partner, of course."

"Of course," Reed echoed. "And hey, you heard Ike in there earlier. If you ever get the hankering to come root around in the mud again, we've got some openings.

"I'm sure Grimes wouldn't turn you down."

"Ha!" Glenn spat, resting her right hand on the door handle. "You've got Greene and Gilchrist ready to ascend. You don't need me around here."

Already Reed had considered both options, reasoning that the 8th could more than use all three, but for the time being he chose to hold that in.

There would be time for such discussions in the future.

"Home to bed?" Reed asked, not making much of an effort to hide the change of direction. He could see Glenn recognize the move, a quick hint of a smile crossing her features, before disappearing, deciding to give him a pass on it for the night.

"Absolutely," Glenn said. "You?"

Glancing over to the clock again, Reed shook his head slightly. "Got a couple more quick stops to make, then hopefully doing the same." He looked up from the clock to Glenn and added, "My computer savant is good, but he doesn't work for free."

"Ahh," Glenn said, cracking the door just slightly. "Tell him I said thanks, too."

"Will do," Reed said, raising two fingers to his brow in a faux salute. "And thank you as well."

Glenn lingered just another moment, the same faint smile on her face, before dropping a foot to the ground. "Likewise."

Chapter Sixty-Two

"Wait, wait, wait," Deek said, holding up a hand from behind his bank of computer monitors. "Before I see whatever you have in that sack there, I have a few things to share."

Reed's eyebrows came together slightly, a crease forming between them, as he glanced to Billie. Never in the years he had known Deek, either on the periphery through Riley or even now in his own right, had he ever known the man to put work before anything.

"Okay, shoot," Reed said.

At just after 11:00 p.m., he could feel the exhaustion of the last few days taking a toll. It seemed like a lifetime ago that he was home watching the Sooners play, being summoned to the hospital to sit vigil for one of their own. In the time since he had barely slept, ate less, working under the singular focus of finding the man that was targeting law enforcement all over town.

"So, after you guys ran off to save the day," Deek said, "I stuck around and spent a little time digging through Anthony Wittek's computer."

In the haste of the moment Reed had completely forgotten that Deek was online, the computer fleeing his consciousness as he ran off to help Kyle Dawkins.

"Oh, yeah?"

"Oh yeah," Deek said, no small amount of enthusiasm present. "That guy was a whack-a-doodle, for sure."

Reed paused a moment, waiting for an explanation, before prompting, "Meaning?"

"Meaning the guy took the term *committed* to a whole new level. He had no less than a half dozen hidden cameras planted in various places, hours and hours of footage from all of them stored on his computer."

Five hours earlier, this information would have been golden. Even now, had Wittek not met his end, it would have been priceless for the prosecution to build a case.

As it was, Reed would be sure to relay the message to the 19th to collect it as evidence for the file, to be sure and grab the various cameras from the crime scenes.

"Every one of them had spreadsheets and documents that corresponded to them, too," Deek said. "What people came and went when, what they drove, everything."

Reed nodded, thinking back to the murders and attempted murders that had occurred over the preceding days. It had been apparent that to pull off any one of them took planning, though what Deek was saying spoke to a new level entirely.

"No wonder if took him a whole year to act," Reed said.

"And another thing," Deek said. "Since I was inside the guy's virtual world, I did a little digging on what you had asked me before, about seeing that woman's Facebook page."

It took a moment for Reed to place what he was saying, a flicker of recognition hitting him, his eyes opening wide. "Amy Hendrix?"

"Right, her," Deek said. "I couldn't remember her name, so I didn't look at her page specifically, but this guy had three different Facebook pages, was very active in local groups. Hundreds of hits every day to various things."

"Local groups, such as?"

"Churches, schools, things like that," Deek said. "Fantastically creepy, even just looking through his history."

"He was scouting," Reed said, his voice distant as he stared off connecting dots. "Somewhere he saw her mention they were going out of town and just like that, he had himself a getaway car."

Considering his background with Sanz and Vazquez, stealing it was no problem, the same with disposal.

"I'll be damned," he whispered, walking forward and extending the brown paper bag in his hand toward Deek.

"Here, you've more than earned this. Excellent job, from start to finish."

For a moment Deek's mouth hung open at the rare praise, his hand rising upward to accept the package. The impromptu wrapping crinkled softly as he peeled it back, the neck of a bottle coming clear before giving way to another handle of whiskey.

"Jim Beam's Devil Cut," Deek said. "Nice. I might even have to start on this before the Johnny Walker."

Reed's eyebrows again rose in surprise at the fact that Deek wasn't already halfway through the first bottle, though he remained silent.

The man had done him a number of solids in the last couple of days. There was no need to insult him.

"You know," Reed said, "this is becoming a semi-regular thing, you lending a hand. I'm sure I could arrange something with Grimes, get you in the payroll system as a special consultant."

His attention still aimed down on the bottle, Deek waved a hand at him, dismissing the notion, before looking up. "Do you have any idea how much money I make doing what I do?"

To this day Reed only had a passing acquaintance with exactly what it was Deek did, no idea how much such skills brought on the open market.

"No clue."

"Well, take what you make and multiple it by about..." Deek said, one eye scrunching tight as he considered the numbers, "10."

He watched as Reed's face relayed pure surprise, bordering into shock, a smile crossing his features. "Exactly. I'm more than happy with the bottles here."

He shook the Devil's Cut once for effect, the dark amber liquid sloshing around inside.

"Besides, this has always been more as a favor to Riley. Even though she's gone..."

At that he stopped, letting his voice trail away, the implication clear.

"Yeah, I always figured as much," Reed said. "I just never wanted you to think I was using that as leverage."

"I wouldn't have helped if I thought you were," Deek replied.

It was easily the most lucid statement Reed had ever heard him make.

A flush of blood colored his cheeks as he looked down to Billie, her stomach pressed tight to the floor, already again retreating to her *rest when you can* training.

"I will admit, though," Deek said, "I was a little surprised to hear you working with a new partner on this."

Reed kept his attention down on Billie a moment, considering the statement, before raising his gaze. "*This* is my partner now."

He paused there, considering the days spent working with Glenn, and said, "There'll never be another Riley. You know that."

Seated behind the desk, Deek opened his mouth as if to respond before thinking better of it. Instead he stood and plodded off into the bedroom portion of the basement, Reed able to hear the sound of items being moved around before Deek returned, his stocking feet shuffling across the bare floor.

Side by side he placed two shot glasses on the edge of his desk before twisting off the top of the Devil's Cut. He filled both before placing the bottle down and taking up the far glass, holding it at shoulder level.

"To Riley."

A moment passed as Reed stared at him, holding his position, his glass outstretched, before he stepped forward and took up the drink that had been poured for him.

"To Riley."

Turn the page for a sneak peek of *The Partnership*, book 4 in the Reed & Billie series!

Sneak Peek

THE PARTNERSHIP, REED & BILLIE BOOK 4

A steady and persistent plume of white rose from the rear tailpipe of the Chevy Caprice as the warm exhaust hit the cold night air, beginning in a concentrated clump and spreading outward before dissipating into nothing. The acrid smell of it bit at The Muscle's nose as he stepped from the driver's seat and walked toward the trunk, leaving the door open behind him, the faint sound of the radio just barely audible.

Motown.

The kind of music they used to make back before computers and synthesizers replaced musicians and instruments. The sort of thing The Businessman would never understand the significance of, would never lower himself to listen to.

At half past two in the morning nobody else was out, the bridge The Muscle was parked on completely deserted, the desolation to be expected on a Tuesday night. The only signs of life were the lights of Columbus reflecting up off the water below, their source equal parts office buildings and Christmas decorations, the Midwestern city in full regalia for the holiday less than a week away.

The heavy soles of The Muscle's boots thumped against the frozen asphalt of the street as he paused by the rear bumper, paying no heed to the exhaust as it moved up the length of him, using his body like a vine climbing a piece of lattice.

On either end of the bridge arches hung out over the roadway, offering support for a pair of yellow sodium lights. Each threw down a harsh cone of illumination, the Caprice wedged into the gap between them, the rising exhaust and the silhouette of The Muscle the only signs that he was even there.

Otherwise the world was silent, just as he knew it would be.

Just as he needed it to be.

Extracting a single brass key from deep in the pocket of his corduroy slacks, The Muscle slid it into the slot just above the rear license plate, the teeth of it letting out a low moan as it passed over the frozen metal. Feeling his pulse rise, The Muscle twisted it quickly to the side, hearing the latch release.

Keeping his free hand cupped atop the trunk, he raised it just a couple of inches before stopping, taking one last glance in either direction.

At this time of night, in this part of town, there was little chance of any law enforcement being around. He was more concerned with the occasional vagrant that was known to frequent the sidewalks and bridges along the Olentangy River, people with eyes and ears that could potentially be his undoing.

This was all meant to set an example, to teach a lesson, but The Muscle had no interest in becoming a martyr in the process.

Not with things going as well as they were, with so much still left to do.

Definitely not with his partner sitting in his suite a few blocks away, shielded from the real heavy lifting of the operation.

Content that nobody was nearby, the bitter December wind having driven everybody away, scattering them to find shelter in the more confined parts of the city, The Muscle released his grip on the hood of the trunk, allowing it to rise upward, the aging springs doing their job pushing it up to full height.

A swirl of cold air pushed into the trunk, replacing the scent of the exhaust in The Muscle's nose, bringing with it the same smell he had spent most of the evening with, the very same aroma that now clung to his clothes, even saturated his hair.

The bitter scent was so strong The Muscle could taste it on his tongue as he surveyed the contents of the trunk, in total only four items.

In the front right corner was a bottle of radiator fluid, a vital necessity for a car with as many miles on it as the Caprice, especially in the face of a harsh Ohio winter.

Opposite it was a tire jack, the black paint on it beginning to flake off, pockets of rust starting to pop up in their wake. Beside it was nestled a can of Fix-A-Flat, the item completely empty, something The Muscle had been meaning to toss out for months but had simply not cared enough to remember.

In total those three things consumed his thoughts for less than a second, his entire focus aimed on the fourth object. Despite being curled into a ball it still demanded the lion's share of the space, just barely fitting inside the empty interior of the compartment.

The Muscle had found that it was easier to think of such things as mere objects, life having ended hours before, humanity months or even years before that. He had no idea who they were or where they came from, in most instances not even knowing their real name.

Not that he really cared to. It wasn't like it mattered.

To him they were simply a means to an end, a product that could be pedaled and profited from, discarded once their usefulness had run its course, much like a greasy box after the pizza inside was consumed.

The only difference between this one and many of the others was her brashness, a brazen disregard for general protocol that emboldened her to not only speak, but to even dare question how things were being done.

Such actions could not be tolerated.

Her death would be a lesson to all, his selection of the dump site deliberate, a joint decision between he and The Businessman, both wanting her remains to be found, needing the story of her demise to travel through the network.

In their experience together it was always better to quash such things before they gained enough steam to even enter the discussion of becoming an insurrection.

By that point, they had found, it was usually too late.

Another burst of wind passed over him, whipping the icy chill up off the water below, causing The Muscle's ears to burn. Muttering softly, he moved forward until his legs pressed against the rear of the car and bent forward at the waist, placing one hand beneath the girl's knees, the other behind her neck.

Using his back and biceps for leverage, The Muscle pulled her toward him a couple of inches before hefting the girl up, her diminutive stature feeling a bit heavier in death than he knew her slight frame to actually be. Rocking himself to full height, The Muscle allowed her to settle against his chest as he stepped up a few inches onto the curb outlining the bridge, feeling the wind get stronger as he got closer to the edge.

A few stray fingers of white could be seen interrupting the surface of the river below, the surface breaks caused by the random felled tree or rocky outcropping. Framing them were the long streaks of orange and yellow from the nearby security lamps, the occasional splash of red or blue from garish decorations filling in the remaining space.

There was no pause as The Muscle walked forward as far as he could, the waist-high barrier along the roadway pressing into him, the cold of the metal passing through his clothes.

Hefting the girl twice in his arms, The Muscle got just a bit of momentum going before tossing her body away from him. There was no ceremony to the action, no moment of reflection, nothing to commemorate her or the life she had led.

For a brief moment her pale form seemed to hang suspended in air, a ghostly flash of white punctuating a dark night, before gravity won out. Just two seconds after leaving his grasp the girl landed with a small splash, the wind carrying away the sound of it, the flow of the water dispersing the cluster of bubbles that collected in her wake.

Remaining in place against the side of the bridge, The Muscle raised his hands to his face. He steepled his fingers together and blew through them, the warm breath doing little to permeate the cold.

Ignoring the stench that seemed ingrained in his fingertips, he stood and stared a moment, waiting for some flash of the girl's body to surface

Only once he was certain that she was gone for good, that he would never have to look at her again, did he turn back toward the warmth of the car, the writhing path of the exhaust still rising behind it.

As he went back, he couldn't help but allow a hint of a smile to form on his face. The mirth he felt was not borne of any joy he felt in the girl's demise, but rather in the knowledge that what he'd just done, The Businessman would never be able to do.

For as long as that were the case, The Muscle knew there was a certain indispensability to his role in the organization, to his place within the arrangement.

And more importantly, he was now armed with new evidence proving as much.

Download *The Partnership* and continue reading now!

Thank You

As a few have commented in their reviews, I know writing this letter at the end of every work is a bit unusual for writers, but I promise it comes with two reasons that are both very genuine.

First and foremost, I cannot emphasize enough how much I appreciate you taking the time to read this work. Storytelling is something I have always wanted to do, and your interest is what makes that possible for me.

Not quite two years ago I put in place something I had always wanted to do, which was feature a dog as a main character. Having read works such as *The Art of Racing in the Rain* and *Marley & Me*, I didn't necessarily want the dog to be a pet, even less did I want to tell the story through their eyes.

It was from there that the idea from Billie was born. Again, thanks to the positive response to her, this is now the third of what I hope to be many more stories moving forward.

The second, and I know this may rankle some folks so please know it comes without the least bit of expectation or pressure, is if you would be so inclined, I would love to hear your thoughts on this novel. As always, I continue to read every review/email that is sent, and definitely take them into account when planning future works.

Again, as a token of appreciation for your reading and reviews, please enjoy a free download of my novel *21 Hours*, available HERE.

Best,
    Dustin Stevens

Welcome Gift

Join my newsletter list, and receive a copy of 21 Hours—my original bestseller and still one of my personal favorites—as a welcome gift!

dustinstevens.com/free-book

About the Author

Dustin Stevens is the author of more than 50 novels, the vast majority having become #1 Amazon bestsellers, including the Reed & Billie and Hawk Tate series. *The Boat Man*, the first release in the best-selling Reed & Billie series, was named the 2016 Indie Award winner for E-Book fiction. The freestanding work *The Debt* was named an Independent Author Network action/adventure novel of the year for 2017 and *The Exchange* was recognized for independent E-Book fiction in 2018.

He also writes thrillers and assorted other stories under the pseudonym T.R. Kohler.

A member of the Mystery Writers of America and Thriller Writers International, he resides in Honolulu, Hawaii.

Let's Keep in Touch:
Website: dustinstevens.com
Facebook: dustinstevens.com/fcbk
Twitter: dustinstevens.com/tw
Instagram: dustinstevens.com/DSinsta

Dustin's Books

Works Written by Dustin Stevens:

Reed & Billie Novels:
The Boat Man
The Good Son
The Kid
The Partnership
Justice
The Scorekeeper
The Bear

Hawk Tate Novels:
Cold Fire
Cover Fire
Fire and Ice
Hellfire
Home Fire
Wild Fire

Zoo Crew Novels:

The Zoo Crew
Dead Peasants
Tracer
The Glue Guy
Moonblink
The Shuffle
(Coming 2020)

Ham Novels:
HAM
EVEN

My Mira Saga
Spare Change
Office Visit
Fair Trade
Ships Passing
Warning Shot
Battle Cry
(Coming 2020)

Standalone Thrillers:
Four
Ohana
Liberation Day
Twelve
21 Hours
Catastrophic
Scars and Stars
Motive
Going Viral
The Debt
One Last Day
The Subway
The Exchange

Shoot to Wound
Peeping Thoms
The Ring
Decisions
(Coming 2020)

Standalone Dramas:
Just A Game
Be My Eyes
Quarterback

Children's Books w/ Maddie Stevens:
Danny the Daydreamer…Goes to the Grammy's
Danny the Daydreamer…Visits the Old West
Danny the Daydreamer…Goes to the Moon
(Coming Soon)

Works Written by T.R. Kohler:
The Hunter